OLD DIARIES AND DAYDREAMS

A NOVEL

ELIZABETH LUEDA AMERINE

ELIZABETH LUEDA AMERINE

This novel is a work of fiction. Any references to real people, events, establishments, organizations, or locales are intended only to add a sense of reality to the fiction. All other names, characters, places, and incidents as well as all dialogue in this book are the product of the author's imagination.

Categories: Literary Fiction, Women's Fiction, Baby Boomers, Friendship, Mystery, Stroke/Rehab, Obsession, Secrets, Austria and Greece, Goddesses and Myths.

PUBLISHER: REED AMERINE PUBLISHING
Author's Contact Information: elamerine.author@gmail.com
http://facebook.com/eamerine.writer

OLD DIARIES AND DAYDREAMS

For Taylor and Emily, my
granddaughters extraordinaire, for all the joy they
have brought me and
in memory of
Zachary, my only grandson

"The diary taught me that it is in the moments of crisis that human beings reveal themselves most accurately."

Anais Nin, essay "On Writing," 1947.

Chapter 1

Every woman should know her goddess. Artemis was Bitsy Bowman's. Tonight she would bring her home. She eased her Mustang convertible onto Highway 35 North toward Dallas. The Foote Gallery's monthly auction would begin in less than an hour. The statuette of the Goddess of the Hunt would fit perfectly in the current window display at her bookstore, Odyssey Books. A daily reminder of her upcoming trip to Greece and of her latest plan to capture the heart of an unsuspecting man, Richard Bennett.

She made her way down a row of folding chairs in the overcrowded room. The pungent smell of expensive and cheap perfumes and summer sweat coated her nostrils. A slight breeze from a fan at the end of the row cooled her damp skin. She removed pink trifocals and wiped beads of moisture from under her hazel eyes. When she put her glasses on again, she caught the eye of a woman who stood in the aisle. Her pulse increased and her hands shook. It can't be Suzie Homewrecker. Twenty years had passed since her second husband left with his young secretary.

Bitsy lowered her gaze and slowed her breath. It's not her. *Suzie Homewrecker may not be in her sixties like me, but she's no longer in her twenties.* The knife sharp cut of betrayal was no longer an acute pain, but a dull ache deep inside her chest cavity, in the ever present emptiness she had been unable to fill. She turned her head toward the fan and closed her eyes. Breathe, count and breathe again.

The sound made by the auctioneer's gavel startled her.

She scanned the display table in front of the raised podium. There it was. Item 189. Her breath quickened. This time pleasure not pain was behind the adrenaline rush.

The murmur of the crowd faded. Lookalike Suzie sat two rows down from her. Bitsy pushed down memories of her years of short lived relationships and shifted her focus to the small porcelain statue of Artemis. An affirmation of feminine strength, guile, courage and prowess. She would find a man to love, one who would love her in return. Her dream lived with each heartbeat.

Her phone dinged. Embarrassed that she'd forgotten to mute it, she looked around her before she glanced at the screen. The message was from her best friend, Anna Tudor.

WHERE ARE YOU? I'M AT THE HOSPITAL. BIG BAYLOR. IT'S JOE.

The man on her right pointed at her phone.

"Sorry, it's an emergency." What happened? This isn't the fun evening planned.

She reread the short text and rapidly typed out an answer.

I'M IN DALLAS AT THE AUCTION. WHAT'S WRONG WITH JOE?

The auctioneer called number 189. Bitsy raised her head. The statuette was walked across the front of the room. Dark blue paint on the gold rim around the bottom read *The Huntress*. She could see the long bow in Artemis' hand. Her phone dinged again.

HE'S HAD A STROKE. CALL ME WHEN YOU CAN.

Bitsy wrapped her hand around the phone. Her Plum Sparkle acrylic nails twinkled under a dozen chandeliers each numbered for sale.

Should I stay or go? She raised her hand to bid.

This was the first time she had attended an auction without Anna who had planned a special dinner for two, for Joe's 65th birthday, at his favorite Indian restaurant.

Romantic dinners never lived up to Bitsy's expectations. Husband or lover, fantasy always turned out to be better than reality.

She didn't say to come. She said call when you can.

The current window display in her store featured books on Greece and posters of the Greek Islands. Bitsy was leaving for Mykonos and everyone in town had become interested in that area of the world. Gossip about her trip had spread like a virus. Less than two weeks of Texas heat before sunrises and sunsets over the Aegean Sea.

She raised her hand and won the piece.

I'll call Anna after I pay for my beautiful huntress.

Bitsy tapped the man next to her. "Excuse me, I need out."

He turned up his palms. "There's no room for you to get past me."

"Will you tap the person next to you? Maybe we can get each one to see I want to leave."

After a few moments of grumbling and grunts, knee bumps and almost losing her strappy sandals, she made her way into the aisle.

Checkout was quick with most bidders still in their places.

With statue cradled to her chest like a baby, she opened her car door. Inside, she placed the goddess on the passenger's seat. Her mind filled with images of the white washed building of Mykonos and the surprised look on Dickie Bird's face when…but, first…

Her excitement evaporated in the steamy air of the car as thoughts returned to Anna and Joe. She turned up the air conditioner fan.

Think I'll wait 'til the car cools down before I call.

She placed her phone in an empty cup holder between the front seats.

Maybe I'll go to the hospital instead of calling.

***

Anna Tudor crossed and uncrossed her legs. The only empty seat in the hospital waiting room was a cushioned window ledge, narrow and too high for her petite stature. She batted her eyelids in the glare of overhead fluorescent lights. Joe had been admitted. Now the wait for tests results and assignment to a room.

Two nurses rushed down the hallway outside the waiting room. One nurse pushed a large metal cart.

Anna leaned forward. Where was Joe? Was the crash cart for him? She looked around the room at other worried faces. She wasn't alone, but was among strangers.

The best made plans came to mind. Birthday dinner, Bitsy meeting them with her win from the auction, nightcaps in celebration. At least, the hope remained for Bitsy to get the figurine and for Joe to have another birthday next year. Tears blurred her vision. The first time she had cried since Joe had fallen out of his chair at the restaurant.

Several loud clangs, beeps and shouts came from outside the waiting room. Anna put her hands over her ears. No peace and quiet in a hospital. How can anyone recover?

"Ms. Tudor?" A tall young woman called from the doorway.

Anna straightened her knit slacks before she stepped away from the window ledge.

"Come with me. You can see your husband now. I'm his night nurse."

Her name tag read Julie. Anna liked that name.

She followed the nurse down the wide hall. The antiseptic smell of the hospital was more pronounced than in the waiting room. She tasted the tandoori chicken she had for dinner and swallowed hard.

At Joe's bedside, she took a rapid and shallow breath. He looked like both a younger and older version of himself, a napping child without worry, but with sagging skin around his mouth and jawline.

"I'm here, Joe." She picked up his right hand. It was limp and lifeless.

"What's wrong with his hand?" she said to the nurse on the other side of the bed, "It wasn't this way when he left the restaurant."

"The doctor will meet with you shortly, Ms. Tudor."

"Can't you tell me? After all, you probably see this sort of thing every day."

The nurse raised the head of the bed without further comment.

Joe opened his eyes and turned to face her.

His mouth hung open and drool rolled down his chin onto his neck.

She took a small step away from the bed.

"What's wrong with his mouth?"

Anna heard steps behind her and felt a hand on shoulder.

"Bitsy, you came!"

***

The sun disappeared behind a string of wispy clouds ahead of an approaching storm. Bitsy stood in the shadows behind the glass entry door of her shop. It had been a week since Joe's stroke. When she saw Anna at the hospital, she looked so weary and frightened. She slept in his room every night before he transferred to the rehabilitation hospital.

A black Mercedes pulled into a slanted parking space across the street. Bitsy leaned closer to the door. Rick Bennett stepped away from his car and stretched his arms over his head. Her breath caught in her throat. The man of her dreams. The target of her hunt for a forever love. *If Rick was hurt or hospitalized would I stay with him? If we were married, if we were dating? Would he let me?* She watched him stand on the sidewalk, hands in his pockets, in conversation with the local barber.

She noticed his silver hair brushed the collar of his blue shirt. He towered over the other man. She shifted her gaze to the statue among the books in the window.

Joe was Anna's life. She has gone to the rehab hospital every day. Could she do that? Give up everything, her freedom, for another person? Artemis championed feminine independence with no need for a man. Need was different than want and Bitsy wanted a relationship with an honest man, a man like Anna's Joe.

She shook her head in wonder and crossed her arms over her chest in a self-hug. The cuckoo clock behind the checkout counter struck nine, time to open. She bit her lip. It was time to take another chance on love. Joe was improving and Anna had blessed her plan to go to Greece.

The earlier clouds had cleared. The sun fell on the figurine situated in the middle of the display window like a spotlight floods a stage. The center illuminated; the background in darkness. Yin and Yang. Good and bad. Seen and hidden.

After the first customer left, Bitsy peeked out the front door. Rick's car was gone. She ran her right hand down her long neck and stopped over her heart. She began to hum, *Some Enchanting Evening,* and waltzed across the wooden floor in front of a display of the latest paperback books.

Her phone dinged.

Time for the daily update. With the phone held out in front of her, she twirled to one of the blue upholstered chairs in the reading area of the store. She brushed long blunt-cut bangs away from her forehead and rubbed the spot between her eyebrows. *Let it be good news.*

The text read: STILL NO SMELL, GARBLED SPEECH. PARALYSIS NOW WEAKNESS. HE'S CRANKY. TEXT ME LATER. I WANT TO MEET FOR DINNER BEFORE YOU LEAVE.

Chapter 2

Anna stopped the ten-year-old Lexus at the end of her long driveway. Her car, the sorry-we-aren't-going-to London-after-all car. She leaned toward the steering wheel, her foot on the brake. Now he couldn't make any travel promises. To the north, dark storm clouds hung low over acres of giant sunflowers, their brown faces turned up toward the overcast sky. The smell of rain, heavy and earthy, wafted through the open windows. The air ruffled her bobbed white hair.

She looked in both directions before turning onto the two lane road. Narrow back roads were her usual route from Middlecreek to the rehab hospital in Dallas. She did her best to avoid highways on good days and never drove them in the rain. And it was on its way.

I love the smell of rain. She blinked away another tearful moment.

No sense of smell meant Joe had no appetite and his unintelligible speech meant frustration for both of them. What if his condition was permanent? When she saw him last she'd wanted to scream, but she saved her screams for the long drive home.

A loud honk behind her took her gaze off the road. She looked in her rear view mirror. A bright red pickup was on her bumper. The driver waved a less than friendly hand gesture out his window. She sped up over a low rise before the road sloped down toward a short bridge. The truck driver gunned his powerful engine and passed her. Faux bull testicles hung off the bottom of a silver trailer hitch.

Country roads, country boys. Not where she wanted to be, not where she dreamed she would be. Joe's promises had always been exciting, but never fulfilled.

The fresh smell of rain disappeared into the stink made by the truck. She squeezed her nose between her thumb and index finger. She raised her window.

A large green plastic container on the passenger's seat contained her famous Hungarian goulash made with the slow cooked marinara sauce Joe loved. He would wait until she moved away from the stove to lean his pug nose over the bubbling liquid. He always said, with a twinkle in his pale blue eyes, "Smells good, hon."

Stop it. She peeled her fingers off the steering wheel. They say he'll recover his speech and sense of smell. Baby steps they call it.

The rows of sunflowers gave way to pasture land. Several cows were under the shelter of a stand of mesquite trees edging the back of the field. A mixture of slate gray clouds and pearl white dust from cement factories in Waxahachie and Midlothian rose up ahead of her. A few more turns and she would leave this quiet country setting as the two-lane Ovilla Road snaked its way through residential developments before connecting with Hampton Road. No highway driving.

She reached for the quilted chintz tote bag nestled next to the goulash. She felt her glasses case, a wallet, a wad of tissues and her cell phone. Joe's tablet was in a side pocket. Ready for a few hours with him. Her recipe: Familiar things in an unfamiliar place. He may not smell the food, but his eyes would spark the memory. He may not smell rain, but he could be told it's there.

She welcomed the vacant parking space close to the front entrance of the hospital as a good sign. This will be the best day yet. Time with Joe, progress celebrated. And then, time away from Joe with Bitsy to celebrate her upcoming trip to Greece. Not Anna's choice of foreign destination. She longed to have British Isles and British Empire entrance and exits stamps in her unused passport. Her daydream.

She stared at the plastic bowl. *Promises not kept, Joe and now maybe they never will be.*

She leaned against the leather seat, pressed her shoulders back and counted her exhales. Breathe and relax. After a few moments, tote and lidded container in her lap, she pulled her compact umbrella from the glove box. The light rain had washed away the country dust and dirt from the hood of her car. A mist covered her windshield.

When she turned to open the car door, the umbrella pressed against the steering wheel. The horn honked. Startled, her pulse raced. Wound tight. *Will I ever relax again?*

"Good morning, Ms. Tudor." The charge nurse waved Anna toward Hall B. "He's in his room. His PT said he used the parallel bars this morning. It's a long road, but small gains, right?"

Anna nodded. Hall B stretched in front of her.

Room 114. Tudor. This was the hard part. Back straight, goulash bowl in left hand, she stepped into the small cramped room. Nothing homey about this place. A large hospital bed, boxy wheelchair, and an assortment of equipment used for treatment: Shiny chrome foot rests, gait belt and rolling iron trees strung with bags of clear liquid. Joe was in bed. He was unshaven, his usual tanned summer skin was sallow and his arms looked skeletal against the rumpled white sheets.

Where was her Joe?

Her footsteps echoed off the tile floor. He turned toward her. His unblinking eyes and an unintelligible growl in his throat took her breath away. She pressed her lips together. She fumbled with her bag and the food container. No clear speech. Not yet they said with an emphasis on the word yet.

Her belongings stacked on a built-in desk next to a tiny closet, she leaned against the edge of Joe's bed. She kissed his dry forehead, and rubbed his left hand against her face.

"I brought you some goulash for later. I brought your iPad, too. Maybe you can use it to tell me what you want, what you need." He refused to use the communication board provided by his speech therapist and seemed to prefer to point and gesture. And growl.

"I bet this'll work, Joe, you haven't forgotten you're a computer genius, have you?"

With a visible effort to turn his body toward her, he growled louder. His weak right side was dead weight. He remained flat on his back.

He had tried. That was good news.

Anna pulled a cream colored hard plastic chair close to the bed. She put the tablet on his food tray and swung it over the bed. With her right hand, she moved his left hand toward the keyboard.

"Now I want you to type something, anything, Joe. Your therapist says you can pick out words using your finger, now I want you to use that finger to write words."

Joe tried to twist his hand free from her grip.

"Come on, you old thing, give it a try. Spell your name for me."

Joe looked at the keyboard.

"I'll help." Anna guided his hand Ouija Board style. It was slow in the doing, but he typed

J-o-s-e-f.

"Josef, what's that? Your name's Joe."

Joe shook his head. He stabbed the tablet screen with his outstretched finger before he turned away from her.

Chapter 3

What to wear? Bitsy ran her right hand along the satin hangers which held her many dresses in an overstuffed closet. She had tried on three perfectly suitable outfits and was still undecided and naked, except for the fuzzy headband holding her bangs out of her eyes.

She slipped on another dress. She turned this way and that in front of the full length mirror on the back of her closet door. One arm on her right hip, she pretended to have a cigarette in her left hand. She had quit smoking many years ago, but she thought a cigarette, held a certain way, was sexy and alluring like Audrey Hepburn holding a long cigarette holder.

She stepped out of the purple maxi dress.

A girl's night out with Anna called for something pretty and fun, something bright. They hadn't seen each other much since Joe's stroke. She missed their lively book discussions. The love of historical mysteries and movie musicals had kept them close friends for almost forty years.

Strange how one or two common interests can spark a relationship that becomes much more than a book club friendship. The wisdom of someone married only once helped Bitsy get through two divorces and she provided vicarious pleasure to Anna with her travel stories and romantic adventures.

"Oh, what to wear?" She tossed another discarded dress across the foot of her bed. The female sex should always look their best. It's an essential part of being a woman, stylish and sophisticated.

Bitsy didn't own a pair of jeans.

The phone rang. She abandoned her search and twirled toward her pink princess phone.

"Hello, Bitsy Bowman."

"Ms. Bowman, this is American Airlines. You had requested a call if we were able to accommodate a change in flight times from DFW to Athens on the 11th."

"Yes."

"You are now booked on Flight 725 departing at 1900 on June 11th, non-stop from DFW to Athens with a connecting flight on Aegean Airlines to Mykonos. Is that satisfactory, Ms. Bowman?"

"Perfect, thanks for the call."

She remained seated at her dressing table. She pursed her lips and blew a kiss toward her reflection in the gold framed vanity mirror. Behind her, the ceiling fan blades made a soothing sound like slow waves on a beach. She closed her eyes and prayed her latest evening prayer.

"You know my heart; I've no more time to waste. This trip to Greece is the opening of a new door. Let it be the one belonging to my forever love. In Jesus' name. Amen."

She returned to her closet. Time to get serious. She fingered the white gauze dress she planned to wear her first night on Mykonos. Rick Bennett was due to arrive the same day. Thank you, American Airlines.

The perfect accidental meeting had been thought out, detail by detail. The gauze dress with its side slits would show off her long legs and the spray-on tan she had scheduled for the day before her flight. Her reserved room at the Hotel Apollo overlooked the docks where large cruise ships disembarked their passengers, but she planned to be strolling the beach when Rick stepped onto the sand.

She wiggled her feet into metallic flip flops encrusted with multi-colored faux gems. A pink peony print dress was her final choice. She gathered up an every ready white fringed shawl from the foot of her bed. Super-hot outside, freezer cold inside. Summer in Texas.

The rain had pushed south. Bitsy put her convertible top down for the drive to Dorsey's Restaurant. Each stop sign offered the opportunity to gaze up at the pink and orange clouds. A watercolor palette sky.

With Middlecreek behind her, Bitsy turned her car toward a manmade lake dredged out of a small creek bed south of town. With no beach area, a proposed recreational park never materialized, but the lake did attract boat owners and a few fishermen. Permanent slips were filled with boats christened with charming and sometimes telling names. Little Bo Peep, Momma's Boy, Lit Up. Country lake, country boys.

She turned into a gravel parking lot. A large white sail was illuminated by her headlight beams. A favorite thing. Boats against the last light of day.

Why doesn't Dorsey's have a back deck? Humid or not, it'd be nice to look at the broad Texas sky with millions of stars twinkling like glitter on black velvet. *And sipping a martini.* She laughed to herself.

Dorsey's was the closest restaurant to Middlecreek with any ambiance and no drive-through window. The yellow painted clapboard farm house offered a mixture of fifties big band music and hearty downhome meals, fried, breaded or killed on the hoof. Oddly, the appetizers were straight from a Manhattan piano bar menu. A tribute to the original owner who was a Yankee transplant.

Bitsy slid into one of the few booths situated along the eastern wall of what was once a large dining room. The high ceilings were made of hammered tin and original to the old homestead. Anna had not arrived.

She knew Anna would want to hear all about the trip. And she wanted to share her plans to meet up with Rick. That would take her mind off her worries, for a little while anyway. Bitsy crossed her fingers under the table, for herself and for her friend.

Anna tapped her on the shoulder. She leaned down to get and give a hug. Her attempt to cover up puffy eyes with fresh makeup had failed.

"Oh, Anna, look at you."

***

Anna didn't want to start the visit with sympathetic comments, but she knew that was unrealistic.

"I guess you can see I've been crying."

"That's to be expected for heaven's sake, but catch me up on Joe's progress and then we'll find another topic of conversation, like the surprise I have planned for someone."

"A surprise. That sounds like something that will dry up my tears."

"It will keep me happy, that's for sure." Bitsy winked.

"Well, Joe's better. He stood for over five minutes today. Stood, not walked."

"What does the doctor say?"

"The physical therapist says he's making progress and I managed to get him to take a few bites of homemade goulash."

"I'm glad he's getting better."

Anna raked her fingers through her hair. "Bitsy, I had to feed him."

Bitsy leaned forward. "But he ate, right?"

"He's not able to get a fork to his mouth with his left hand without dropping food. And his right hand's useless."

Bitsy leaned against the leather booth.

"You need a drink."

"I need a miracle. No, Joe needs a miracle. But a drink sounds good."

"Vodka martini?"

"You bet."

Bitsy motioned to a passing waiter. "Two very dry vodka martinis."

With drinks ordered, both friends studied the menu.

"Want to share an appetizer?" Bitsy said. She peered over the menu, her reading glasses perched on the tip of her nose.

"Sounds good to me. I haven't been very interested in food lately. I've cooked Joe some of his favorite meals. Did I tell you he can't smell? Anyway, after I cook for him, knowing he probably won't eat, I don't want to eat either."

Someone in the booth behind Anna let out a loud hoot. She took in a quick breath.

"This is making you sick, I can see it." Bitsy reached for her hand. "You need to take care of yourself, too."

Anna had heard similar words before. She listened when Joe's treatment team suggested she limit her time at the hospital during therapy hours. They talked about family members becoming ill themselves and the benefits for Joe to regain a sense of independence. Don't baby him was the message. *Maybe after today, I'll take the advice and stay away.*

She put her head down, her hands covered her ears. Noise wasn't what she needed.

"Let's talk about something else, okay. Anything else."

"Something happened today, didn't it?" Bitsy said. "Something new that has you even more upset than usual."

Anna looked up. She moved her hands from her ears to the table top.

"I had Joe type on his iPad, told him to type his name and he typed Josef, spelled like the German J-O-S-E-F. That's not his name; he's just plain J-O-E."

"What does that mean?"

Anna shook her head. "I don't know, I just don't know."

"Did you mention it to the speech therapist?"

"No, I wanted some time to think."

"Maybe it's because of the stroke. His language problems?"

"No, Bitsy, I saw the look on his face, the way he poked his finger at the screen. When I moved the tablet away from him, he turned his head away from me. He shut down, kept his eyes closed. Ignored me."

Drinks arrived and the conversation turned to Bitsy's trip to Greece. Anna found herself looking over her friend's shoulder, out the double paned tall windows at the far end of the dining room. She could see lights strung on several sail boat masts as they made their way back to their slips. Every now and then she would nod her head or say, "Right."

"So?" Bitsy sat up straighter. "What do you think about that?"

"What? Another martini?"

"No, Anna, I was talking about Dickey Bird, Richard Bennett."

"I'm sorry. Not very good company, am I?"

"Even at your most distracted, you're more likely to hear me than anyone I know. So, what do you think about me and Rick?"

"I didn't know there was a you and Rick."

"That's the fun of it, he doesn't know either!" Bitsy tilted her head and her long hair spread over her shoulder like a wrap.

"Okay, I'm all ears. Start at the beginning, the one I missed." This time Anna signaled the waiter.

***

Before she could begin her tale of "Bitsy Finds Love in Greece," the appetizers were placed on the table. Marinated mushrooms, calamari and chunks of Double Glouster and Swiss cheese were served in a divided straw basket lined with napkins printed with the restaurant's logo, a trombone and a saxophone each blowing out the name Dorsey's. A separate plate of cocktail rye bread and saltine crackers circled a mound of red grapes.

Bitsy speared a mushroom.

"What do you say, let's load our plates? Then I'll tell you my plans."

Anna hadn't moved. Her hands were folded on the table and her head was bowed.

Bitsy stopped mid chew. "Sorry, forgot the prayer."

After a moment, Anna said, "That's okay, I've been praying more than usual." She transferred calamari to her small plate.

Once Bitsy had sampled each of the appetizers, she folded her napkin and placed it on the table.

"Okay, here's what you missed earlier. I purposely chose to attend the bookseller's conference on Mykonos because Prissy Modine, told me Rick came into the bookstore looking for anything we had on Istanbul, Mykonos and Milan. Prissy was her usual curious self and found out he's flying to Istanbul to purchase some old Cadillac for a classic car exhibition in Milan, but after he buys the car, he's making a stop on Mykonos for a few days of vacation." Breath depleted, Bitsy sucked in some oxygen before she continued. "So I get there the same day he arrives. What do you think?"

Anna's face showed no reaction to the plan to snare Rick.

***

Anna loved her friend, but found it hard to understand her methods or, quite frankly, her interest in starting up some new relationship with a man. From her perspective, Bitsy had everything. She was a stunning 60 year old with Ann-Margaret hair, a recognizable waist and no jowls. She owned her own business, could come and go as she pleased and traveled to interesting places at least three times a year. Worlds apart from being stuck on the so-called Tudor Ranch in the company of two goats and a cat while Joe wined and dined big shots in big cities.

My waist has all but disappeared, my neck sags and my white hair almost glows in the dark. Spooky.

"I've lost you again to the obsessive chatter about me."

"I think you're great, Bitsy. And I think your plan's terrific."

***

It was Bitsy's turn to daydream, to ponder her choices. She had opened Odyssey Books after her first divorce, forty years ago. She kept too busy to mourn the loss of her marriage, although she had never actually liked either of

30

her husbands. Both cheated in business and in marriage. She attended her first international bookseller conference the first year her shop was open. Friendships with many female booksellers with similar interests had bolstered her independence and fueled her interest in ancient myths, goddess lore, and her love of Artemis. *Others may see me as Aphrodite, but they're wrong and I see Anna as Hestia, hearth and home.* That assessment would be wrong, too.

The table was cleared of leftover food and empty martini glasses. Bitsy clinked Anna's espresso cup.

"Here's to more good news tomorrow."

"Here's to safe sex." Anna's face flushed. Her cup wobbled in her outstretched hand. "I mean, here's to safe travel."

"I say here's to all the above." Bitsy raised her cup above her head. "Guess we need to call it a night."

"I'll call you tomorrow. Tonight, I intend to find out more about this Josef thing."

Chapter 4

Anna was propped up by several pillows. Again and again as the night passed, she glanced toward her nightstand. Midnight, then 1:30 a.m., now 3:30. Although she had dosed on and off, deep sleep was elusive. It was the questions. She turned onto her stomach and buried her face in her pillows. Still questions slaughtered sleep.

What was she missing? Joe's mute, but adamant gesture was unmistakable. He meant to tell her his name was Josef. *Where's his birth certificate?* When she met him he told her he was born in England and that his family moved to the United States when he was a toddler. He was 22 years old when he came into the Southern Methodist University Student Bookstore looking for textbooks on corporate law and finance. She worked there during the summer break from her college course work. He was in town to assist in two mergers and acquisitions of Texas companies by a New York corporation. *I never met any of his relatives, but I didn't have any for him to meet either.*

She could still remember their first conversation.

'I don't know much about Dallas. Maybe you could suggest a lunch place.'

'I love Campisi's; it's not too far from here. Best pizza around.'

'Do you get a lunch break?'

She had surprised herself by accepting his invitation. It was during that lunch, he told her where he came from and that his parents died in an automobile accident when he was twenty. She shared her loss of both her parents. Her dad in Viet Nam in 1965 and her mother from asthma in 1968. *Neither of us had siblings. We were on our own.* Was that part of the instant attraction?

What has he failed to share, what's missing?

She swung her legs over the side of the bed. Her cat, Tuppence, leaped onto her lap.

"Whatcha need girl? Some lovin'?" She held the cat up in front of her then wiggled her nose into her soft fur. "How about a snack?"

Tuppence purred all the way to her chintz porcelain dish nestled in one corner of Joe's home office.

His desk was against one wall of the glassed-in back porch. Gunmetal gray with silver pulls and a large month-to-month calendar centered on top, it was stacked with piles of reports, statistical print-outs, city planning maps and financial records of some extremely successful companies. Joe hadn't retired, but worked at home rather than maintaining office space elsewhere. His desk was a testament to his reputation as one of the country's most sought-after business minds. His expertise was in turning companies from financial failure to money-makers.

Anna pulled out his thirty year old leather executive chair and sat in front of the desk. Where to begin?

She leaned forward on folded arms. She scanned the cork board hung behind the desk. It was a myriad of colored push pins with scraps of handwritten notes, old photographs, advertisements and losing Lottery tickets captured under their sharp tips. Her vision softened and her mind drifted back to the promises Joe had made her when they were dating. He promised if she would support his career plans and have dinner waiting for him every night, he would take her to Paris, London, Rome, wherever her heart desired. After they married, his business travel increased and she had dinner alone most of the time. Promised trips never happened.

She opened the right hand desk drawer. The cash box inside was never locked. She opened it and on top of other important papers, like the deed to their small ranch, was her passport. She kept it current in case Joe's promises and her dreams came true. She flipped through its empty pages. *No entry or exit stamps.* Rifling through the rest of the box, she realized Joe must not have a passport. She found no birth certificate, other than hers, at the very bottom of the box.

She opened the left hand drawer and was surprised to find Joe's collection of pipes. He stopped smoking when she quit cigarettes. She had never paid much attention to his pipes. She knew he prized them as heirlooms passed down from father to son. When he had smoked, he kept his collection in a circular wooden holder around a lidded amber glass container that held the aromatic tobacco. After he stopped smoking, the pipe holder disappeared from the living room mantle. She assumed he had packed it away, along with his pipes, in the attic filled with other obsolete items.

Her bedroom alarm clock made its usual 6:00 a.m. jarring sound. She scooped up the pipes. Their smell reached her nose before she made it to the bedroom. She inhaled, exhaled, inhaled deeper. Such a sweet smell, so familiar. She stretched out on the bed, pipes lined up on her chest. Tuppence lurked at her feet.

"Don't pounce on me, Missy."

She raised one pumpkin colored paw, her green eyes unblinking. She stretched her body and curled it around Anna's toes.

Anna slept until a gust of wind rattled the loose shutters outside the bedroom window. A reminder of another of Joe's unfulfilled promises.

When she turned to push herself up from the firm orthopedic mattress, the pipes fell to the hardwood floor with a thump, thump. She had been dead to the world.

Tuppence bolted off the end of the bed.

Anna bent down and retrieved the pipes. She rubbed her fingers along and around their stems, all were carved. Two had elaborately carved bowls.

She moved to the breakfast room and switched on the light. She spread out the pipes on the small glass top table where she and Joe started their day with coffee and dry rye toast. Routine was at the top of Joe's agenda. Never any spontaneity with him.

She slid the rattan chair from under the table and sat on the chair's edge. She examined the pipes. She noticed manufacture's marks along the back of each pipe stem. She reached behind her and rifled through the top drawer of the rattan buffet next to the table. Her fingers found the magnifying glass.

The pipes were from Germany.

Anna gunned the car's engine, a habit she started when, earlier in the year, the car stopped in the middle of a busy road without warning and she was almost hit from behind. Somehow revving the engine before leaving home made for a more relaxed drive. She had decided to see Joe between his morning therapy sessions rather than waiting for the afternoon when he spent more time in his room. She had his pipes in her tote and a list of questions in her mind she hoped he could answer using his tablet.

Before she turned left, she saluted the American flag she had painted on their roadside mailbox. God Bless America.

Joe sat in his wheelchair. Anna noticed he had more control over his posture than when he first arrived for rehab. No visible lean to the right side. His weak right hand was splayed on the wide laminate tray attached to the wheelchair. He wore a gait belt over his Dallas Cowboy tee shirt.

"Hi, sweetheart," she called from the doorway. "Glad to see you up." She hoped she sounded cheery, she wanted his cooperation.

Joe looked toward her. No growls, only silence.

The blinds were raised which allowed for a view of the landscaped lawn. Morning sunlight filtered through the row of manicured crepe myrtles along the wide sidewalk that circled the hospital. Hundreds of pink, purple and white blooms peeped out among thick green leaves.

She noticed that Joe followed her gaze. She walked up behind him and kissed his neck.

He stiffened. She walked around him and pulled up a chair. He pointed to the tote bag she had hung on the chair back.

She reached around her shoulder and pulled out the iPad.

Joe shook his head and continued to point to the tote. His finger moved up and down and back and forth as if some awful thing was stuck to his finger that he couldn't get rid of. Then, he did something that caused Anna to drop the iPad back into the bag and scoot her chair closer.

He rubbed his nose.

"You can smell!"

He nodded and made an effort to speak. A garbled "es."

Anna literally leaped from the chair toward his lap. The wheelchair tray kept her from her goal.

"Honey, you can smell," she said, her hands all over his face.

She sat back in her chair.

"And, I heard you say, yes, well, almost yes. That's a beginning, right?" She had forgotten what had started this tentative conversation.

Joe hadn't. He went back to pointing.

She realized he had smelled his pipes.

Chapter 5

Bitsy wedged her car into one of the parking spaces in front of her bookstore. She honked the horn. Nothing happened. No Prissy. *She's likely to be eating breakfast in the break room.* She gritted her teeth at the image of crumbs and powdered sugar on countertops.

Bitsy managed to wrap both arms around the stack of heavy books she had borrowed from a physician friend. She kicked at the door of the shop. Nothing. After a twist here and a shift there, she managed to turn the door knob. The overhead bell jangled.

"Prissy, come help me." She wedged a foot between the door and its frame. "Where are you?"

Prissy emerged from the back storeroom, a jam spreader in her right hand.

"Sorry, Ms. Bowman, I was…"

"Never mind, what you were doing, come help."

Prissy held the door open with her left hand, spreader still in her other hand. Orange marmalade fell onto her wrist and a bigger glob landed on the hardwood floor barely missing Bitsy's exposed big toe.

"Watch it!"

"Sorry, Ms. Bowman." Prissy looked from one hand to the other. She pushed her back toward the door and moved the jam spreader behind her. Marmalade now decorated the cover the latest issue of Vogue magazine.

Bitsy pushed passed her.

"Clear off the coffee table so I can put these books down."

Prissy rushed around the sofa and into the back room. When she returned she had a roll of paper towels in her hand.

Bitsy stood next to the coffee table. "Any day now," she said.

Prissy put the paper towels on the trestle table and shoved several magazines and pamphlets into a pile on one end of the coffee table. She moved closer to Bitsy, who placed a few books onto her outstretched arms.

"Are these text books?"

"Not exactly. They're medical books on neurology, rehabilitation and a research manual, "After a Stroke: The Compromised Brain", about treatment and recovery."

"For your friend, Anna?"

"Knowledge is power, Prissy."

Bitsy moved from the coffee table to the back room. "Thanks," she shouted.

She took a paper plate from a free standing cabinet, put two croissants on it and filled her favorite Breakfast at Tiffany's mug with fresh, hot coffee.

Things are going to work out for us, Anna, for both of us. I just know it.

She would be gone for at least ten days, maybe more, if Rick was receptive to her planned proposal to spend a few weeks together in Greece. She had brochures of several small oceanfront rental houses not far from Athens.

She stopped before leaving the back room. Paper plate and coffee in her hands, she took a deep breath. *Anna faces that time alone, her husband in a hospital and where will her best friend be? In Greece.* She walked to the front room couch and stood over the medical books lined up on the coffee table. Her eyes scanned one book to another.

My trip to Greece. A good idea or not?

The trip was for business. It was a deductible business expense. It was an annual conference held in different locations each year. But this year more than one thing was different. Rick, Anna, Joe.

"Prissy, I expect Anna to call and if I need to do anything for her, I'll need you to handle things here."

All the smeared and dropped marmalade had been removed and Prissy had placed the damaged magazine underneath the front counter. She sat on the tall cushioned stool next to the cash register.

Bitsy left the medical books where they were and returned to the back room.

The antique brass doorbell clanged. A burst of sunlight changed the dark hardwood floor from chocolate to caramel. The first customer of the day stepped across the threshold.

Bitsy stood just inside the opening to the break room.

"Good morning," Prissy said before she looked up from the New York Times. "Can I help you?"

***

Anna didn't move. The silence following Joe's struggle to communicate was like a heavy woolen blanket, smothering. Joe had stopped pointing. Their eyes were locked. Neither blinked, neither looked away.

A scream from down the hallway broke the silence. Anna turned her head away from Joe and saw two nurses rush past the door.

Joe touched her leg with his good hand. When she turned back to him, he raised his hand in the direction of her tote.

"Okay, Joe. Let's talk about the pipes."

His face remained without expression, but his shoulders lowered several inches.

"I searched through your desk last night after you wrote J-o-s-e-f on the iPad. That threw me. I found the pipes in the drawers. Now I'm more than confused, I'm afraid. Who are you? Joe or Josef? The pipes are from Germany. You spelled your name as if you're German. This is news to me; you told me you're English from England."

Joe lowered his chin and mumbled a response.

"Look at me, Joe, so I can try to understand what you say. Say it again."

He raised his eyes to hers before shaking his head. His facial droop made him look like a stranger. Foreign to her in more ways than one.

She stood up and her legs knocked against his knees. She stumbled over the wheelchair footrests. "I'll be back." She left the room and took a few steps toward the nurse's station. She flattened her back against the wall and rested her head against it. "God, give him back his voice."

The speech therapist stopped in front her. "Are you alright?"

"Not so much." She pushed herself away from the wall. "I know I've asked before, but do you think Joe will be able to talk again? He seems to be trying to speak, making some word sounds. But it's mostly unintelligible."

"As you know, there're no crystal balls to predict complete return of function after a stroke, but you've noticed he can produce some sounds. I think it's likely he'll recover his speech although it may be different than before the stroke."

"How so?"

"He may retain some slurring or a lisp and his speech may be slowed. Patience is the key for you and him."

"I had him try to communicate using the iPad yesterday."

"Good idea. He also has a communication board in his closet. It has pictures he can point to to help him communicate his needs."

"He refused to use the board when I put it in front of him during one visit. I don't remember how long ago that was. My days are running together."

Anna turned back toward Joe's door.

"Try again. Yesterday, he used it for me."

Communication board on his lap, Joe used his left hand to spell answers to Anna's questions. Josef Trost was his birth name. His grandmother was Austrian and moved to Germany when she was young. His grandfather was German. His father immigrated to England because of Hitler's annexation of Austria. His parents moved to New York after he was born in England. He learned his birth name as a teenager. He was told to keep it secret.

Anna sat silent for several moments. *What can't he tell me using this board?*

She had more questions. She wanted more details, but she could see Joe was exhausted. The slow effort to spell each word letter by letter had drained him.

He motioned for the call button. His right arm was pinned against the wheelchair by his weak torso.

"Let me move you."

She pushed him up and away from the arm rest and stuffed a pillow from the bed in the space. "There, is that better?"

The physical therapist knocked on his open door. "Time for therapy, Mr. Tudor."

Anna stayed behind Joe, her hands on his shoulders. . *Mr. Tudor, not any longer, actually not ever.*

She swung her shoulders toward the therapist's voice.

In four strides, the PT was at her side. She placed her right hand on Anna's left arm.

"He's going to have mat work and some walking in the parallel bars, if you want to observe."

"I don't think so, not today." Anna managed to produce what she hoped was a pleasant grin.

"I need to get back home. Exterminator's coming today. Mice. Don't want to miss him."

The therapist took Anna's place behind Joe's wheelchair and leaned over his shoulder. "Looks like you were having a conversation with Ms. Tudor. Communication boards are great."

Joe raised his left hand and pushed the tray with the board away from his wheelchair, knocking it against the end of the bed.

"Now, Joe, I'm sure you did a fine job, right Ms. Tudor?"

Anna hesitated.

"He managed to tell me a lot of things today, but not nearly enough." She stopped at the door. "Go do your therapy. I'll be back tomorrow."

***

The outside temperature approached the century mark by the time Anna pulled up in front of her house. There was no exterminator coming. She had the house to herself, herself and Tuppence.

She sat in the car for a few minutes before opening the door. Time in the car had become the place to sort through any confusion she had either before she saw Joe or after she left him at that place, that not home, far away from home place.

She replayed the answers to her questions, which, unfortunately, led to more questions. In the moment before the therapist entered the room, Joe had attempted to speak. The best she could tell he said "attic" and he pointed to the picture of a book on his communication board. Anna looked across the passenger's seat and scanned the open field next to the house. It needed mowing. The prairie grass was already yellow in the June heat. She needed to water her vegetable garden and flower beds.

First, I need to find the portable fan. I can't go into the attic without a fan.

She turned off the ignition. She grabbed her tote and pulled herself up and off the front seat of the car. She was certain Joe had been saying attic. She tossed her hair and slammed the car door.

What's in the attic? More evidence of lies or the answer to all my questions?

The attic was floored with two by fours covered with various outdated, soiled and mostly ugly rugs kept for that purpose. Anna plugged in the fan cord and set it on medium speed. She directed it toward the back corner where two trunks had gathered dust in front of two tall bookcases filled with, not only books, but porcelain Knick Knacks, empty tobacco tins, fancy liquor bottles, also empty, and shoe boxes holding miscellaneous items. There was a dormer window midway along the back roof and two dormers along the front slope. Not enough light came through these never cleaned windows to see much more than shadows and brightly colored objects.

She had turned on an unadorned overhead bulb and she wore a ball cap with a built-in LED lights. Joe's hat. He used it when he checked the stables at night, when they had stables. Lately, he had used it to check the perimeter of the house before bedtime. There had been a report of feral hogs in the area that had masticated neighbors' gardens, lawns and even toppled saplings.

She flailed her hands in front of her eyes. Spider webs separated her from the trunks. She had decided to ignore the stacks and rows of books on the shelves and start her search in the trunks. These two trunks belonged to Joe before they were married. When, as a young bride, she had asked about them, he told her they were full of archived financial information and business proposals that he was required to keep by the government for at least ten years.

He had sounded so important, her chest swelled then, now she slumped down on her knees in front of one of the trunks. She let herself fall further to the floor. A small cloud of dust pushed out from under her navy crop pants.

The larger of the two trunks was approximately four feet tall, made of leather with brass findings and opened like a closet. The smaller one looked more like a chest than a travel trunk. It was made of stained wood with a flat hinged top. She opened the smaller trunk. It was lined with cedar and the smell brought tears to her eyes.

I never noticed smells so much. This smell takes me back to my childhood and my grandmother's quilt chest where she kept old clothes as well as her handmade quilts. Many days I spent playing dress up and smelling like Christmas.

The trunk wasn't full of papers, important or otherwise. The first layer seemed to be uniforms, wool jackets with gold trimmed lapels and cuffs, still shiny gold buttons engraved with initials and trousers with a strip of gold running down the outer legs. She uncovered a sword in a heavy metal scabbard gilded in gold and set with what must be faux pearls and rhinestones. Under the sword were a plumed hat, its feathers matted, and a cape with gold braid.

She flung the clothes behind her and dug deeper in the trunk. Her hand touched something hard. She had found a book. She raised herself up onto her knees and leaned over the trunk, the LED lights casting a cone shaped beam directly over the area where she had felt the book. She pushed more clothes up and away from the spot and saw on the bottom of the trunk two books, side by side.

"Ouch!"

She automatically put her bleeding index finger in her mouth.

"Must be another sword in this darn trunk."

She took off the hat and shined its light on her hand. A small and smooth slice of skin hung like a limp flag from the tip of her finger. Blood pooled at the crease before big droplets fell onto her knees.

Hat back on head, she pushed herself up from the floor and searched the nearest bookshelf for something to wrap around her finger, something to stop the bleeding. Everything was caked with dust.

On the bottom shelf shoved behind a dusty chalk elephant, she found a quilted sewing basket. Inside she found several fabric remnants, clean and the right size to use as a cloth bandage. She had moved away from the fan and sweat began to collect on her upper lip like a wet mustache.

"Misery, misery," she said under her breath.

Bandage securely in place, she returned to the opened trunk. This time she removed the items gingerly, one at a time, until the two leather bound books were the only objects left to remove.

Sweat now trickled down her back and dripped from her ears. She rubbed one ear and then the other against raised shoulders. It was time to go back downstairs where she could look at the books in the comfort of her air-conditioned kitchen.

She turned off the fan and held the books in one hand. They were small enough and light enough that she could safely carry them down the attic stairs. She had always been physically active. Once with the horses, then with the llamas, and now with the goats, garden and a few chickens. She also loved to dance and Joe had obliged her that hobby when he was in town. At 62, she was still light on her feet.

At the kitchen table, she ran her right hand over the red leather cover of the larger of the two books. She turned the spine toward her. It was tooled into diamond shapes with the initials EAH centered in the middle of the spine. She turned the book around before she put it on the table. The tooled leather design on both the front and back of the book showed two stylized birds with wings spread and interlocked at their tips. There were cascading tuffs and plumes over and around their bodies. She gently opened the book. It measured about 8 inches by 6 inches and the pages, yellowed by time, served as a neutral background for the still vivid black ink. There was no author, no date.

The book was filled with page after page of handwritten script with the look of calligraphy, graceful and stylized. Writing reminiscent of a bygone era. Interspersed in the text were numbers, those pages looking like a time table or some sort of schedule. *A personal diary or a journal and in a foreign language.* Although she didn't speak any language except English, her voracious reading habits had allowed her to recognize various foreign words. For the most part the language in the book looked like German although she noticed some passages in what might be Italian or French.

She moved that book aside and looked at the smaller, rather plain book in a black leather binding edged in gold. The handwriting was less elaborate, but with a gracefulness not often seen in the digital age. A front piece bore the name Marta with no surname. There was a date at the top of each page, beginning 26 December, 1888.

A young girl's diary and an unknown author's book looking to be of more importance.

She turned in her seat and pulled open a drawer in the rattan server behind her. She chose two large dinner napkins from a stack of linens. Each book was placed and wrapped in a napkin.

It's time to call Bitsy and have her take a look at these books before I see Joe again.

***

The phone rang and Bitsy abandoned her day dream of Rick, ouzo and sand covered limbs.

"Hello, Bitsy Bowman."

"Bitsy." Anna's voice was high pitched and wired. "What do you know about old diaries?"

Bitsy cradled the phone between her chin and shoulder and reached for the glass of iced tea on her coffee table.

"Old diaries? What's up?"

"Joe told me to check the attic for books…"

"Wait a minute, Joe can talk?"

"No, not really, but he tried and pointed to the picture of a book. But, the question is can you tell me anything about two old diaries I found in the attic? Old German diaries."

"Does this have something to do with Joe being Josef?"

"I don't know what it means, but he wanted me to find the books and now I want to find out about them. One is dated 1888. Will you take look at them before your trip? In fact, maybe you could take them with you to your bookseller conference."

"Of course. Sounds intriguing, mysterious. Want to try the new tea room across from Odyssey tomorrow?"

"Can we do it today? I've already been to see Joe and I'm not going back."

"Ever."

"Not today and maybe not tomorrow."

"We could meet for a drink at Dorsey's after I close up for the day," Bitsy said.

"Can't you take a few minutes off for coffee at the tea room?"

"Anna, it's a tea room, silly, they serve tea," Bitsy had returned to her fantasy of Rick on the beach. She was striking poses on the circular couch. Right leg crossed over left or left over right.

"Oh." Anna's voice had all but disappeared.

"Sorry, Anna, I know you're stressed to the max. How about meeting for a four o'clock tea? I hear the scones are delicious."

"I'll be there, books in hand."

"You might want to handle them with care, in case they're valuable. Don't open them without gloves on, okay."

"But, I have…"

"Don't open them again. I'll bring the gloves I wear when handling antique books."

***

The Rose and Crown tea room was crowded. All but two of the small round tables were taken for the traditional English tea. Anna had wrapped the books in a soft silk scarf and now placed them in front of her on the white linen tablecloth. There would be little room for a tea pot and a platter of biscuits and pastries.

She signaled a waitress in a drab cotton dress with a ruffled apron and wearing a bonnet pulled down over her ears.

"Good day," the waitress said. She put a plate of scones and tea sandwiches on the edge of the crowded table. "You might want to remove your scarf so as not to stain it, ma'am.

"I need to keep this scarf on the table. If you could remove the flowers and condiment tray, I would appreciate it."

"Shall I take away the refreshments, too?"

Anna shook her head and held the books to her chest. "You can leave the plate and please bring me an individual cup of tea, not a pot full."

The waitress picked up the condiment dish in one hand and the flower arrangement in the other. She nodded her head and swung around toward the kitchen area.

Her mutter could be heard as she walked away. "Takes all kinds, don't it?"

The cottage-styled front door opened and Bitsy waved as she stepped over the threshold.

"Nice place," she said. "Love the shelves of old books and tea cups and the ivy and trellis painted walls, don't you?"

Anna looked around her and noticed for the first time the quaint and charming room. The rough brown cross beams spread from slim bookshelves which displayed old English books and china pieces. Any other time, she would be babbling about Agatha Christi's Miss Marple and enjoying the feel of an English cottage. She loved Miss Marple or more to the point, her adventures.

Bitsy sat across from her and reached over the plate of tea cakes and sandwiches for the books.

Anna unfolded the scarf onto the table top and handed Bitsy the small black diary.

"What have we here?" Bitsy took the book and turned it over in her hand before placing it on the table in front of her. She opened the plain leather cover. The front piece was as Anna had described, inscribed with a female's name and 1888. The first entry was also dated and written in the European fashion, 26 December 1888.

She had forgotten to put on her curator gloves, her manicured plum polished nails shone under the overhead lighting.

"I do believe I'm losing my mind," she said. She reached into her trademark tote bag and pulled out a pair of white cotton gloves.

"The language appears to be German," she said while she looked through the first few pages of the book. "Of course, at the time of this diary, many different countries spoke German besides Germany, like Austria-Hungary and Alsace. It'll take some time to have it translated."

She moved the small book to the side and reached for the red leather diary. She rubbed her fingertips over the embossed cover and looked up at Anna.

"This book's important." She lightly tapped the cover with her index finger.

"Bitsy, you haven't even opened it. What makes you think it's important?"

"The birds. I've seen these bird figures or some similar to these either as a family crest or on an old tapestry somewhere. Old royalty, I think. You said the diary is written in German, so maybe German or Austrian royalty."

"I guess just being written by some royal family member makes it valuable, huh?"

"I don't know if it has any real value, but it should, at the very least, be interesting reading. It could divulge something important."

Anna cocked her head to the right and scrunched up her nose.

"Well, it could," Bitsy said.

"We both have read too many mysteries."

Bitsy rubbed her cheek with her left hand and stared up at the beamed ceiling.

"I've got it," she almost shouted. "I saw a sketch of these birds on a compendium book list sent to me by a German bookseller. He's the one I've mentioned who's always trying to foist raggedy old German biographies on me. He can't comprehend the size of Texas. He thinks Middlecreek is near New Braunfels, which was an early German settlement."

"So, these bird figures are on books from Germany?"

"On something from Herr Hegel. The book list, a letterhead, something recently." She shook her head as if that would clear her vague memory.

The waitress stood quietly at the edge of the table before placing one cup of tea near Anna's elbow which was propped on the table.

"Anything else?" she asked.

"I'll have a cup, too," Bitsy said without looking up from the book.

She took her time turning the pages and examining the numbers as well as the elaborate penmanship. Every three or four pages, she would look up at Anna, nod her head and return her gaze to the book.

"I'm about to jump out of my skin," Anna said when she looked up again. "What do you think, what do you see?"

"I see a puzzle. A puzzle meant to be a puzzle, if that makes sense."

"So do you have any idea where to go from here?"

"Well, there's a man I'll see on Mykonos. He's the curator of the museum there, and he's well versed in antiquities, especially antiquarian books. He'll know something, I'm sure of it."

Anna relaxed against her chair and cupped both hands around her steaming cup of Earl Grey. "Bitsy, since the book discussion is basically taken care of for now, I want to change the subject."

Bitsy wrapped the books in the scarf Anna had provided and slipped them into her tote. She leaned into the table. "Tell me."

"I can't decide what to do about Joe. I mean about his lies. He's so vulnerable right now, but I'm so angry I just want to smack him across his face. His sagging face."

Tears welled up in her eyes and when she lowered her chin they dropped like rain onto the linen table cloth.

"There must be a good explanation for his family to change their names, to distance themselves from their past, their heritage. Does knowing he's German instead of English really matter?"

"It's not that, it's the betrayal. It's the elaborate false backstory. I'm his wife, his wife." Her breathing sounded heavy as it escaped her chest.

"I wish you'd come with me to Greece, get away for a while. Joe's recovery's likely to be long and slow. Why don't you come with me?"

"I can't. I'd feel worse if I left him, in his condition, even for a week or so."

She leaned down and picked up her purse from the floor.

"Thanks for meeting me. I know you need to get back to your shop."

"I can stay and talk if you want."

"Just knowing I can talk to you is enough. I think I need to go home and snoop some more."

"I don't know if that's such a good idea. You're upset enough and Joe can't really explain much right now. Come back to the bookshop with me. We can visit between customers and I've got better cake than this." Bitsy waved her hand over the untouched plate of scones and sandwiches.

"Bitsy, I'm so glad you invited me to spend the afternoon here. The break from sleuthing was just what I needed."

"I'm glad, too."

The two friends hugged each other before getting into their respective cars for the drive back to their homes.

***

Bitsy lived in one of the city's few townhouse complexes. They were built during the 1980s, complete with community swimming pool, Jacuzzi hot tub and jogging paths. A city dweller compared to Anna's life on the outskirts of town.

"Hey, Anna!" Bitsy waved her left arm above the windshield of her open convertible. "Think about what I said. A trip to Greece."

Turning away from the downtown square, her mind zeroed in on decisions she still needed to make about what to pack. She needed to stand in front of her closet to be reminded what she had in her wardrobe. *Some people think I shop too much, but what is too much?* She cranked up the radio. The Rolling Stones were singing *Start Me Up.*

Chapter 6

A Shakespearean program was on the local PBS channel and Anna wasn't going to miss the four hour program. While she preferred Agatha Christi, she had read all of Shakespeare's work, in college and then on and off while Joe was away on his business trips. Her attempt to relive lost plans to teach comparative literature as a college professor. The dreams of youth. The dreams of a lifetime.

The opening credits of the program scrolled by unread. Anna was drowsy and dozing before the first segment of the series ended. Her brow relaxed and her breath slowed. She fell into dream sleep. Sleep had become her only real refuge from worry and anxiety after Joe's stroke and was even more needed after his recent revelations. She wished for fictional mysteries not real ones. This wish wouldn't be granted anytime soon.

***

Bitsy took her iPad to bed with her. She found a plethora of information on the Internet about Germany and Austria at the end of the 19th century. The language in the largest of the books, which was the most interesting, was written primarily in German. She found the bird figures were similar to that of the Hapsburgs of Austria and she found mention of museum archived diaries of several royal family members. On another site she found an article about the custom of monarchs keeping private diaries.

While she was mostly looking forward to being with Rick, she was also excited about seeing other booksellers she knew and delving into Greek mythology, now she would need to take these books to the one person she knew who could give Anna some answers. Peter Gallenos.

The good news. The conference was at his museum. The bad news. She didn't want the books to interfere with her agenda. *First thing, I'll turn these diaries over to Peter. That's the ticket.*

She put the iPad on the nightstand and reached for her sound machine. She pressed the button for Waves.

"Soon," she whispered, "I'll be falling asleep to the sound of the Aegean and, hopefully, to the sound of Dickie Bird's heartbeat."

The night reached its darkest point. Bitsy tossed and turned. She pushed against her bed's iron footboard, her pillow mushed up under her neck. Her dreams revolved around pursuit of Rick. She saw herself singing *I've Got*

You under My Skin in a Mykonos blue mosaic tile shower with Rick covered in sand stepping under the water. This scene changed and Prissy was standing in the bathroom tossing the latest best sellers into the shower with her. Rick had vanished. Bitsy shot up in bed. The clock read 4:44 a.m., the hour of the wolf.

Shortly after her second divorce, Bitsy celebrated with a weekend retreat to an abandoned monastery on the California coast. The retreat was led by a Jungian analyst who insisted the participants take a pledge of silence for the first day and night. She slept in a small cell once used by the monks. The second day focused on dream interpretation and the collective unconscious with a special and individual journey held that evening. Each participant was instructed to leave the monastery building and find an isolated spot on the heavily treed grounds to spend the night alone. This exercise was called Night of the Wolf with an emphasis on personal awareness of the Hour of the Wolf. Fearless and able to face both exterior and interior truths.

Bitsy turned her back to the clock wanting to resume her dream of Rick sans Prissy. Soon it would be time to take care of last minute chores before leaving for Greece.

The sound machine morphed into an alarm clock and beeped at 6:00 a.m. She reached over two plump pillows to turn it off. She stretched her body full length under the soft pink sheets before she opened her eyes. She let her legs drop over the side of the bed. She used her bare feet to search for the slippers she had left beside her bed last night. Her mind whirled. She tossed her loose hair. So many last minute things to do, not the least of which was going over her rules and regulations for running the bookshop with Prissy. Her interest in books was a plus, but her interest in hot dogs, French fries and popcorn was definitely a minus. Last year there were smears and smudges around the store after she returned from her annual two week trip in spite of Prissy's promise to refrain from eating in the store.

The International Bookseller Conference was the only time she was gone for two weeks. She took a one week time out four times a year and closed the shop during those times. Two weeks, even ten days, were too long to close the store, especially with more and more people buying books on line. She had to remain competitive and accessible. The conference itself was less than a week long, but she always counted on staying longer with some new friend or heading to her favorite getaway, a small hotel in Venice.

She used both hands to pull back her tousled hair and held it in a low ponytail. First the bathroom routine, then coffee and an aspirin. Thinking about Prissy was a headache maker.

***

Peter Gallenos, the curator of the museum on Mykonos, closed the plaster covered door of a metal lined wall space designed to hide prized objects. He turned back toward his small and sparsely furnished living room and removed the curator's gloves he wore. He picked up his glass of retsina and stepped out his balcony door. His gaze fell on the row of terra cotta pots filled with geraniums and bougainvillea perched on the wooden balcony railing. Reverently, he looked to the darkened sky, one hand on the cross around his neck. The moon appeared larger than before he had poured over the antiquarian books he brought home from the museum. *Perhaps my eyes are only opened wider.*

He loved old things: objects, books, stories and folktales. But he wasn't looking forward to this year's bookseller's conference in what he considered his museum He had been curator there for over twenty years. While this year's focus was on Greek myths, the emphasis was on the feminine roles in mythology, the Goddesses. Peter was an Apollo man, a Zeus man, an Odysseus man.

He caressed the thick blue tinted glass of wine. In the kitchen, dolmas had warmed in a toaster oven. They would be cold by time he ate them. He took another sip of the retsina. His thoughts were on the hundreds of women spouting the importance of the Goddesses. He choked on the strong drink. *Will there be only women this year?* He could already hear the chit, chit, chattering and giggling. Of course, he would need to be solicitous, smile and grasp the hands of them all. He knew the role he played.

Sitting with a stiff spine on the edge of his outdoor chaise, he smelled the fragrance of the flowers tinged with the salty outdoor air. His vision blurred while he concentrated on the gray stone floor where it met the wooden door frame. He blinked rapidly when his gaze fell on the stark white Flokati rug covering his living room floor.

Tomorrow I must dust off the large paintings of the triple Goddess. He spit a mouthful of wine back into the blue glass. The museum committee insisted the paintings be in the museum foyer to greet the attendees. The committee president had said, "In the spirit of this year's

Goddess focus we should show off this unusual acquisition." Peter spit again.

"*Merda!*"

Chapter 7

Time evaporated. Bitsy hadn't finished packing and departure was in a few hours. Her headache, after spending the morning with Prissy, had gone from a dull throb to intermittent searing pain from ear to ear. A martini would be welcomed if the packing was done. She had talked briefly with Anna about the timing of her pickup for the airport. A road trip might be the best thing for her. Middlecreek to DFW qualified as a road trip.

Bitsy rubbed her temples. Tears welled up in her eyes. It had been hard for her to go out on her own after her first divorce and Anna had been her rock. Now it was her turn and she was jetting off to an exciting adventure Anna had never had.

Oh, I wish she would go with me. She swallowed hard and tasted tears in her throat.

She tossed new royal purple espadrilles into her carryon. Anna's two antique books wrapped in a Bob Mackie scarf were tucked into a hidden slot designed for laptops. She paused before she opened up her vintage train case. *Tonight I fly away for not only the conference, but for Dickie.* She selected several perfumes and lotions from an elaborate jeweled box on her vanity table. Her spray on tan would shimmer and her pulse points would be covered with exotic smells.

As time passed, her mind fell away from worries about Anna and toward her hopeful adventure in Greece.

Chapter 8

Anna stood in the middle of Joe's hospital room facing the opened window blinds. Her arms were crossed over her chest. She rolled her shoulders in an attempt to relax after hours in the attic and hunched over the computer keyboard. She had poured over numerous internet sites hoping to fill in the blanks, her blank head and heart Joe had filled with lies. Today, she would be included in his speech session. She would watch him eat and be taught prompts to give him for swallowing. *I don't want to be a caregiver.*

She walked closer to the window. Landscapers, on their knees, planted flowers along the sidewalk. Their bright fuchsia and white blossoms momentarily lifted her spirits. Life continued, the seasons cycled and Joe would improve. And she would adjust. Her anger and hurt would subside. Joe Tudor was the center of her life. But what about Josef Trost?

Joe's wheelchair knocked against the door frame. It was time to show her interest in his recovery. Time to pretend in front of strangers that she was a dutiful spouse even though, for the first time in her marriage, she wished she was single.

I need time away from all this, but that's not likely to happen. She turned toward Joe and his speech therapist.

"Ms. Tudor, I'm glad you could be here for family training."

The therapist patted Joe on his shoulder.

"Your wife will learn some important techniques to help you with your eating. After our session, the case manager will talk to you both about discharge plans."

Anna didn't move from her position by the window.

"I can see he has made gains, but I'm concerned about discharge from treatment. I'm not sure I can care for him at home."

She hugged herself again.

"Not to worry, the case manager will explain options available to you."

Anna stood next to Joe's lunch tray and the therapist began to explain safe swallowing techniques. She nodded here and there. Her eyes focused above Joe and the therapist, her mind on Bitsy's trip to Greece. *I'm going to miss her, her enthusiasm in all things; her indestructible attitude that all is possible if you believe.*

"Stop it," she whispered.

"I'm sorry," the therapist raised her eyes toward her; "Did you say something?"

She shook her head. "You're doing good, Joe." There was no enthusiasm in her voice.

She returned to thoughts about Bitsy's ability to follow her heart, make her own promises to herself. *No need for anyone else. Lessons to be learned.*

When Anna arrived home, she promptly called her minister. She wanted information about her church's senior day care program. Joe was scheduled to discharge from the hospital before the end of the month and she wasn't going to be trapped by his disabilities. She knew she needed to forgive him before she took on such responsibilities. The time to act was now before he came home. Her call went to voice mail. Her message was to the point.

THIS IS ANNA TUDOR. JOE CAN'T TAKE CARE OF HIMSELF YET. I CAN'T TAKE CARE OF HIM 24-7. PLEASE CALL ME ABOUT THE SENIOR DAY CARE OPTIONS OFFERED BY THE CHURCH. THANKS.

Time to act as chauffeur for Bitsy. This act didn't seem like a responsibility, but a much wanted pleasure. An hour with her, not another hour with Joe.

During the short drive to the other side of Middlecreek, Anna replayed long ago promises she made to herself, B.J., Before Joe. And those made by him after they met. Virtually all were broken. She didn't become a college professor, a world traveler, or even a mother of three, her ideal family size. When she saw Bitsy straddling an oversized purple paisley suitcase on the curb ahead of her, maudlin thoughts disappeared as if erased from a school blackboard, but leaving a smudge of dust in her brain.

She pulled up next to the curb and rolled down the passenger side window.

"What are you doing outside in this heat?"

"Just excited I guess." Bitsy stood and stepped away from the luggage.

"Need help?"

"No, just pop the trunk."

"You look beautiful, Bitsy and ready for another of your adventures abroad."

"I've been thinking that after Joe recovers, you and I need to go on a girl's trip, anywhere you want to go. What do think about that idea?"

"You're the best and it would be a dream come true, but I'm afraid I'm obligated to be a caregiver. You know the "in sickness and in health" vow."

"There are people you can hire, so don't give me this no choice stuff. We'll talk about it when I get back. Don't dismiss the idea yet."

Anna agreed to think about it, but she shook her head, no. Old disappointments had been overridden by new disappointments. Believing in a trip now was ludicrous.

Bitsy blew kisses toward Anna from the underground American Airlines departure area. Her cheeks blushed from more than her rosy rouge. Her eyes twinkled under the glare of the fluorescent lighting. "See you in a couple of weeks. Wish me luck."

"Safe travels and good luck with you know who."

Anna did wish her luck with Rick. *I can't wait to hear about her trip and her fun. Fun, I want some of that, too.*

Chapter 9

Bitsy's first view of Mykonos from the plane's window enhanced her sense of adventure. White stucco buildings seemed to sprout out of Mediterranean blue white capped water filled a variety of boats. Rick would arrive later in the day. She tried to pick out her hotel, but she hadn't been here in many years and the number of structures on the island had grown along with the number of tourists at this port-of-call. More than a dozen luxury cruise ships bobbled in the sparkling sea. Which one was Rick's?

She looked away when the flight attendant began giving landing instructions. She clutched her tote bag with both hands and began to hum *I'm in the Mood for Love.*

"Pardon?" The man next to her, who had been silent during the hour's trip from Athens, touched her left arm.

"I was humming a happy tune, monsieur." She tilted her head and smiled. *Almost time.*

She unpacked the largest suitcase opened on the bed. Her fingertips tingled as she shook out the dress she would wear to the beach later. She held it up in the sunlight streaming through open balcony doors. Her body shivered in anticipation of meeting Rick. She took a very deep breath. *Dickie.* She exhaled and raised her face to the wicker ceiling fan. *Dickie, tonight.*

She had requested a room with a balcony overlooking the bay. After she emptied her suitcase of its contents, she stood on the private balcony and surveyed the crowded shore dotted with both ancient and newly painted boats, a smattering of dangerous looking rafts, and exquisitely decked out yachts. A short distance away was anchored the center of Bitsy's attention, an Epirotiki Line cruise ship.

She leaned against the marble balustrade that bordered her balcony. Thanks to the overhanging canvas canopy, it felt cool under her hands. Her eyes focused on Rick's ship as it rocked gently in low rolling waves making their rhythmic way to the beach. Gulls squealed overhead, but she kept her eyes focused on a particular ship-to-shore open bed ferry pulling away from the *Argonaut.* A shiny white classic Cadillac could be seen strapped down in the middle of a crowd of tourists. The boat made its way toward a wide wooden dock on the southern side of the bay. *He's almost here.*

She stepped back into her room. The immediate difference in temperature caused goose pumps to cover her bare arms. She rubbed them away. Draped over the back of a chair, her white gauze sundress caught her eye. The dress purchased for this day, this hour, this man. She had been a sun worshipper when it was the thing to do. Now she settled for either tan towels or the spray-on tan she had purchased two days before the trip. Bronzed skin would electrify the whiteness of the dress and suggest more tanned skin just below the gauzy material.

She slipped the dress over her head, grabbed her favorite floppy straw hat and her tote bag containing all manner of important items she could not do without. She almost leaped out the door and into the simply decorated white hallway. White on white on white with a touch of bronze. Mykonos, the white jewel of the Aegean would be her place of joy for a few days. Or so she thought on this first day on the island.

She heard the ferry bump up against the dock even before she turned the corner at the end of the cobbled stone street and had a view of the bay. She flipped up the ends of her hair, pushed down the crown of her hat and wished the wind would subside before she crossed paths with the extremely handsome and widowed man of her desire.

The beach area around the docks serving cruise ships was always filled with taxi drivers, hotel personnel, and local children looking to grab a bag or two for tips. For ship passengers, the scene looked much like any other island stop until they looked up and toward the town and caught a first close up view of hundreds of white-washed buildings, brown tiled roofs and the profusion of bright pink bougainvillea cascading from built in planters outside windows and on porches across the island.

***

"Watch it!" Rick could be heard above the den of voices around him. "That's my pride and joy, folks, my first Caddy." He turned back toward the ferry. He squinted into the afternoon sun beginning its descent toward the horizon. The chrome trim around his car glinted with like a silver halo.

He was fit for 64 years old. A successful advertising executive, he had shifted from early years as an art director to the marketing side of the business. His recent interest in classic cars had led him to Istanbul. This stop on Mykonos was only a stopover on his way to Milan for the annual International Classic Car Exhibition. He stepped back as his car was loaded onto the back of a trailer.

81

"I'll be by to check on my Caddy after it's secured," he said to the group of men tying down the car.

***

Bitsy shielded her Ray Ban shaded eyes with her right hand. Her breath was shallow and she felt beads of sweat form and slide from her shoulders to her unrestrained breasts. Without looking, she knew her nipples had hardened. *Everything works.* She moistened her lips. She held her espadrilles in her left hand and stepped onto the sand.

She was within ten feet of Rick when he turned and saw her. A slight frown creased his sweaty brow. He shook his head. His crooked smile revealed a small gap between his front teeth that caused him to produce a slight hissing sound when he spoke certain words.

"Why if it isn't Bitsy Bowman standing right here in front of me?"

"Hi, Dickie." Her usual smooth alto voice sounded like something had constricted her vocal cords. She coughed and tried again. "Nice to see you…"

The space between them narrowed quickly due to Rick's long strides.

"But imagine seeing you here," she said. She fluttered her eyelids, but realized the dark lenses of her sunglasses prevented any effect.

"What brings you here, Bits?" Rick reached out to shake her extended hand.

She dropped her chin and removed the Ray Bans.

"Oh," she said, "I was told you were tramping around Europe with a stop here on your way to Milan and the car thing. I thought it might be fun to surprise you." She let go of his hand and took a step back. She pushed her hair behind her left ear. "And I'm here for a bookseller's conference." She hesitated then bent over to put on the espadrilles in her hand.

The sand was difficult to balance on while holding her tote bag in one hand and trying to tie the ribbon strap around her ankle. She looked up at Rick; the sun caused him to look like a silhouette. She wasn't able to make out his features. "Would you…?" she began.

He got down on one knee, took her right foot into his left hand and slipped the shoe on with his right hand. She noticed he had stopped wearing his wedding ring. She slipped her sunglasses on again and looked toward the sky. She silently berated herself for thinking that was a good sign. *But it's been two years, right?*

"There you go, all fixed up," he said. He stood and regained his full height, towering over her five foot four stature. "So, how long have you been here?" He raised his gaze toward the town away from her eyes.

"I arrived today and will be here for a several days or longer if I decide to stay after the conference is over." She turned toward the town and stepped ahead of him. Soon they were out of the sand and on a solid ground. In front of them a slew of restaurants and bars with chalk board signs advertised the day's menu and usual specialties of the house.

They walked side by side toward the main road that cut through town and headed to other villages clustered along the shore line.

"How about a drink?" she said.

"Maybe later after I see to it that my Caddy is safe and secure." Rick stopped in the middle of the road. "So, I'll give you a call. Nice to see you, Bits."

He started back down the street toward the beach when Bitsy realized he didn't know where she was staying. "The Hotel Apollo," she called. He raised his right hand in a wave delivered without turning around.

She made her way up the street to the turn off to the hotel. She swung stiff arms up and down like a solider on parade. Her scowl threatened to frighten a small group of children asking if they could carry her tote bag.

"No, I can do it. Go bother someone else."

She pushed between two older women into the hotel lobby. *I made a fool of myself, at my age.* She pursed her lips.

She punched the elevator button repeatedly. The first to enter the elevator, she leaned against its back wall. She hadn't taken a deep breath since she saw Rick move away from his car. She didn't let go of her breath until after the doors closed on a packed elevator. *All these people and I'm alone. Not what I envisioned.*

***

A dark skinned man moved next to Bitsy, his unusual ring flashed under the oval lights recessed in the mirrored ceiling. A ring engraved with the profile of a heavily plumed bird, enameled blood red. The man had noticed Bitsy's large tote bag and the International Bookseller Conference flyer protruding between the bag's straps. His gaze rested on the gilded edges of a red leather book stuffed into an outer pocket. While he could not see the entire spine of the book, he saw two gold-leaf letters, E and A. He took out his Blackberry and made some notes before he slipped it back into the front pocket of pleated white linen trousers.

"Excuse me?" The man leaned toward Bitsy. Chin toward chest, he lowered his eyelids. "I could not help but notice the brochure in your bag. You must be going to the conference at the old museum, up the hill, no?" He leaned closer. "I am, too." His hand reached out toward her bag.

Bitsy pulled the bag up and hugged it against her chest.

"Yes, I'm going to the conference." She moved a step away from him, her eyebrows raised. "Who are you anyway?"

"Oh, I am so sorry if I offended. My name is Constantine Verone. I am a bookseller from Rome. And you?" Again, he moved toward Bitsy. This time she didn't back away.

***

"My name's Elizabeth Bowman. My friends call me Bitsy." She seemed to murmur in tune with the elevator music. "Sorry if I was abrupt with you, but I'm not use to strange men standing so close to me." She laughed. "Oh, I didn't mean that you're strange." She put a hand over her mouth.

He's not unattractive and seems to be interested. Well, if Dickie's going to ignore me, this could be your lucky day, Signore Verone.

Chapter 10

The interior of the Hotel Apollo paid homage to ancient Greece with tall pink marble Doric columns, mosaic rimmed quarry tile floors and wall niches displaying small masks of Greek Gods. The only nod to Modern Greek design was the use of blue linen covered chairs and couches edged with a white Greek key design. The Hotel Apollo was the oldest hotel on the island and was always filled with guests loyal to its traditionalism.

Bitsy stepped out of the elevator onto polished white tile quarried from an area outside Athens. Her room was only a few steps away, but she slowed down and actually stopped in the hallway. After her interaction with Rick she felt silly and stupid. She shook her head and continued to her room. She slipped the electronic room card into its slot and heard a distinct click. *Beautiful island, not-so-bad-looking me and he only has eyes for an old Cadillac! What is it with men and their cars?*

She dropped the card on a small bistro-styled table next to the double doors leading to the balcony. Before anything else, she called room service and ordered two large, very dry vodka martinis with three olives each. She took off the uncomfortable espadrilles, removed her dress and put on short sweats. She pulled her hair into a ponytail and sat barefoot on the small balcony waiting for her drinks. *My new plan, get pleasantly tipsy.* She jumped when she heard the knock on her door.

***

Once his Caddy was stored away from the sea salt and sand, Rick called his office in Dallas to rearrange his itinerary. Things had changed when he saw Bitsy standing on the beach. He decided to extend his visit on Mykonos. It had been a two long years since he held a woman in his arms, no one since his wife's death. Bitsy seemed willing, he thought. He remembered her flirtatious looks and obvious interest in seeing him.

"Hello, Millie," he said to his secretary, "What's up in Big D?"

***

Bitsy perched on the edge of the blue and white striped canvas chaise lounge wedged against the balcony railing. She slowly sipped her martini and tried hard not to blink. She didn't want to miss the actual sinking of the marmalade sun into the paled but sparkling sea. The last spreading rainbow colors beyond the shadow relief of the ubiquitous windmill silhouettes on shore. She tipped her nearly empty martini glass between two fingers. Her thoughts were on the material she had read for the first class tomorrow. A study of the once matriarchal world, when the feminine was honored and the female ways were worshipped.

Wrapped in the splendor of a Greek sunset, she knew she had forsaken her long ago study of the ancient myths. She wondered if her pursuit of a man's attention had separated her from her authentic spirit and soul. Would a soul mate expand or shrink her independent spirit? Could the feminist in Bitsy, the young woman who burned her bra and marched for the Rights of Women awaken from her deep slumber brought on by sexual desires? Could she honor both aspects of woman?

She closed her eyes to block out the expansive sky as it began to show its night face, the twinkle of a million stars. She imagined Rick's arms around her. She heard a noise on the balcony next door. She imagined a mysterious stranger only a few steps away. *What's wrong with me?* She jumped off the chaise and stepped into the dark hotel room.

OLD DIARIES AND DAYDREAMS

Can I enjoy a romantic interlude with Dickie or Constantine and really be an independent woman? A modern day Artemis?

She deposited her empty glass on the bedside table and picked up the waiting second martini. Raucous laughter and Greek music could be heard from the outdoor bar below her balcony. *I'm in no mood for a crowd of exuberant tourists circle dancing behind a waving white handkerchief.*

She waved her drink in front of her and returned outside. She hoped the sound of the waves would relax her, but the harsh ringing of her room phone interrupted her troubled reverie. When she twirled toward the sound of the phone, she stumbled on the uneven stone floor. She reached down toward the end of the chaise for balance and noticed, out of the corner of her eye, a man standing on the other side of the louvered partition between balconies. A shiny cuff link in his hand twinkled against his dress shirt, a dab of ochre on a white canvas. She saw the tips of a bow tie under his bent chin. It was Signore Verone. How convenient, she thought. She slipped quietly into her room. She felt every drop of the vodka in her system with each rapid heartbeat.

Her phone continued to jangle.

She leaned across the queen sized bed and lost sight of her neighbor.

"Bitsy Bowman here." She slid the martini glass onto the nightstand.

"Hi, there, Bits." Rick sounded like he had been drinking, too. "Thought I'd call to see if you wanted to go out to dinner tonight. The Caddy's safe and I'm feeling a little bored and hungry. What do you say?"

She didn't answer right away. On the one hand, she had come to Mykonos to spend time with this man; on the other hand, she wanted an invitation without alcohol talking. A thought crossed her mind before she responded. *What if he uses alcohol to drown his sorrow or to be with another woman other than his wife?*

"Dickie." She licked her lips before she continued. "It's been a long day for me. I have an important class to attend tomorrow and I want to do some reading before then. How about a rain check?"

***

Rick straightened his spine and ran a hand through his hair. *Did I miss read her come on? Hadn't she been the one who wanted to get together?*

"Fine, girl," he said, "Get with you later."

"Thanks, Dickie, maybe we can get together tomorrow after my class. At the Apollo pool or the beach."

"Sure," he agreed, without picking either place. "See you tomorrow. 'Night."

He turned over on his bed. He held up phone receiver and said, "I wish she wouldn't call me Dickie!"

Several minutes later, he picked up the Room Service Menu. Nothing looked good.

***

Constantine hadn't realized Bitsy was on her balcony until she moved into her room. *What fortune.* He put his Moroccan leather wallet into his inside jacket pocket. He picked up a blue hued glass holding the remainder of his first Glenlevet of the night. Neat. With one swift motioned he downed the last swallow. One foot into the room, one on the balcony, he swiveled his hips toward Bitsy's room and leaned closer to the partition. *I must find out about the Dickie fellow.*" Inside his room, he said to the darkened walls, "No one can interfere with the successful completion of my mission."

***

Local families and foreign travelers on holiday filled the lobby. Bitsy snaked her way through them. The effects of her two martinis prompted her to give up preparation for tomorrow's class. Turning down Rick like a school girl wanting to seem hard to get added to her need for major distraction.

Let the shouts of Opa begin.

She entered the large, open air bar on the sea side of the Hotel Apollo. She dressed for the evening out in white linen wide-legged pants with a bosom enhancing crisscross knit blouse in aubergine. She wore her brown leather Zorba sandals. Her frosted white toe nails were a throwback to the 1970s, her era. The Era, as far as she was concerned, a time she and other women celebrated the return of the feminine, even if only among themselves. Sleep overs and night's out were spent sharing stories of strong and independent females which soothed several broken hearts. She still kept a generous amount of Goddess books in her bookstore. A few of the local area high school teachers provided an opportunity for girls to explore the matriarchal myths and not only the Apollo, Odysseus and Oedipus sagas.

When approached by the bar hostess, she told her she wanted a table in the dark, in the corner, in the back. Tonight she wanted to be an observer, not a participant.

Chapter 11

Constantine slipped quietly into Bitsy's room. The lights were out and only the beam of his flash light kept him from knocking a large makeup case left on the edge of the unmade bed to the floor. He side stepped over a pile of clothes near the bathroom door. The narrow shaft of light showed the conference flyer on top of a pile of books on the dresser. He sorted through the books with a stubby fingered hand while he kept the flash light beam close to his body. He expected to feel the luxury of very old, very fine leather. Nothing but ordinary books. The diary wasn't there.

"*Merda, Merda!*" He spit the words under his breath. "What has that old woman done with the book?"

He whirled around on nimble feet, swung the flash light beam in a circle, decorating the walls and furniture with brief moments of complete illumination before a return to darkness. He didn't see the hint of red he looked for, a spot of blood red, nor did he smell the hint of musty

ancient leather. No diary. *She must have taken it with her.*
Does she not know the significance of the book?

"*Merda*," he said again. "If she knows what she has,"
he said leaning over to look under her bed, "she should
protect it from the elements." He stood up empty handed
except for his now limp flashlight resting on his linen
covered thigh. *Nothing here of interest.*

He walked back to his room. He knew he shouldn't
confront her in public. He switched on his room light
before he closed the door. He stood on the threshold for a
few seconds, leaned his head into the hallway, no one was
at the elevator, no one was to be seen. He made his way to
his bed where he sat staring at his reflection in the dresser
mirror. His thoughts drifted back to the day his father
invited him to sit with leaders of the secret Grand Dukes
Society in the stone cottage, behind Mayerling, deep in the
Vienna Woods.

He had been thirteen and shaved for the first time
before the meeting. A symbol of his adulthood, his father
had said, and of his entrance, as a novice, into the Society.
The Grand Dukes Society had been formed for the sole
purpose of finding the legendary diary of Emperor Franz
Joseph of Austria-Hungary. Talk of such a diary had been
on the lips and minds of a wide range of groups since the

death of the heir to the empire in 1889. Its existence, according to Constantine's father, was confirmed by the red enameled gold rings passed down generation to generation, depicting a plumed bird of prey similar to those of the Hapsburg family crest. He was told there were sketches of a book cover found in the archival papers of the Emperor and, most importantly, a cipher was kept under lock and key by the President of the Society. A cipher given to Franz Joseph's closest confidant.

He knew who to call and he knew the call couldn't wait until he had found the book seen in the Bitsy's bag. The book he believed to be the missing diary. He knew if anyone else saw the rumored book, it could be disastrous for the Society's mission to preserve the glory of the Hapsburg dynasty. More powerful groups were interested in the diary and some of those were more ruthless. *I must retrieve the diary; take it away from the American woman. And transport it to Vienna.*

***

Bitsy slid into the back booth. She faced a crowd dancing in a circle to recognizable Greek music. The instruments used, the rhythms, the almost voice-like strains roused the senses and seemed to give feet a life of their own, forcing a person to the dance floor. Music that

97

evoked an abandonment enjoyed by the listeners as well as the dancers. The island mantra was: Life is to be savored and enjoyed. She tapped her finger tips on the table top in time to the music and waited for her martini to arrive.

Why did I turn down Dickie's invitation? She reached for a handful of toasted pita chips, noticing a brown spot on her right hand. An age spot, one her expensive concealer didn't cover on her relatively smooth hand. She spread her fingers in front of her. Her routinely manicured nails and the multitude of rings on her hand called attention to the spot. *It's getting harder to find myself attractive. My looks have been my currency, my value. How can I call myself a feminist?* She scanned the room for other older women. At least, she thought, I no longer compare myself to the young and beautiful.

The night life on Mykonos had changed dramatically since Bitsy had visited in the 1970s. More of a mixture of people came to the island these days, not just wealthy American tourists and retirees. Did the college crowd and twenty something's have an interest in Greek mythology or did they merely revel in the beach, food and music with no care about the history of this windswept island nestled close to the sacred island of Delos? She raised a fresh martini. Did they know of a time when females were worshiped and viewed as powerful deities in their own right? The twirling white handkerchief held high above the line of dancers passed by her table.

"Opa!" she shouted.

She sipped her drink and mentally argued with herself about how her beliefs didn't seem to be reflected in her behavior. She dunked a fat olive into her martini.

What would Artemis do with a man like Rick? Fleet of foot, swift with the bow and arrow, Artemis could easily stop a mere mortal man in his tracks, but would he be killed in the process? Would he submit from fear rather than desire? She gulped down the remains of her drink. The DJ changed the music from lively instrumental Greek songs to Nana Mouskouri's love songs. She gathered up her purse and shawl to return to her room. The lonely, white washed, sterile room. She scooted to the end of the booth. On the other side of the room stood Rick.

She hesitated to get up from her table just long enough for him to notice her change of mind. He waved and made his way through the tables around the dance floor toward the dark corner Bitsy had chosen earlier.

"What's up, my dear Bitsy girl?" He showed off the attractive gap between his front teeth. "Want to buy a hurt and thirsty guy a drink?"

99

"Hurt, huh?" She narrowed her eyes. She felt her cheeks flush. "Do women always have time for you when you want?"

"Okay, okay." He leaned in toward her. "Maybe I've been rejected before, but not in Greece, in June, by Elizabeth Bitsy Bowman."

He stood up and moved toward the opposite side of the booth. He slid onto the leather seat like a smooth skinned snake with gleaming eyes and a quick tongue. He had changed from his earlier yachtsman clothing into khaki shorts, what once were called Jesus sandals and a bright Greek blue and sunset orange shirt that reminded Bitsy of Hawaii except for the Greek key pattern in the fabric.

"I was just about to go to my room. As I told you earlier, it's been a long day." She scooted to the edge of the booth, her canvas bag held to her chest with one hand. "I asked if you wanted to meet me tomorrow."

"Right." Rick reached across the table. He gently pushed a stray strand of hair away from her eyes. His wide hand came to rest on her cheek. She felt his soft warm skin. *What would Artemis do?*

She turned her face away from him. He raised his hand above his head. "Okay, okay," he said. He got out of the booth before she managed to stand up. "Have a great night, honey."

Something clutched at her stomach. For one long moment throwing up was the only thing on her mind. All those lovely martinis and olives and pita chips. She took a sip of water and after plunging a hand into the glass, she sprinkled her face with droplets. She held her head back and closed her eyes. *Get me out of here.*

She gathered up her belongings and slid out of the booth.

Tomorrow I'll be surrounded by a group of women who know what Artemis would do. What wise women do with their lives and it's about time I get wise with my life at 60!

Shafts of daylight spread across the foot of her bed, creeping closer and closer to her half covered naked body. She had kicked off the crisp cotton sheet during the night, exposing a rounded hip and her lean back. She slept on her side with her slim arms crossed over her breasts as if sheltering them from the ocean breeze wafting across her bed. Gauzy drapes made whispering sounds against the tile floor and outside the open French doors the muffled sounds of fishermen clamoring into their boats could be heard over constantly lapping waves.

It would likely be another glorious Mediterranean day of sun, sand, retsina, lamb gyros, and other island delicacies. For the tourists it would be another lazy, restful day without the harried rush or the brutal busyness of home, wherever home might be. For some waking this particular morning, the day would be filled with the joy of mingling with like minds and learning new things. For others the day would be filled with a sense of ancient purpose unfolding toward completion.

In less than 24 hours two very different agendas would collide.

Chapter 12

Constantine wiped his sweaty forehead with one of his many hand stitched Irish linen handkerchiefs and waited for a string of clicks that indicated his use of a specific electronic devise that would route his call from Mykonos through Zurich to Boston and then to Milan so the caller ID would indicate the call was from Dr. William Stuart of Boston College.

He hummed to himself. The clicks sounded like a woman's stiletto heels crossing the marble floor of the Hotel Apollo lobby. *Women, my bane today.*

He noticed a swarm of colorful butterflies layering the hot pink geraniums bursting from the confines of worn terra cotta pots in one corner of his balcony. The scuffed tile floor showed years of wear and bleaching from the afternoon sun as it passed over the island toward a sea sunset. The morning was warm and he felt damp under his arms and in the middle of his back.

Click, click.........ring, ring.

"Hello, William," Francesca Campelli sounded breathless like a runner at the end of a race.

"I wish I were Dr. Stuart," said Constantine, "I am but his student assistant for the summer. He asked I call you about the Triple Goddess paper you promised him. He needs it before the fall semester begins. My name is George."

"Yes, George." Francesca's voice had regained its usual deep, resonating sound. "I suppose he's anxious to read it before I present it in September, right?"

"You know the Professor better than I do, Dr. Campelli, I am but the messenger." He cocked his head toward the ceiling thinking about Hermes and even Eros. Francesca was a beautiful woman and he thought of all women as objects of pleasure to be owned in any way possible.

***

"I do know him well, George. Tell him I'll have the paper to him in good time. Tell him also I'll be out of my office for a few days. I'm attending a conference on Mykonos to gather more data for the paper. Many women booksellers will be presenting their research on the Greek Goddesses. In fact I'm leaving later today. I hope my answer calms the nerves of William."

She looked around her office and drew in a deep breath. She savored the smell of the familiar leather bound volumes and musty parchment-filled folders she would take with her to the conference. She never tired of the feel of old books in embossed leather bindings, the texture of thin parchment and engraved pamphlets where fingerprints could be seen from years of handling before becoming a relic of the past and needing tender care to prevent disintegration. These were the things that always brought a mixture of tears and a twinkle to her large dark brown eyes.

***

"Yes, Dr. Campelli," Constantine replied, "I'll pass along your answer and have a great time at your conference. A bunch of women, huh, maybe I should attend." He laughed into the phone while pouring himself a scotch. "Dr. Stuart has left for a short trip, too, so no need to call him or email him. He'll contact you after he's read your paper."

"You would be welcomed at the conference, George; we women always enjoy educating men about our matriarchal past." She laughed, too. "Arrivederci and good luck to you, young man."

105

Instead of pushing the end button on his disposable cell, he stayed on the line.

After a few seconds, he said, "Are you there?"

"My dear, Constantine," the voice was deep and steady. "You always find a woman for your own purposes. This will catch up with you, I'm afraid."

He could hear the familiar arrogant tone of the current President of the Society, Johannes Myrick.

"What news from Mykonos?"

"I believe I have spotted the diary." His speech was rapid. When there was no immediate response, he repeated more slowly. "I believe I have spotted the diary."

"Where is it?"

"I caught a glimpse of it in an American woman's bag, one of those large bags they carry with them everywhere. Written on it was the name Odyssey Books. That's the name of a bookstore in Texas. Elizabeth Bowman is the American woman's name."

"Enough, answer my question. Do not give me unimportant information. If you spotted the diary as you said, your answer should have been, 'I have it.'" Johannes voice was raised. "Did you not retrieve it from her?"

"I haven't gotten close enough yet, but I'm working on it, sir. I did speak with her in the elevator and my room is next to hers. Fortuitous, no? "

"If I am hearing you, Constantine, you think you have found the diary and yet you do not have it. Some woman has it. What is it you are waiting for?"

Constantine wanted to slam the phone against the stucco wall of his hotel room, instead he said, "I'll get it."

After he heard the disconnecting click, he tossed the phone into his leather attaché case.

It landed next to his copy of the flyer for the bookseller's conference. There would be classes and discussion groups, renowned authors and speakers from all over the world and plenty of books and souvenirs to purchase. The four day Goddess conference, as he called it, would start later today with additional Summer Solstice activities for those who purchased the extended stay on Mykonos. He patted both his cheeks several times with his left hand. *There will be one woman who will be otherwise engaged long before the Summer Solstice.*

***

After the two cell phone hang-ups, Francesca gently placed her office phone in its cradle. *This trip may answer the mystery of Mayerling over one hundred and twenty-five*

107

years after the deaths. She tossed the items she was taking to the conference into her briefcase. She would call Washington, D.C. after she reached Mykonos and reacquainted herself with Bitsy Bowman.

Chapter 13

Pamela Jones arrived the evening before the conference and went quickly to the Mykonos museum to meet with the curator. She was the designated chairperson of this year's conference, which meant hours of preparation before the doors opened. From the backseat of the taxi, she leaned forward to catch a glimpse of the sea. Her breath slowed. Thoughts sifted through upcoming agenda items both at the conference and the plans for a special night for a few colleagues. She imagined sitting in a Sacred Circle on thickly tufted cushions embroidered with the signs and symbols of the seven primary Greek Goddesses.

Francesca had called her before she left England to let her know of the rather secret event. Seven women would leave Mykonos for Delos and each would be asked to focus on her own inner experiences as they relate to being feminine. While this year's conference at the museum would offer the study of Greek mythology in today's world or the study of the Greek Goddesses, the evening event would honor the Goddesses.

She paid the taxi driver and stood at the quarry rock curb for a few seconds before she approached the double doors of the museum. Inside the doors, she passed by icons and crosses attached to the walls.

When she first was introduced, as a student in Rome, to the differences and similarities between Greek and Roman Goddesses, she promised herself she would visit Greece. Years later she discovered this museum on Mykonos. It was small by usual museum standards. Its walls were of white quarry stone. Niches carved out of the stone held small treasures. Scattered rectangular wood tables held glass cases of precious metal objects, jewelry pieces and chards of mosaic covered clay once part of some ancient temple floor. The tables were arranged so that visitors could walk among them.

A carved wood desk, where visitors sign in and pay a nominal fee to enter the larger part of the museum, sat directly opposite the front doors. On her first visit, she was drawn to three paintings of a beautiful American hanging above the desk. Each portrait was painted at a different time in her life and depicted the three stages of a woman: Maiden, Mother and Crone, the Triple Goddess within all women. Upon her death, a few months before Pamela's first visit, this woman, who so loved Mykonos, donated the paintings to inspire women and to remind men of the regenerative nature of the female. Not one person throughout life, but three distinct entities circled together to represent birth, life and death/rebirth.

That was the beginning of her journey to make the myths relevant to today's women and empower them to treasure the feminine. Her bookstore in Sussex, Ladies in Reading, was dedicated to women's writings and the myths and fables of the feminine.

Today, she noticed these paintings were leaning against a side wall. *What's up with that?*

She knocked on the ornately carved door bearing a small gold sign with black letters that read, "PRIVATE." She knew this was Peter Gallenos's office even though he had another room where he met with visitors. Besides being curator, he was a Greek Gods and myths scholar and he had shown mild interest in learning more about the Goddesses which she appreciated as an indication of his respect for her.

What a difference from London boys and so called gentlemen, she thought. Her problems there pressed against her heart. She was hoping for some sort of peace among women friends. *This is a vacation, no worries here. Time to be refreshed.*

She knocked again on the thick wooden door. *Where can Peter be? He knew I was coming.* She looked right and left down the dark hallway. She had expected to see him scurrying around in order to finish up the display stations for tomorrow's opening.

***

Peter sank to his knees in front of a prized statue of the Virgin Mary in an adjacent room to the main chapel attached to the museum. He was a man of ritual who sought and found solace at his many altars. This particular altar reflected his mother's Catholic upbringing, an altar at his home honored his Russian heritage and the altar in the Museum Chapel was Hellenic with an emphasis on the Gods of the sea and fishermen.

"Hear me, Mother Mary, I ask for a successful gathering and the opportunity to be in the presence of great antiquarian books that are the foundation of my life and, if it is to be, that I may hold for my own a new possession from long ago. You know I will never do harm to any object that pleases me."

He placed his right hand on the altar's edge and pushed himself up from the kneeling position. While his health was excellent, he had become weak with age and feared the time would come when he couldn't bow down at any of his altars. To bow and ask for God's forgiveness.

Chapter 14

The first day of the conference began with a blue topaz sea sparkling under the cloudless sky. A morning where the reflections of the Aegean would be felt on brown arms and legs, on carafes of Blood Marys, as well as on the lips of early drinkers. Bitsy smeared moisturizer over her sun-kissed face. She had packed her ditty bag for classes and presentations and ordered a simple breakfast of oatmeal and fruit from room service. The opening speeches at the museum were scheduled to begin at eleven o'clock with a break for lunch before the actual conference began at two o'clock.

Before the welcoming speeches, her mission was to find Peter. She wanted him to take responsibility for Anna's books. She worried they could be damaged or lost. She had kept them with her when out of her hotel room and under the bed pillow during the night. *Only when they are out of my hands can I relax.* This was, after all, a vacation of sorts and she didn't want to think about someone else's stuff, even her best friend's. Peter was an expert in ancient and very old texts and he spoke five languages. She believed he would be able to shed some light on the origin of the books and even translate the writings. He might even offer an appraised value for them.

***

Pamela put the finishing touches on her makeup before leaving her hotel room for the conference. After she searched the museum yesterday for what seemed like an hour, she found Peter in a small chapel addition on the side of the ancient building. He stood there in silence and turned toward her when she entered the room. Within seconds his wide grin changed his usual solemnity to show pleasure in seeing her. She asked him if he would attend her lectures on the feminine in Greek myths. Francesca told her he had requested a balance of lectures between her female focus and classes on Apollo, the Sun God, Jason and Paris.

She knew his focus was on male deities and she didn't want to alienate him with her strong beliefs. She hoped for an opportunity to win him over. She began the visit by asking him about the Triple Goddess paintings. He told her he was disappointed the administrators of the museum insisted he remove them from storage for the conference and hang them in the main foyer.

115

As she punched the elevator button, she thought about the rather misogynous comments he made. *He showed me a different side of himself today. One I don't like.*

***

Bitsy decided against her strappy espadrilles and slipped her lotioned feet into silver Nike's to better handle the cobblestone walk up the hill to the Museum. Swift of feet was Hermes, but so was Artemis. She tried to schedule a meeting with Peter before 11o'clock, but was told he was unavailable until the lunch break at noon.

She hung up the phone.

"Rats!" She took one last look at herself in the large oval mirror on the back of her hotel room door. *Another day and looking good.*

***

Shiny blue glazed terracotta pots filled with bright fuchsia colored geraniums edged the winding walkway toward weathered wood double doors. Tall iron plant stands of trailing pink bougainvillea were placed in front of the opened doors. Impressive for a small museum. Greece's blue and white flag, attached to a gold colored pole that extended from the stone arch over the entrance, made soft slapping sounds in the ocean breeze.

Conference participants were greeted by Peter in the

square foyer. He wore an elaborate long black robe trimmed in gold braid with an embroidered Greek key design down the front panel and across his shoulders like epaulets. An oversized silver cross etched with grape and fig leaves hung around his neck.

He was a layman and the museum had never been used as a place of worship, but he preferred to dress like a priest while there. The small building attached to the rear of the museum, furnished as a chapel, was there at his insistence. Over the years, many visitors took time to pray and reflect in the quiet, cool interior of the chapel with its rough stone walls and three rows of rich patina darkened wood pews. Glittering silver icons of Christ were surrounded by small votive candles on an altar draped in rich black velvet cloth.

Peter straightened his spine, pushed back his shoulders and raised his chin. He always assumed this pose when greeting visitors. His profile, a personal disappointment, didn't approach the classic Greek or Roman. His Russian heritage showed in the sharper edge to the tip of his nose.

"*Kalispera*, welcome." He waved one hand in the direction of the registration table. "Most pleased to see you here this morning."

The first of the booksellers crossed the threshold and into the foyer.

They formed a line to pick up name tags and conference schedules. Peter remained at the door, hands clasped behind his back. His smile widened briefly as he acknowledged each individual crossing into the museum, then his affect returned to a practiced blank, not happy or sad, absorbed or vacant, interested or bored. He knew most of the participants from many other conferences he had attended over the years. Gatherings throughout Europe and the Baltic area.

His eyes glazed over with memories that transported him away from the chattering women who poured into his museum. Memories of another time and place. The time and place where his quest for older and older historical treasure began. His breath became shallow. His eyelids closed.

"Mr. Gallenos," a woman's voice breathed in his ear, "Are you falling asleep?" She laughed as she tapped his shoulder. "I promise booksellers aren't boring." Several women had pushed closer to him. When he opened his eyes all were grinning and batting their eyelashes.

***

Bitsy met up with Pamela in their hotel lobby and now they both waited in the museum foyer for Francesca. *I do love my female friends, but my heart is set on spending time with Dickie.*

A whistling sound behind her swept away her day dream.

"Bitsy," Francesca called from the walkway, "and Pamela, my two favorite bookworms!"

Chapter 15

Bitsy rested her hands on the granite table top and waited for Peter to return with a carafe of retsina. Lunch at an out of the way, non-tourist, beach bar was a nice respite from thoughts about Rick and Constantine. Thoughts that interfered with her ability to attend to Francesca's opening speech about her afternoon relationship class centered on Demeter and Persephone.

She watched Peter standing at the bar. In his mid-70s with unruly, thick hair as white as the common white washed buildings of Mykonos, she wondered about his love life. *What are you doing, Bitsy? Leave the man alone.*

He stood next to her to pour her a glass of the bitter wine. She looked up into his deep brown eyes that popped out of his leathery face. *Some women might find him handsome.* Before he put the carafe on the table, he patted her bare shoulder. His hand was soft. She knew he wore the ubiquitous white cotton gloves when he handled old and delicate museum books and objects. His hands were several shades lighter than the rest of his skin. *Is it too late for me to benefit from daily glove wearing?* With the carafe of wine in the center of the table, Peter sat down opposite her.

"Ms. Bowman, I must tell you about my latest find, an illustrated volume comparing Greek and Turkish symbolism used in folktales."

Peter called ancient stories folktales rather than myths.

"That sounds interesting, but I'm curious your choice of words. Folktales rather than myths? And please, call me Bitsy.

"I didn't want to offend. Bitsy. A name that suits you."

"Thanks. But back to my question. You're the curator of a Greek museum, on a Greek island, just a few miles away from the birthplace of Apollo and Artemis, where Hercules killed the Giants of Mt. Olympus. It's one of the Sacred Isles. Myths surround you."

"It's my Russian ancestry. I grew up on folktales. You must have read some as a bookseller. The Snow Maiden, for instance."

"I thought it was the Snow Queen."

"A fairy tale, not a folktale. In Russian lore, it's a maiden."

After the waiter removed the empty wine carafe and replaced it with a pot of espresso, Bitsy reached into her tote bag and pulled out Anna's two books.

"I'd like you to look at these old books, Peter. They belong to a friend, well, actually, to her husband and had been concealed or packed or forgotten in an old trunk in their attic. She, my friend, is interested in their origin and value. I am, too."

She moved the coffee pot and a small crystal vase from the middle of the table and set the books in front of Peter, side by side.

He opened the smallest book.

"Not much here," he said, "I've seen many of these diaries over the years. It's old, but old doesn't mean valuable."

Bitsy chewed on the inside of her cheek. *Old doesn't mean valuable. Is that true about me?* Peter read a sentence or two of the small book.

"This diary's dated in the late 1800s, as you know, and is from Austria. The writer mentions Wien, Vienna, in the first entry. It appears to be the record of an important time in the life of the author, probably meant to pass along to her heirs. The end the 19th Century in Austria was splendid indeed, with art, science, politics, and literature in reach of the common man. Many kept diaries of those exhilarating and changing times." Peter closed the book and set it aside.

"So this book isn't museum quality?" Bitsy dropped a dollop whipped cream into her espresso. "Too bad. I was hoping to retire."

"Oh no, we need smart booksellers like you who are willing to find new and forgotten books to offer in your bookshop and at our conferences, but let me look at the other book."

His right hand stopped an inch above the red leather book. He looked up at Bitsy before he picked it up in his the gloved hands. He held it up at arm's length. His eyes glazed over, as if hypnotized. His lack of movement and outstretched arms attracted stares from others. He didn't notice.

"Are you alright?" Bitsy reached her hand across the table and grabbed one of his wrists.

"No," he whispered. He hadn't blinked since picking up the book. "No, my dear, I'm not alright. I must take these books safely to my house. Immediately."

He pulled the red leather book to his chest. Using only his legs, he shoved his chair away from the table.

"What's wrong?" Bitsy gripped the edge of the table top as she followed suit and pushed her chair from the table.

He turned his back to her and quickened his pace toward the street.

She tossed some money on the table. The small book remained where Peter had left it. She dropped it into her tote bag.

"Wait for me."

When she caught up with him, he placed one arm around her waist and again whispered, "We'll talk once we are in my home."

***

Peter's house was one of the closely built white stucco homes lining street after street on Mykonos. All had brown or blue painted wooden doors, wide planked shutters, baskets and baskets of bougainvillea on the front landings, the balconies, and planted in a variety of window boxes. Inside, color continued to have a place. Blue, the most prominent, with touches of bright yellow and vermillion. He surprised her with the suggestion they share a split of champagne.

While he got the wine and glasses from the kitchen, she wandered past a wall of books to admire his collection

124

of sea shells under glass on a large coffee table. She moved toward the double doors leading to his balcony. Out of the corner of her eye she noticed something shiny behind an ornate folding room divider. She peeked around the screen and saw an altar with Russian looking icons on the wall, standing jeweled crosses and candles of descending size on a lace table runner. A kneeling bench was tucked under the altar.

Peter's voice from the kitchen caused her to swing back toward the balcony doors. *Did I see something I shouldn't have, something private or secret?* She didn't want him to catch her snooping.

"Under different circumstances, I would suggest we sit on the balcony," Peter said. He placed a silver tray with two glasses of champagne on the coffee table next to the red leather book. "Please come sit." He emptied his glass before Bitsy took her first sip.

"This may be a long sought after diary; one many have not believed existed while others have been dedicated to find. Over the years the tale of the missing diary has become part of a legend, a mystery that has yet to be solved." He paused before he continued. "The true story of the death of Crown Prince Rudolph of Austria-Hungary."

He took a deep breath. His shoulders shook. "Do you know the story of Rudolph and his mistress, Marie Vetsera?" He laid a hand on the cover of the book as if it were a Bible. A book of truth.

"I know there was a murder-suicide at a hunting lodge called Mayerling and that the ruling Hapsburgs were left without an heir. Are you saying this is the diary?"

"It looks like the diary as described in rumor and folk tales. The red leather, the birds, the initials on the spine."

"That doesn't sound like a scientific or forensic way to know if this is the diary, Peter."

"Ah, but there's much more." He opened the book and motioned for Bitsy to move closer. "The use of Italian as well as German is right, the use of numbers as code is right, and even without dating the paper and ink. I believe this could be the personal diary of Emperor Franz Joseph."

"You said personal diary. I read about secret diaries kept by some monarchs. And this could be one?"

"The story goes that Emperor Franz Joseph, Rudolph's father, kept a diary, in which he documented his son's affairs of the heart, other indiscretions, including the number and names of illegitimate children and his fears for the dynasty due to his son's affiliations. Most importantly, rumors suggest the diary contains a detailed account of what happened at Mayerling when Rudolph and Marie died. This wasn't the Royal Diary to be displayed in the Schonbrunn Palace after his death. This was a diary no one was to read."

"So what do we do next?"

Instead of answering, he asked, "Who else knows about this book?"

"Well," she hesitated. "We know." She made a tittering bird like sound and looked over his head at a woven rug hanging on the wall. "Anna knows and her husband, of course…" Her voice trailed off until it was only one rapid breath after another.

"You didn't show it to Pamela or Francesca? I know they're friends of yours."

"No, I just wanted to get rid of the books, to get them to you and go on with my holiday."

"What about hotel employees?"

"You're making me nervous, Peter." Bitsy wriggled her body to the edge of the couch. She bent over her legs and hugged them.

"I really do need to know, Bitsy, so try and remember."

"There was a man in the hotel elevator, who said he noticed my conference flyer. It was in my tote bag. And when I looked where he was looking, the red book was sticking out a little bit."

"Enough for him to see the birds?"

"Probably." She sat up and scooted away from him. "What's this about? So what if this is the diary of a long dead Emperor. The world has gone on without this book or the Hapsburg dynasty, for that matter."

Peter stood up and began to pace the room. "The importance of finding the Emperor's diary is to be determined." He ran a hand through his thick hair, "How do I help you to understand?"

Abruptly, he sat down so close to Bitsy, she had to lean back against the arm of the couch to avoid his hitting her. "Believe it or not, there are many people who are willing to go to great lengths to find and confiscate royal memorabilia, many people wanting to rewrite history."

His eyes had grown bright, his pupils were dilated. His words seemed to catch in his throat. "I think I fail to explain myself."

"So it's about the contents not the age and royal provenance? It's the death details. Wow!"

"Time will tell. Obviously, no one living knows what was written in this book, but it's likely to describe a family in turmoil and the ultimate heartbreak of losing a child." Peter wiped his forehead with the back of his gloved hand.

"So can you translate?"

"It will take some time and I have no time until after the conference."

"No worries, I hoped you would keep the books until I leave for home and I hope to stay for several days after the conference ends."

"I'll put both books in the museum safe this afternoon. Don't worry, but I must ask you not to tell anyone about the diaries."

"You're scaring me again, Peter. Am I in some sort of danger because of these books?"

"Just be cautious, as I said, there are people, groups, who are capable of all sorts of behavior to attain their goals. And that means finding the diary."

Chapter 16

Anna poured another cup of coffee. She reread Bitsy's text message sent before she left DFW last night. WILL MISS YOU. REMEMBER TO TAKE CARE OF YOURSELF. AND WISH ME LUCK WITH DICKIE.

She let go of a sigh. She put her phone down, but kept her hand on it as if that kept Bitsy near. She wanted to hear her voice, her words of encouragement to limit time at the rehabilitation facility with Joe.

She knew Bitsy would be busy, likely smoozing with colleagues and maybe smooching with Rick. She hoped she would text or Facebook as she usually did when she was on one of her trips.

She needed her more than ever this time.

Anna admitted she still felt obligated to daily hospital visits to show the rehab therapists she was invested in her husband's treatment. His speech continued to improve and he was able to use a walker as long as the therapist held him up with a gait belt. When discussing his upcoming discharge, she was informed a wheelchair had been ordered and she would need to be trained to assist him when transferring from bed to chair and toilet.

She wanted to be anywhere but Texas. To be on her own, to be free of responsibilities to others, namely Joe or Josef.

Her coffee had turned cold. Time to make another trip to Dallas.

She sat on a plastic chair against the tile wall of the rehab gym. Joe finished his walking exercise and stood grasping the frame of a silver walker. His tight fists turned his pale skin purple as if bruised. His loss of weight was concealed under a baggy sweat suit. He needed a haircut. His occupational therapist continued to monitor his morning shaves. *Another new task for me.*

"Anna." Joe said. He lifted a hand off the walker to wave.

His therapist tightened the gait belt. "Take it slow, don't lose your balance."

Anna stood up and pointed to his wheelchair. "I'm going to take you back to your room."

"Good." His smile was crooked, his facial muscles not completely restored. His voice didn't sound like his. It wasn't slurred anymore, but was deeper, more guttural than normal. It sounded like he needed to cough, all the time.

In his room, she tried to get comfortable in the faux leather recliner jammed against the window sill. Joe sat in front of her.

"I'd like to go to bed."

"No, Joe, you're to stay up, work on core muscles." She pointed to her ribs. "Besides, you have another therapy session in thirty minutes."

A frown stretched from temple to temple. He stuck his tongue out like an angry child and rolled his wheelchair closer until their knees touched.

"I know you want to talk about my name, my family history. Did you find the book in the attic?"

Anna nodded her head. He was being so matter-of-fact as if nothing had happened that would disturb her or their relationship. He sounded as if they were about to discuss his last business trip. She swallowed a scream.

"Yes, Joe, I found the book or books, I should say, and I sent them to Greece with Bitsy. What do you think of that?"

"What do you mean? There was only one book for you to find in the attic. A Bible, my family's Bible. Is that what you sent with Bitsy?"

"I didn't find a Bible. I found two very old dairies. Written in the late 1800s."

He gripped the arm rests of the wheelchair. He spoke slowly, exaggerating each syllable and each word as if she didn't understand English.

"There is a Bible in the attic. It lists all the names and the dates of family births and deaths. I thought it would satisfy you about my real name, my family's heritage."

Anna was sure that if he could stand on his own, he would have been in her face. As it was, he could only spit words out and keep a grip on the arms of the wheelchair. His eyes bulged and his cheeks were puffed out.

"I'm telling you what I found when I searched a small trunk in the attic. I didn't find a Bible, but I did find two very intriguing books that may be valuable. Bitsy's going to show them to an expert at her bookseller's conference."

Joe's color went from a flushed pink to ash. He slumped against the back of his chair.

"I never went through the entire trunk after it was left to me by my grandmother. I opened it once and found layers of old military uniforms, molting feathers, and braided epilates. Where were the books?"

"At the bottom. I had to practically empty the trunk to get to them. And, by the way, no business papers were in there!"

"Don't be angry at me, please. At my grandmother's request, I agreed to leave the trunks undisturbed. After looking at the first layer of old uniforms, I never opened the trunks again. Does Bitsy think they're worth something?"

"That's what she's going to find out. But, I'm more interested in hearing about just who you are. The books only add to what I'm calling the mystery of Josef Trost and his…"

A knock on the door stopped her in midsentence.

A med nurse came in with cups of pills and a pitcher of water. As she left, Joe's attending physician came in for daily rounds. Anna looked at the room clock when he left. Less than fifteen minutes before Joe's next therapy. Not nearly enough time for the discussion she wanted.

"Look, Anna. I know nothing about these books. What I know of my history is this: My father left Germany for England when Hitler annexed Austria. My grandfather was from Berlin, but my grandmother and great grandfather were Austrian. He first married a Russian opera singer he met in Vienna. They had no children. She returned to

Russia shortly after they married and got an annulment. My parents, knowing there were rumors of a Russian link in our family, changed our name when I was a toddler in the early 1950s because they wanted to move to the United States. McCarthyism scared them so they took a very English name. All the important dates and names are documented in the family Bible."

For a moment or two, silence filled the stuffy hospital room. Anna checked the clock again.

"I'm going now. Your OT will be here soon. We can continue this conversation later."

"You're going to Google this information, aren't you?"

"What do you think?"

"I think you should go back up into the attic and find the Bible."

"I don't care about names and dates written in a Bible, Joe. I care about the people, your family members who decided to alter reality, to fabricate a history, to teach you to lie."

A knock and then the usual greeting from his therapist signaled Anna's visit was over.

Chapter 17

Pamela's cheery "hello" greeted Bitsy as she made her way down the aisle in the museum auditorium.

Bitsy settled back against the tufted chair. After she took her seat, she motioned for Pamela to sit next to her.

"I will when I finish stacking these papers for Francesca's class."

Her class on Demeter. Just what I need to hear. I need to find my fearless self if those old books actually put me in danger. "Surely not," she whispered to herself, "Not over old books."

"What did you say, luv?" Pamela slid into the seat next to her.

"Nothing, really, just I'm looking forward to this class. And yours on Artemis. She's my favorite Goddess."

"I love Athena. Like to think of myself as creative and, of course, wise."

The lights dimmed to indicate the class was about to begin. Bitsy patted Pamela's hand.

The worst thing Peter had said was that she couldn't tell anyone about the books, nothing, and for her this promise would be difficult to keep.

Maybe I'll text Anna. No, I don't want to put her in danger, if there is danger. What a bother!

***

The first day of classes wound down. Brief hugs and blown kisses were dispersed to recognized acquaintances and friends. Bitsy wanted only to stretch out on her hotel bed, order a martini and review all that Peter had told her. To her surprise, as she passed through the museum's double doors, her thoughts returned to Rick. And the long evening ahead. Another evening alone on beautiful, romantic Mykonos. *But maybe not. Hope springs they say*

She hummed a happy tune. Rather than waiting for a taxi, she decided to walk back to the hotel. She was free of the books and wanted to celebrate.

The geraniums outside her hotel nodded heavy heads in the last slice of daylight. She could see the setting sun between buildings as it floated toward the sea. She crossed the marble floor of the hotel lobby. Someone called her name in a thick foreign accent. She spun around. The concierge waved a hand above his head. He motioned for her to come to the desk, but he met her mid lobby.

"Did you call my name, Bitsy Bowman?"

"Oh, yes, Ms. Bowman," said Nikko Pappas, his shiny gold name tag was large enough for her to read without her glasses. "I have an invitation for you." He held out a pale blue envelope embossed with an anchor and bearing her name in graceful script.

"My, my. Who could this be from?" She took the envelope and pressed it to her heart. Her thoughts full of mischief and easily shifted from Rick to the mysterious Constantine Verone and back again. *Maybe an evening with a man will help my feminine goddess express herself.*

Thoughts of Peter and his warning surfaced. *No danger from Rick.* She nodded her thanks to the concierge and turned toward the lobby bar. She forgot about going to her room, but she paused in mid-step. Her thoughts on Constantine. *Is he a danger? What would he care about old Austrian books? I'm sure he's Italian.*

She stifled a giggle. At this point in her so called vacation, it didn't matter if it was Rick or Constantine sending her a written invitation to ask for her company, even though such a thing was hardly the current custom. These days people unfriend each other on Facebook and lovers send Dear John texts. She clutched the blue envelope tighter and entered the hotel bar.

She slid into one of the black leather booths and flung her tote onto the seat beside her. She decided to wait until her drink arrived before she opened the envelope, to savor her romantic fantasies awhile longer. Rick had been a loss to this point and she wondered if she was up to a dalliance with Constantine.

Her usual vodka martini was placed on the table. She pulled her glasses from her tote. She fingered the envelope for a moment before opening it.

The note was handwritten in a stylized script, a mixture of cursive and printing with enough gracefulness to indicate a female hand. She sipped her drink.

You are invited for an overnight excursion to the Sacred Island of Delos. The evening will be for seven women to experience and learn about the seven major Greek Goddesses through ritual and a pre-Summer Solstice celebration. You will need to be at the western most dock at 8:00 this evening. As this is a unique event, you are asked to tell no one. See you there,

Francesca Campelli.

Bitsy turned the note over and over in her hand. She wasn't sure what she was looking for. A logo. A phone number to RSVP. But nothing was there except the handwritten note from Francesca.

I wonder why she didn't mention this today at the conference. She finished her drink before she searched her tote for her cell phone. *Rats! Francesca said she's staying with a local friend and I don't know her name.*

Back in her hotel room, Bitsy ordered a pot of coffee. The martini at the bar had been followed with a glass of ouzo. *What was I thinking? Too strong a drink before a boat trip.*

She attempted to call Peter to get Francesca's local phone number, but he didn't answer the museum phone. She did talk to Pamela to ask if she had been invited.

As she waited for the coffee, she surveyed her unpacked clothes folded neatly on the blue cotton bed quilt. *Pamela made this excursion sound intriguing, after all Delos was the birthplace of Zeus's twins, Apollo and Artemis, a sacred island.*

She began to sort through her choices of outfits. Her mind on her favorite goddess's story. The mythological twins who were said to be the personification of the moon and sun. Artemis, the divine Mood Goddess and Apollo, the Sun God. The male was described as strong and highly intelligent while the female was depicted as a strong hunter and protector of the night. Their myth suggested Delos was a place surrounded by protective strength and a charged energy which could be felt among its lasting ruins.

This could be a life changing trip, like the time I slept among the red mesas of Sedona where extremely powerful forces are said to calm some and agitate others. It was there I found the strength to get my first divorce. Maybe, a night on Delos will free me from my search for a man.

The most pressing dilemma was her usual one. What to wear. And in this case, what to take for a sleep over without a hotel accommodation. Pamela was more laid back and casual than she was and more likely to have the perfect outfit to wear. Francesca, for all her glamour, had spent several months hiking through the jungles of Central America. *I'm the unprepared. No sleeping in the nude tonight and no way I'll take my lace nightie either.*

She tossed aside several gauzy palazzo pants and skimpy tops she had selected for Rick's pleasure and since he hadn't cooperated with her fantasies, her enthusiasm for a celebration on Delos grew.

She stepped out of the sultry off the shoulder black dotted Swiss dress she wore to the conference and the sandals she had carried in her tote. Her Nikes would be fine for the stone and dirt paths and mosaic floors she remembered from a previous visit to Delos. None of the clothes she had stacked on her bed were appropriate. She turned and sorted through the dresser drawer where she had placed her most casual and least favorite travel clothes.

A pair of cargo pants and a T-shirt with Austin City Limits printed in block letters over the silhouette of a flying bat caught her eye. She, momentarily, remembered a lovely evening with a former lover, sipping champagne and watching the nighttime exodus of the bats from under the bridges in Austin. She pushed a strand of hair from her eyes before she shook out the wrinkles in the shirt. She raised and lowered her tense shoulders. She looked at the dreary clothes and questioned her decision to go on this overnight trip, but being alone was worse than looking like a refugee.

She zipped up her duffle bag. What would the locals in Middlecreek think about a sleep over with ancient lions guarding modern day Goddesses? She checked her lipstick in the mirror and ran a hand through her hair. *There's no way I'm homesick. But I worry about Anna and her Joe.*

On the elevator ride to the lobby, she texted Anna.

HEADED FOR A NIGHT ON DELOS. SACRED ISLAND.
SOME SORT OF GODDESS CELEBRATION. SENDING HUGS
AND PRAYERS FOR YOU AND JOE. NO CELL COVERAGE ON
ISLAND. MORE LATER.

Tourists must leave Delos before the sun set, which
explained Francesca's desire to keep the trip secret. Pamela
said city authorities would frown upon the plans if
informed, and Peter would get into trouble since he helped
with the arrangements. Another secret with Peter, she
thought.

Chapter 18

The phone rang in Bitsy's room moments after she closed her door. The tinny, vibrating ring created a grating sound in Rick's ear. He cradled the phone between his shoulder and chin as he finished buttoning his fresh linen shirt. He planned to leave Mykonos tomorrow afternoon to accompany his classic car to Piraeus. Tonight he wanted to see Bitsy and entice her to bail out of the conference and sail with him to the mainland for a day or two in Athens. She was a little forward for his old fashioned taste, but she was attractive, intelligent and seemed interested in him.

His business persona as an advertising mogul was that of a hard driving, ruthless alpha male. Many people thought his only interest beyond making and spending money was adding notches to his belt, either from client takeovers or wooing the ladies. He laughed at this thought of wooing ladies. *Does anyone use those words anymore? I guess I am old fashioned.* He nodded his head and pressed the phone closer to his ear. His call was transferred to the front desk. All calls transferred after six rings.

When asked if he wanted to leave a message for Ms. Bowman, he hesitated. Her angry tone when she refused his apology and invitation for sharing drinks replayed in his head. "No, no message."

I'll catch up with her in the morning and try another apology.

***

Seconds after Rick's call, Bitsy's phone rang again. Constantine tapped his right index finger on the marble topped credenza in his hotel suite. *Where are you, my sassy looking woman? As you Americans say, I'm getting roiled up.*

He stopped drumming his finger and reached up to smooth his slicked back hair. He was due to leave Mykonos on the morning ferry to Piraeus to meet his superiors at the King George Hotel in Athens. *I'm supposed to arrive with the diary.* The diary he didn't find in the Bitsy's room. And he hadn't seen it in her tote bag during the conference classes.

When the operator picked up his call, he slammed the receiver down. The phone bounced off the credenza and crashed to the tiled floor.

"*Merda*! Now I need to find a woman as well as a book." He picked up the phone and threw it across the

145

room. It landed outside the open balcony door. He shivered although his room was still warmed by the evening sun. Above his balcony railing, he saw lights of several boats bob among gentle waves. *Oh, to be fishing, fishing in the sea with a Greek nymph at my side.*

He stepped onto the balcony and bent to pick up the phone. When he stood up, the sight of the sea reminded him that if he didn't find the diary, he might find himself among the fishes. "So, where are you off to, my American lady?" he said to a pot of geraniums balanced on the thick balcony rail. "Where?"

***

Rick made a few business calls before he went downstairs. His solo plan was to have a drink, return to his room for a room service dinner, and cap off the evening with some ouzo and a good book.

Constantine had other plans. He must find Bitsy. He knew he couldn't rest until he did.

Chapter 19

The faded blue painted boat was smaller than Bitsy would have wanted under usual circumstances, but her excitement erased any fear. She sat squeezed between Pamela and Francesca.

Francesca told the group that Peter had agreed to provide the boat and boatman and indicated he would take any heat from authorities if it came to that. She said she had recruited a local folklorian to preside over the group and a pre-Summer Solstice celebration.

Bitsy looked at her. She wanted to ask why she was invited, but, as the boat was pushed away from the dock, she decided to just go with the flow.

"I'm sure many of you have questions about why you were selected for this trip and what to expect from a night on Delos." Francesca raised her voice above the boat motor and the strong waves clamoring to be heard and felt. The spray was cold even in the warm air. "All will be known after we arrive at the sleep over site."

"You look like the Cheshire cat that swallowed the canary," Bitsy said. The other women laughed.

A large wave slapped the front of the boat as it dipped toward the water.

She grabbed Pamela's arm. "I don't like this."

Pamela nodded her agreement, but didn't speak.

The boatman adjusted the motor and the rocking motion eased. Sighs filled the air space. In the relative quiet, Bitsy began to reflect on what a privilege it was to be able to spend the night among relics that were present where Artemis was born. *My goddess, the warrior goddess.* A new resolve rose up in her. She sat back against the side of the boat and her eyes rose toward the evening sky. She watched lights on the wing tips of an airplane cross overhead.

The boat sliced into small white caps. She shifted her body and placed a hand on the outer rim of the faded skiff. Her hair whipped by the wind.

"Dear Lord, thank you for your hedge of protection," she said under her breath. The wind picked up. She wiped hair from her mouth and turned back to the group of huddled women.

"How much further is it to the island?" Pamela shouted.

"We'll land soon," Francesca said. "You'll notice a change in the sound of the motor when we slow for landing and, perhaps, you'll be able to see in twilight the twin lions placed on the island to protect Apollo and Artemis."

The guardians of Delos remain. The ancient lions and the mysteries of the Greek islands increased Bitsy's immediate level of courage. A new found calm seemed to grow with each dip of the bow and slap of the dark water against the small blue boat.

Courage and strength would be needed in the hours ahead.

Chapter 20

"You're the concierge. Why cannot you tell me the whereabouts of Ms. Bitsy Bowman?" Constantine's voice was several octaves higher than usual. "She may be lost on the island or at sea." Again, he shivered at the thought of the endless sea outside the hotel doors. "I'm a new friend of Ms. Bowman. We were to have dinner together this evening." His teeth snapped shut.

***

Constantine's shouts were heard across the lobby where Rick stood near the opening into the bar. He caught Bitsy's name. He turned to see a man with clenched fists leaning over the concierge's counter. Menacing was the word that came to mind. In three long strides, he stood next to him, invading his space. He put one large suntanned arm on the marble counter.

"Couldn't help hearing you ask about a friend of mine, Mister. Maybe I can help you. Why don't you come with me into the bar and we'll talk over a drink?"

Constantine pushed himself away from the counter and away from Rick's outstretched arm. He faced Rick and put his hands behind his back. He rocked onto his heels.

"I beg your pardon, were you speaking to me, sir? I do not know you and I have no business with you, I doubt. Please to excuse me but I have reason to worry about a friend."

"Funny fellow, my longtime friend never mentioned you, so I'm wondering just what's going on here?"

"It's nothing to you. I have recently met the charming Signora Bowman and I expected to see her this evening. But sorry I've been told she has left the hotel. I hope I am not saying this to you without her welcome. If you are indeed her friend, perhaps you could tell me her location."

***

Constantine watched as Rick's grin disappeared and deep furrows blanketed his forehead. His piercing blue eyes glinted in the bright lobby lights. "You must be mistaken, Mister, if Ms. Bowman were leaving the island I would know about it."

"Well, not a bother. I'll continue on to my dinner. If you will but excuse me." Constantine stepped away from the counter. He straightened his shoulders and ran flat hands down the front of his white linen jacket.

"No problem." Rick took one step toward him. "I'm just putting you on notice, stay away from my friend."

"As you wish." Constantine bowed his head toward Rick as he backed away.

***

Rick turned toward the concierge who had kept his head down during this confrontation between the two hotel guests.

"I need to know who that man is, he makes me nervous."

"I'm sorry Mr. Bennett; I'm not permitted to speak of the guests of the hotel. I'm sure you understand this privacy rule."

"I just want to know if he's a regular guest or here for the bookseller's conference at the museum."

"Again, I cannot answer your personal questions. Perhaps you can ask those at the conference you speak of."

Rick found a seat at the bar in the hotel lounge and ordered a Crown and Seven. He wondered if the bartender knew what a Seven was. He reached for the basket of pita chips and looked into the bar mirror to see if he could glimpse the tables in the adjoining dining room. No sign of Constantine and none of Bitsy.

"Keep them coming," he told the bartender. He shook his drained glass. *This is going to be a long night.*

Chapter 21

Anna opened a can of Tuppence's favorite tuna soufflé gourmet cat food. She pulled a chintz patterned bowl across the cool granite countertop. Her movements were slow; many thoughts circled in her head like a fair ground carrousel, each one a horse of a different color. Joe was Josef, she wasn't a Tudor but a Trost, all the lovely English traditions she embraced as part of her life were meaningless, now merely reminders of her husband's lies.

What had replaced those treasured traditions? Questions. Germans and Austrians replaced the British heritage with rumors of a Russian consort. She was now part of a family who fled Austria. Why? What other secrets could be uncovered? Were they communists? And who was the Austrian great-grandfather? The one alive when the diaries were written.

The empty bowl on the wood floor rattled. Tuppence was hungry, her paws scratched the rim.

"I'm hungry, too, my sweet, hungry for answers, for understanding, for compassion." She had none of those things this morning.

She opened the screened door to the back patio and made her way to a green and white striped glider. Its canopy fluttered in a soft warm breeze. She tugged at the deep pocket of her quilted rose colored robe and found the wad of tissues she kept handy. So many tears. It was difficult to distinguish between tears of joy at Joe's improvement and tears of sadness that he wasn't 100% recovered and tears of self-pity. She didn't want to be saddled with a disabled spouse. Her merry-go-round thoughts always came back to the most important questions.

Who was Ms. Anna Trost? And did she want what Anna Tudor wanted?

She picked up her delicate china cup from the wrought iron side table, at the bottom a sheen of lemon juice floated atop the last swallow of Earl Grey tea. She wrapped her hands around the cold cup, covering the familiar china pattern. Buttercup, her favorite. Very English. She slid the cup onto its saucer. She tucked her hands under her legs and counted to ten. Her breath slowed with each count.

A cardinal sped by her ear before it landed on a lichen covered princess statue holding a small mirror. She had watched it many times fly from tree limb to mirror and back again. She believed the bird was captivated with its image. A frenzied attempt to get to its reflection.

Who do I see in my mirror? Can I be the same happily married woman when the life I counted on has been shattered?

Something foreign and frightening had accompanied Joe's stroke, something more damaging than coping with his physical deficits. *I've been betrayed by my own denials, my own fabrications.* She covered her eyes with both hands. *There's nothing to see except the emptiness of a life without dreams or trust.* She fumbled in her pocket for a tissue.

When she stood up the startled bird dashed across the back yard and was lost from sight deep within the lush leaves of an oak tree. Fly away, she thought, that's exactly what I'd like to do. Her emotional compass spun from despair to wild fantasy. Caregiver to world traveler. She stepped inside. It was time to dress for Dallas.

She stood in front of her bathroom mirror and dabbed her favorite English rose perfume behind her ears. While she dressed she decided she would make another trip to the attic before her trip to the hospital. Maybe the Bible Joe thought she would find would answer some questions. *He seemed to think the answers were there.*

The morning was surprisingly cool for June in Texas and she left the fan off and went directly to the bookcase next to the old trunks. The overhead bulb now free of dust illuminated the hundreds of books and objects stored or, more accurately, discarded there. *Why would he leave the Bible here? What didn't he want me to know? Oh, yeah, his family's origin. Or is it more than that?*

She brought a duster with her and began to swipe it across the rows of books. After a minute of two, she rubbed her itchy nose. The dust laden air caused a sneezing fit.

She stood back from the shelf and scanned the area she had cleaned. There it was. A large, thick Bible in faded black leather, a gold cross peeling off the spine. She pulled it from between what looked like text books. Its edges curled upward and there was a deep scratch across the front cover. It smelled of mildew.

This is awful. No way to treat a Bible. Oh, Joe, what were you afraid I'd find?

She waited until her coffee machine produced another cup of tea before she opened the Bible.

She had almost dropped it when she climbed down the attic stairs. Her heart rate increased and hadn't slowed down. While she waited for her tea, she ran her hands over the cover. The leather was stiff, but she could feel the depth of the engraved words, *Fresch Family Bible 1880 Austria-Hungary.*

Tea cup in one hand, she opened the book to the presentation page. It read, PRESENTED TO HELMUT FRESCH BY EMPEROR FRANZ JOSEPH ON THE OCCASION OF HIS BIRTHDAY, 5 OKTOBER 1880.

Her cup fell to the floor. Tea spattered on her shoe and shards of porcelain scattered in all directions.

Another name. Great-grandfather?"

Not sure she had read the inscription right, she put a finger on her nose. Yes, she had her glasses on.

Joe's from a royal family? Or this ancestor was close to a royal family? He failed to tell me about the Fresch name. Blew me off with the tale of a Russian love affair and Hitler's Germany. I know there's more to the tale of Trost to Tudor.

She closed the Bible without reading the entries of births and deaths. Getting to the hospital was her priority.

She wiped up the spilled tea and swept the broken glass into a dust bin. She checked her phone for messages as she always did before leaving her house.

Prissy had left a voice mail last night asking her to come by the bookshop. A delay of her trip to Dallas would have been welcomed before this morning's discovery.

Drat. At least Joe's a captive audience and will be there when I get there. The moment that thought raced across her mind, she stopped in place. Captive wasn't a word to banter around.

"Have you heard from Bitsy?" Prissy called to her from the open door of the bookshop.

"Yes, she texted me yesterday." She called as she closed her car door.

Prissy moved to the sidewalk. She rocked back and forth from one foot to the other.

"What's got you so antsy?"

Prissy went back in and waited by the door. She closed it after Anna crossed the threshold.

"It's just that I've had lots of calls about the book club, Ms. Tudor and Bitsy didn't tell me when it would start up again. I'm overwhelmed with the calls and the messages."

"Let's sit." Anna walked past the checkout counter and sat down on the curved couch in the center of the room. "Take a couple of breaths and try to gather your thoughts." She patted the cushion next to her.

"You're right, Ms. Tudor, I'm probably upset about nothing. My momma says all the time, 'Prissy you'd be upset if there wasn't anything to upset you.' That's what she says. But, all those calls and I have no answer."

"I know Bitsy called each and every one of the book club members before she left and told them she hadn't decided when the club would meet again. They're just bored or, maybe like you, look for something to worry about."

For a moment, Anna felt like herself again. Focused on someone else's worries. The easy going steady helper.

Prissy got up from the couch and faced her. "I can be so silly. But I wish Bitsy would text me."

"Her text to me was all good. It sounded like she has wrapped herself in the culture around her and is having fun. She mentioned a celebration."

Anna followed Prissy to the front of the store and offered her a hug before she left.

"Thanks, Ms. Tudor, thanks for coming."

She waved from her car as she backed out of the parking space. How many times had Prissy called her Ms. Tudor? Everyone in town, everyone in her life, for the last 40 years, called her by that name. She turned her car away from Middlecreek toward Dallas. For the first time, she was glad she didn't have children. The name stopped here and the games did, too.

She called Bitsy's number. The call went directly to voice mail. *Now who's silly? She told me she wouldn't have cell service for a while.*

She parked outside the hospital and looked up the phone number of the Hotel Apollo on her iPhone. She tapped in the number.

"*Kalispera*, may I help you?"

Anna was grateful for the English, but the connection wasn't good. She heard clicks and buzzes every few seconds.

"Hello, I'm calling from the United States for Elizabeth Bowman." She spoke slowly into the phone.

"Please to hold," said the male voice that identified himself as the night manager. "I am sorry to say she is not answering her room phone, Miss. You may leave a message on her phone or you can leave one with me."

"I'll leave a voice message, thank you."

She heard several short beeps before a long beep signaled she should start speaking.

"Bitsy, it's me. I know you're on Delos, but I want to talk to you. Nothing very urgent, but please call me when you can. Hope you and Rick found each other. You didn't mention him in your text."

She dropped the phone into her bag. Some have Greek vacations and liaisons; others have cold rooms with hard floors and all the trappings of a rehab hospital.

She fluffed her hair and licked her lips. Joe would be in his room for the next hour. Enough time for another interrogation.

Chapter 22

Constantine sat in a tall booth. He nursed a glass of retsina and rehearsed what he would tell his superiors when he arrived in Piraeus. *Bitsy removed the book from her room. When she attended the convention, I watched her and didn't see her pass the book to anyone. She spent some time in the restroom, but I checked after each visit, no book in the stalls. I didn't find her during the lunch break, but she wasn't gone long and returned in the company of two women.* He scratched his head. Bitsy had spent all her time with the Brit and the Italian. He found an opportunity to look into their large tote bags. No diary.

He took a sip of the wine. His mission was like a search for the Holy Grail. *Women are not worthy for a task such as mine. My job is for men only. For men who can be devoted to a legendary cause.* He turned in his seat. No sign of Bitsy in the restaurant or in the lobby. *Where is she and where is the book?*

A group of women passed his table. One woman asked the others if they had heard about the secret sleep over on

Delos. Constantine slid out of the booth. He followed the women to the outdoor taverna. He sat down in a chair near the table the women selected. They were dressed in sheer, flowing white dresses and wore flowers around their necks. He sniffed loudly. *Stupid women, this isn't Tahiti or Nepal.* Then he remembered, the Summer Solstice next week when celebrations to the Sun God Apollo were held throughout Greece. Good, he thought, these wanton looking women would be reminded of male dominance when women behaved as women without ambition. He waved his right hand toward a waiter. An ouzo to celebrate Apollo.

He put both elbows on his table and leaned forward. His ear was as close as possible to the women's table.

"I overheard the concierge tell a bell boy a group of women left before sunset for Delos," said a thin, freckled faced, red-headed woman.

"I thought Delos didn't have any overnight accommodations," said another of the women.

"Me, too," said the only older woman in the group. "I know for a fact, there are no hotels on the island, only ruins."

Constantine rubbed his chin. *Is Bitsy on Delos?* He pushed his chair back from the table with such force his foot slipped on the polished tile floor. *Do not cause attention.*

"Hello, beautiful ladies," he bowed toward the group and swept one of his hands out to his side as if he held a toreador's cape. "I could not but hear your talk of an excursion to Delos." He tucked his chin down toward his chest, but kept his eyes on the women.

"Oh, my," said one of the women, "I'm so sorry if we disturbed you, monsieur." Glitter on her eyelids twinkled under the overhead string of lights.

"Marsha," said one of her companions, "It's not monsieur. That's French. I don't know what Mister is in Greek."

"Never to mind, ladies." Constantine moved close to the edge of their table. "I only need to ask but one question of you. Do you know who is taking this nighttime trip to Delos?"

The red haired woman spoke first. "I only know it was a group of women from our bookseller's conference."

Marsha said, "I saw Pamela and Bitsy leave with duffle bags. They weren't dressed for dinner. In fact, now that I think of it, they were dressed for a camp out!"

"You are too kind," he bowed his head again. "Bon soir."

He wanted to rush to out of the taverna, but chose to make a slow exit. He heard one woman say, "That was French. Maybe he is French."

He snapped his fingers. *Things are looking good.*

***

Bitsy was first off the boat. To the west, an enormous pumpkin colored sun was setting. Its lingering heat warmed the sea breeze. Clouds spread over the eastern horizon. *Oh, please no rain!*

She hadn't moved away from the wooden dock even though the others stumbled up a rough stone covered path with their overnight gear in tow. The local sailor who had ferried the group to the island came toward her, gesturing with both hands.

"You, lady, you left your bag," he shouted. "I must leave. A storm may come and my small boat must be secured on Mykonos."

Pamela came down a path toward her. "Hurry," she said.

"Sorry, sir," Bitsy said, "I didn't know I…"she trailed off. The man had turned away from her. There was nothing to do, but follow him back to the boat. *What have I gotten myself into? No bed, no room service, no baggage handling and rain!*

"Hurry, Bitsy," Pamela called. "The evening ceremony is scheduled to start when the sun sets."

A Litha fire and a guide would lead the group of participants in ancient chants and dances to celebrate the Moon Goddess.

The seven chosen women gathered at the bottom of a slight hill where they left their bags and shoes. Melena, their guide, passed out circlets of flowers to be worn as crowns. The air was filled with their heavy scent; a mix of gardenia and bougainvillea. Bunches of rosemary sprigs were intertwined with the blossoms. Silk ribbons in a rainbow of colors had been fastened at the back of each circlet designed to fall to each woman's waist. Modern day goddesses in cargo pants. What's next?

Melena pulled gold and silver robes from a large tapestry bag. They shimmered, like liquid flames, in the remaining light.

"Pamela." Bitsy touched her arm. "Have you done a Summer Solstice ceremony before?"

"I went to one at Stonehenge, a long time ago with a group of tourists."

"A small group like this?"

"No, the group was large and boisterous. I didn't feel any magic that night. I think magic requires a certain amount of stillness, like the hour of the wolf."

"Are we supposed to feel magic?" Bitsy mentally made the sign of the cross, even though she was Baptist by birth. "I don't believe in magic although that sounds rather ridiculous since I believe in myths."

"Relax, my Texas friend. This is about symbols, feminine symbols that have been around for millennia, not to be forgotten. It's about the empowerment of women to embrace who they are as females in today's world." She hugged Bitsy. "With a little help from the wisdom of ancient stories."

"Guess we should put on our robes and flower crowns." Bitsy bit her lip and looked over Pamela's shoulder. The bottom half of the sun had disappeared over the horizon. "Are we having fun yet?"

Chapter 23

"What is this you say to me?" Constantine asked the concierge. "It cannot be too late to charter a boat!" He gripped the phone with both hands. "I must go to Delos tonight."

"Signore Verone, no boats go to the sacred island after dark. There are no accommodations, but you can sign up for a day excursion. If you wish, I will be happy to add your name to the first one tomorrow morning. There is one seat available."

"No, no, no, I will find a boat." He squeezed the room phone. His fingers turned red and his manicured nails dug into his palm. Sweat soaked his silk Pucci-like print shirt. He felt droplets stream down his temples.

He replaced the phone receiver in its cradle on the bedside table. A flyer for boat rentals next to the room service menu caught his eye. He grabbed the phone receiver again. He called the first number listed on the back page of the flyer.

***

Georges Poppelkia, in his late 70s, had ferried tourists to Delos and other surrounding islands since he was sixteen. Tonight he was stretched out in a hammock on his small balcony, happy the work day was done. A bottle of ouzo sat on an outdoor table. Six boats loads of tourists to Delos was a good, profitable day. *More headache than backache.* In the silence of the evening, he sipped his drink, its licorice flavor reminding him of the tastes of the Mediterranean region where food is lively like the music and dances.

His mind drifted to images of his youth, leading many a circle dance, white handkerchief in hand. His eyes refocused on his glass. Empty. He poured another cloudy drink. In the east the sky had darkened. *A storm would be welcomed to wash clean our white buildings and leave fresh the air.* "Opa!" he sang to the stars hidden by the blanket of clouds.

Inside his open door, an old fashioned black telephone rang. He hesitated while the phone rang again. He had no family on the island and those on the mainland never called. It's those flyers, he thought, my lady friend Caromina's idea. *Trouble.*

He wiggled out of the hammock. *What did I say to her, I don't want more business.* He picked up his drink. He swallowed the last of it before he lifted the thick phone receiver.

"*Yia sas.*"

***

"Hello," Constantine said, "I have your flyer and I want to charter a boat to Delos, tonight." He pushed the phone against his ear.

"No way I take you out tonight, sir. No one can go to Delos after dark and, besides, a storm is on its way."

"I have money, lots of money, you can buy a bigger boat if you want, you can take a long vacation. I must have a boat tonight."

"You want to buy my boat? Did I hear you want to buy my boat?"

Constantine heard the man smack his lips.

"I will pay you a reasonable price, but I must meet you now."

Georges put down his empty glass and sat down on the low iron framed cot he used as a couch during the day. He only spent money on things that had to do with his business. His wife left him for the mainland and took his one child, a daughter. He stopped caring about where he slept, how he dressed or the choices he made. His life was

171

the sea and this man was offering him a chance to own a bigger boat.

Constantine could hear feet tapping in rhythm to the sound of the waves in the background.

After a long pause, Georges said, "Meet me across from Zorba's Bar on the Beach. Go to the end of the boardwalk where boats are secured for the night. My boat bears the name, *Jason*. It is blue. The name is in white. It will take me a short time to find my registration papers."

This was the break he needed, a man who would sell his boat. He ended the call and immediately entered the number for the Hotel Wien. He wasn't sure where Johannes or Karl was, but he knew one or the other was likely to be at the Vienna hotel while others waited for him at the King George Hotel in Athens. He had been told to keep them informed about his progress. Now he needed to ask them to meet him in Piraeus tomorrow. *I'll have no book, but I'll have a way to get it.* He could hear his own breath between rings of the hotel phone. He rolled his eyes. *If Johannes had trusted me with his cell...* He spit into one of his linen handkerchiefs when the call was answered.

"Good evening, Hotel Vienna. This is the front desk."

Chapter 24

Constantine expected dire consequences if he didn't produce the red leather book. He had heard stories of other members' humiliation in front of their fellows for failures. He knew one member disappeared from his small apartment in Vienna, never to be seen again. He heard he had refused a research trip to Siberia. When he asked Johannes if the story was true, he had responded with "Who? I've no memory of him."

His own loyalty to the Society had been forged by hot tears after his father, within minutes of death, had demanded that he, his oldest son, fulfill the mission to find the Emperor's diary. His father had been the only Italian in the Society. His family had included a physician who tended to the health of the Hapsburg family in various royal locations and who was on hand when Prince Rudolph died.

The book must be mine to claim. This thought beat like a drum in rhythm with his heavy footsteps. His smooth stride carried him quickly down the weathered wooden boardwalk across from Zorba's Bar. He kept his face away from the lighted terrace filled with diners. His dark eyes scanned each boat tethered along the dock. He passed several blue boats with white lettering. *A joke on me, all the boats look the same.*

He stuck his hands in the pockets of a black windbreaker. At the end of the dock, he turned back toward the restaurant. He stopped just outside the beam of a large metal pole lamp. He found no one on the dock.

"*Kalispera.*" A short, stocky man wearing faded jeans and a navy blue shirt with white epilates passed through the light and stood in front of him. Constantine hoped this man was the man who would sell his boat. *The man who solves my dilemma.*

"I am Georges and I have a boat to sell, for a price."

"And I am a buyer of a boat." He shook the man's hand. Smooth hand holding rough hand.

"You look at boat, this one," Georges said. He pointed to a much larger boat than what Constantine had envisioned. It wasn't one of the small skiffs seen carrying passengers to Delos. It was a cabin cruiser, able to carry twice the number of passengers a skiff could and was perfect to secure and hide someone below deck. A spirited bout of bargaining ensued before papers and boat keys were passed from one to the other.

"May all the fish of the sea rise up and take your bait," Georges said, "And may all the women on the beach rise up and take your bait."

Constantine laughed. He nodded before he stepped onto the gently bobbing boat.

Fish or female, both do respond to bait. My catch doesn't know what comes in the night to catch her.

He dropped his black leather duffle bag onto the floor of the deck. Arrangements for his possessions to be sent to an apartment in Vienna had been made before he left the hotel. The cost of this service was minimal to him. The room service waiter he paid had been more than happy to accommodate him.

In the boat's cabin, he pulled yellow plastic worry beads from his pants pocket and toyed with them. He opened doors, looked into the head, and sat on the one of the berths. Topside, he examined the boat from stem to stern before he familiarized himself with the instruments.

"I have piloted many a boat between Milan and Corfu," he said as he moved his hand around the smooth wood steering wheel. He put on a faded captain's cap he found in the cabin. Settled on the blue vinyl covered pilot's chair, he maneuvered the boat away from the dock into a pitch black night. The Society and his surprise would succeed when so many other groups had failed. *Failure, no. Success, yes.*

Once away from the dock and out of sight of the party goers at the taverna, he cut the engine. He fingered the ignition key, but left it in place. He slid away from the controls and made his way into the cabin below. He opened his duffle bag. He spent some time looking through the items he would use for this mission to Delos. Satisfied he was completely prepared; he took a hammered steel flask out of the bag. Fortification. He had never kidnapped anyone before.

The midnight sea was like India ink. The wind had vanished into the blackness and all was still. All except Constantine. He rocked from foot to foot behind the pilot's wheel.

It won't be long. For what? That's the question. For Bitsy to be accosted. For me to be reprimanded by my colleagues for going to these links to get the diary. My colleagues. Ha!

He reached again for the flask now wedged between instruments on the dash. *I've never felt accepted by the other members of the Society. My heritage isn't pristinely*

Germanic. But I dare say I'm the one who'll get the glory for finding the diary.

He imagined the cottage in the woods where Bitsy would divulge the whereabouts of the Emperor's diary and he would be celebrated by his peers. A hero.

He would tell his social friends of his status and the history of the Grand Dukes Society. The society that used a stone cottage in the Vienna Woods for their meetings. The cottage, adjacent to Mayerling, built after Crown Prince Rudolph turned Mayerling into a royal hunting lodge in the late 1800s. The cottage that housed a separate grounds keeper to track the deer Rudolph and his guests hunted, in the hopes the Crown Prince would always have targets and return to Mayerling with a kill.

Over the years, after the death of the Crown Prince, the cottage fell in disrepair, used primarily to store obsolete and unwanted items belonging to the nuns who moved into Mayerling several years after the tragic deaths. Emperor Franz Joseph, in his grief, had decreed that no one in his family or household could set foot in the hunting lodge again. He banned it from public view and would have had it burned to the ground if not for the large number of paintings and gifts from other heads of state housed there. A close confident suggested he transform it into a convent. The nuns would act as caretakers for the treasures found there, keep their silence and pray for Crown Prince Rudolph daily. The cottage in the woods was all but forgotten. The nuns confined themselves to the main buildings.

In the 1920s, the Society petitioned use of the cottage. The path there was overgrown with brambles and overhanging tree limbs whipped to the ground by frequently damaging mountain winds. If allowed to use the cottage for its semiannual meetings, each member pledged to clear away the dead and decaying debris and return the cottage to its original condition. There was no mention of the purpose of their meetings, their mission to find the personal diary of the last Emperor. Each of the members signed the petition with notations describing their ties to the Hapsburgs in hopes knowledge of their family backgrounds would persuade the nuns.

Guidelines for membership called for connection to the Hapsburg dynasty and that all participants would induct their first born son into the Society at age 13 to ensure the continuance of the group and their mission. Members became booksellers or collectors of ephemera. They attended book conferences and scoured flea markets around the world. Because tales of the Hapsburg empire and the mystery of Mayerling was passed down from father to son, the members of the society knew the diary existed and if found, by someone other than them, could be sold to the highest bidder. Groups who lost powerful pre-World War I positions or those who want the contents of the diary to remain secret and would distort or suppress the Emperor's words.

Constantine's grip on the wheel tightened when a gust of wind rocked the boat sideways.

Those groups who would shame or sell out the Emperor remain active, but we, the Grand Dukes, remain true to our heritage. Finding the diary will put an end to all the conspiracy theories and the multitude of rumors still on the tongues of many.

The existence of the red leather, bird embossed, personal diary of the Emperor and the legend that it contained the truth of the death of Crown Prince Rudolph and Marie Vetsera had been debated for over one hundred and twenty-five years. For the Society, there never was need to debate its existence. They had the ciphers.

Constantine scratched his thick eyebrows close to the center of his wide forehead. *They'll be surprised and pleased. I will be lauded.*

The wind returned and a strong gust blew his cap from his head. It lodged underneath his feet.

Merda! He shivered in the warm night.

He reached down to retrieve the cap. When he rose up he saw flames in the distance. They appeared to be on Delos. *What are those women doing? Burning down the ruins?*

He shoved the wayward cap down over his furrowed brow. "No matter, ladies," he said aloud. "I come no matter what."

Chapter 25

Peter handled the Museum acquisition fund which received part of the proceeds of book sales during the conference. The first day was a success both in attendance and sales, but he was happy it was done. In fact, he would take pleasure marking off the day on a large calendar that hung in his kitchen. Two more days of the women and the Triple Goddess.

He turned off the lights in the foyer on his way to the auditorium. He would continue to turn off lights until he reached the small chapel where he always stopped to thank God for the day past and the day ahead. This nightly ritual soothed his spirit and prepared him for his usual hours of home study. He had always preferred solitude to both social gatherings and group study. When he could, he avoided classes and presentations given during conferences.

He locked the back entrance to the museum. He stepped off the landing and into the unlit parking lot. He reached under his loose fitting robe and felt the red leather book tucked in an inside pocket. No one was about. He removed the book, and felt again the embossed leather cover. He tucked it under his arm. Inside his car, he placed the diary on the passenger's seat.

As usual, he checked his rearview mirror before turning toward his home. *You can never be too careful.* He didn't turn on the car radio; rather he took this quiet time to review his conversation with Bitsy. By the time he neared his house, he wished he had taken a better look at the small black leather book. *It was in German, it was from the late 1800s, it was found with the diary. A companion book?*

He turned his car around in the middle of the street and headed back to the museum. The small black diary was in the office safe. After thinking about it, he believed it could be another important account of what happened at Mayerling. He didn't want to wait to find out. He nearly jumped the curb in his haste to get back to the museum. *Take care, take care.*

The area around the museum was essentially vacant at night. No tavernas close by, no residents, no late night businesses. He passed the darkened windows of the local library, then the whitewashed stone fence surrounding a private school. He turned into the pebbled drive between a closed florist shop and the museum. The back of the museum was in darkness, no bright beams of security lights like the ones on the front of the building. This was his fault. He never seemed to remember to have the rear lights replaced until the day was over and all he wanted to do was go home where a glass of ouzo or retsina waited along with his latest study material. Tonight, he was glad for the dark.

Chapter 26

Bitsy did a pirouette. Her silver robe glinted in the fire light. The crown of flowers and ribbons looked like a tambourine in her right hand. She held it above her head a moment before she put it in her hair. A few other women danced in a circle around the growing flame of the bonfire. The Litha fire of legend. Mead offered in gold goblets had lessoned her worries. A soothing stillness in spite of the whoops of the dancing women filled her heart with calm. The storm never materialized and the wind had died down. The edges of the robes lifted in the gentle breeze and the drink fueled dance steps. Scattered flowers that fell from the crowns decorated the ground.

She stepped away from the bonfire and looked toward the beach. She didn't hear any loud whooshing of waves as if the sea was relieved the sun had eased its way over the horizon and left it to slumber until sunrise. She walked a few feet up a small hill to a Goddess altar the guide said was prepared for the upcoming Solstice celebration. She leaned gently against one side of the arch constructed over three stakes where the ceremony would take place. She closed her eyes and visualized the brilliant blazing orange sun that turned the horizon into colors of turquoise and peach before it plunged into the unending sea.

The group had gathered here to watch the sunset before Francesca struck the match to their fire. Bitsy breathed in the salty sea air and swallowed wrong. Her cough broke the spell she had been weaving. She wrapped her arms around her chest. The night had cooled and would get cooler. She turned back toward the ceremonial fire. *Give me some heat.*

***

Melena placed seven silk pillows of different colors in a semi-circle around the fire. Each one was marked with a symbol representing one of the seven major Greek Goddesses. Artemis, goddess of the hunt and the moon. Athena, goddess of wisdom and craft. Hestia, goddess of the hearth and wholeness. Hera, goddess of marriage. Demeter, goddess of grain and the maternal archetype. Persephone, maiden and queen of the underworld. Aphrodite, goddess of love and beauty. With the pillows on the ground, Melena held up a golden chalice filled with more mead to be shared.

As each woman came forward for their sip from the cup, she directed them to their pillow. Bitsy put her left hand behind her back and crossed her fingers as she held the cup in her right hand. *Let me get Artemis.*

Melena pointed to the purple pillow.

Bitsy ran her hand over the embossed bow and arrow, symbols of the Goddess of the Hunt. She picked it up and squeezed it to her heart.

Francesca rose from her tufted pillow to help pass food around the group. Skewers of lamb, grape leaves stuffed with spiced rice, and soft pita bread covered with a black olive tapenade was accompanied by more mead.

Bitsy sat between Pamela, on a yellow topaz Hestia pillow and Francesca, on a blue sapphire Athena pillow. Melena began storytelling during the dinner. She made her way around the semicircle providing insight into each Goddess symbol and associated color.

When she returned to her place next to the fire, she closed her jeweled story folder and suggested the women move away from the collapsing pyre and find a place to settle down for the night.

"The time has come to sleep and dream and prepare for life tomorrow and beyond. We'll return to Mykonos around 9:00 a.m. I wish you mystical dreams."

Everyone moved inland away from the smoldering embers. The ceremonial pillows were left behind. Duffle bags or overnight travel cases were retrieved. Bitsy found a sleeping spot next to Pamela. She spread out the Hotel Apollo blanket she had packed. After she sat down, she checked her cell phone. No signal here. The celebration was over and the isolation of Delos was sinking in. She tapped Pamela's shoulder. She was stretched out on her Tartan plaid blanket.

"Any mead left?"

"Sorry, luv." Pamela sat up. Her answer was echoed by a few other women who overheard her question.

Bitsy lowered her voice and suggested the two of them return to the hill area to talk for a while. "I'm not drowsy, even with all the mead," she whispered. She was antsy about her secret and wanted to tell someone about the Peter's warning and the books.

"What's up?" Pamela whispered in return.

"Let's wait 'til we're alone."

Before Pamela pushed up from her blanket, she pointed toward Bitsy's bag. "Take a sweater; it'll be cold on the hill with no fire."

Bitsy grabbed a purple fleece jacket.

"Let's go to the far side of the fire site near the Solstice altar." She tied the jacket around her waist.

Pamela followed a step behind toward the sea. At the bottom of the small hill topped with the altar, Pamela shook out her blanket and sat crossed legged with her back to the stakes.

Bitsy waited until she was situated to join her. Both faced the glowing embers. The hill shielded them from the full force of the wind off the water.

"I need to share something," Bitsy said. She told her about the books, Constantine and Peter's warning that unscrupulous people, interested in the red leather diary, could be dangerous.

"I believe Constantine was friendly with me because of the diary. Do you know him?"

"I've met him at other bookseller gatherings, but I don't actually know him."

"Does he seem sinister to you?" She reached across the blanket for Pamela's hand. "I shouldn't have told you. What if the books really are dangerous?"

"Bitsy, books aren't dangerous," Pamela squeezed her proffered hand. "But, anyone who reads the paper or watches the news knows that people can be."

"I know." They held hands for a few moments.

"Do you believe a couple of old books could spell international intrigue? Maybe, Peter's deluding himself, wanting to believe he's found something remarkable. I think he's someone who needs to feel important. I mean, look at the way he dresses in long black robes as if he's the priest of the museum. Not that I don't admire him for his intelligence, but I'm just saying." Pamela stretched her legs out in front of her and leaned back on her arms.

Bitsy leaned closer. She didn't want her words carried on the breeze as if it had ears to hear and a mouth to spread her words back to Mykonos. "All I know is he told me not to tell anyone about the books. Enough of my secret. Let's have a look at the altar?" She stood up.

The wind was stronger at the top of the hill. Both women covered their ears.

Neither heard the subtle change in the rhythm of the lapping sea a short distance away or the small splash of an anchor dropped into the water.

"Pamela, look, someone put their flower crown on one of the stakes. I bet these stakes represent the Triple Goddess, right?"

The night sky had cleared of earlier clouds now dispersed to the west. Millions of stars twinkled above

189

their heads. The silk ribbons on the crown shimmered with each graceful movement.

"Yes, the stakes represent the three stages of a woman's life. Traditionally, Maid, Mistress and Crone. I prefer the modern terms, Young Woman, Mature Woman and Wise Woman." Pamela's smile was illuminated in the star light.

"Might that be because we've reached the third stage of life?"

They shared a laugh.

The two friends stood on the uneven altar stones and faced the middle and tallest stake adorned with the fragrant flower crown. Bitsy pointed to the horizon. A shooting star fell in the direction of the mainland of Greece. She made a wish.

"Guess it's about time to call it a night or, should I say a midnight?" She stepped off the altar stone. "Be careful, these stones wobble."

Pamela moved behind her.

Bitsy heard a quick intake of breath before she felt something brush her back and hit her ribs. She stumbled sideways and tried to regain her balance. She looked down and saw Pamela slumped on the ground, her right hand stretched out in front of her. In the moment it took her to take in the scene, Bitsy felt a strong arm across her throat and a soft cloth mashed against her nose and mouth. She reached up to fight off the attacker. She thought she would die when the stars above her blurred like a watercolor in the rain.

***

Constantine left the unconscious Pamela at the altar. He carried a limp Bitsy to his boat. *No worries. The tide has changed, my American woman.* He would secure her in the boat and get her to tell him where to find the book. *Accolades ahead. You're a mere annoyance.* He straddled the side of the boat and heaved Bitsy onto the narrow bench that ran around the perimeter of its deck. He wanted no more than to deposit her in Piraeus, give Johannes the location of the diary and return to Vienna and his latest companion. *A woman who knows nothing about Goddesses.* He whistled a Viennese waltz under his breath.

He would reach Piraeus in the early morning hours at a secluded and secure dock historically used for transports outside the law. He had been told to check in hourly with his superiors, but there wasn't a signal here. *Cheap phone or bad location.* He fingered another throw away cell phone in his jacket pocket. After Bitsy was tucked away in the cabin and they were further away from Delos, he would

191

make the call. *There must be a satellite over this vast ocean.*

His whistle changed from the waltz to a Broadway tune, *The Impossible Dream.*

Chapter 27

Anna dug into her rose velvet makeup bag. Her fingers wrapped around a lipstick tube. She applied the shimmery magenta Madame Dew Berry before quickly dabbing her lips with a tissue. Bitsy had suggested the shade. It was on trend and would give her pale face a pop of color. *I miss her more than I imagined I would.*

She looked in the mirror over Joe's hospital sink. He was in bed. His dinner tray across his chest like on a child's high chair. His eyes were on her rather than his food. She dropped her gaze into her opened tote bag. She scrabbled around its bottom with both hands. *Where are my keys?"*

"I'm going to go, Joe." She slung the bag on her shoulder and jiggled the keys.

"I don't know why you can't stay while I eat."

"Because I'm having an early dinner with Eleanor Peck. You remember, my high school friend."

"Where did she come from all of a sudden?"

"She's a Facebook friend. We've reconnected."

"But, Anna, I hate to eat alone."

Joe's lower lip turned inside out showing soft red tissue. He shoved the tray toward his knees. "I didn't want this awful stuff anyway."

"I don't have time for this, Joe. I'll see you tomorrow."

She didn't look back as she left the room. *Things are going to be different, for me and for you.*

She stopped at the nurse's station.

"I want to schedule an appointment with Joe's case manager." She propped her tote bag on the counter in front of the unit secretary.

"I'll leave her a message to call you, Ms. Tudor."

"Thanks, I'd appreciate that. Tell her I need to see a list of in-home caretakers, the 24 hour a day kind."

The evening had cooled more than usual. Anna hurried into the Mexican restaurant on the interstate frontage road near Waxahachie. She didn't drive at night, Joe was the driver. She didn't drink and drive no matter the time of day, Joe did. But a margarita called her name.

It's about time you move out of your comfort zone, kiddo.

She stretched her back and rolled her shoulders against the ladder back chair. *Will I recognize Eleanor?* Facebook photos were not necessarily recent. Hers wasn't. She preferred to post throw back pictures of a time when the world stretched out in front of her and all things were possible. *At 62 I can see the horizon and it's not that far off. The end of chances to fulfill dreams.* Who said the 60s were the new 40s?

A tall, brunette waved to her from the hostess station. These days few women were au natural with their hair color. Anna ran a hand under her bob before she waved back. She would have known her high school friend anywhere in spite of some weight gain and the neck. She always checked out the neck. Some tighter than hers, but some could be called the dreaded turkey neck.

No getting away from negative thoughts. Where had her inherent optimism gone? The way of her unrealistic dreams?

Chapter 28

Constantine pushed the boat away from the shore. His first goal was to secure Bitsy before the chloroform wore off. He had placed her on one of the two small berths in the cruiser's cabin. The raised beds ran along opposite sides of the room at an angle with a small wooden table top nestled between them at the footboards. A closet was on each side of the ladder from the upper deck. One was the head and one was for gear.

He removed a coil of thick rope and a bronze handled fisherman's knife. He pricked an index finger on the razor sharp tip of the serrated blade and sucked the bubble of blood away before he cut two lengths of rope and returned the knife to the closet shelf. Bitsy was on her back, her head turned away from him. He tied her wrists together. He pushed her up onto her left side toward the small window above the berth. He grunted with the effort. *Such a bother you are.* He pressed his knees against the wooden side of the bed and rolled her over onto her stomach. He tied her ankles with the remaining rope. *Sleep well, my American woman, your sea voyage begins now.*

He hesitated then turned her onto her back. *Better that you have adequate air; I don't want you to smother.* He pulled on the knots in the rope on her wrists and then on her ankles. In his youth, he hunted deer and rabbits in the Vienna Woods with his father. He prided himself on his skill with a knife and in tying deer securely across the hood of his father's old Mercedes. His weren't nautical knots, but they would hold a small woman. He closed the window curtains above both berths and took one last look at Bitsy before he climbed the ladder.

Time to weigh anchor. Piraeus waited. A greeting committee waited, too.

He stood behind the wheel in a wide stance and turned the ignition key. The engine rumbled to life. He glanced back toward land. He saw no one, but he didn't increase the engine's power or turn on the running lights. He would wait until he couldn't see Delos.

He felt the bulge deep inside the left pocket of his windbreaker. By now someone would be in Piraeus to meet him. *When the cell works, I will make the most important call. I will report not what I bring, but whom.* Johannes had tacitly agreed to the use of physical force to get the diary. There had been no discussion about a kidnapping. A kidnapping without the book.

The sea was calm, but his knees felt strained as he kept his balance on the swaying deck. He had seen a cruise ship pass to his left, miles away but looking like a holiday house with strings of lights outlining its upper deck and superstructure.

He tapped in the number Johannes had given him. He dreaded the probable reprimand. He gritted his teeth at the first ring.

"Hallo."

"Hermann, it's you." Relief flowed through tense muscles like warm red wine. "It's Constantine. I'm in transit to Piraeus. Estimated arrival time is 7 a.m. Gods willing and waves allowing."

"Constantine." Hermann coughed then cleared his throat. "Johannes has been frantic not hearing from you on schedule." He added, "I wouldn't be you for all the beer in Germany."

"Sorry, didn't hear that." He wiped sweat out of his eyes. "Tell them I have a way to get the diary. Tell them I bring it with me."

"I'll pass your message to the others. Good luck."

The call ended before Constantine could ask who would be waiting for him. He twisted away from the wheel and looked into the cabin. *Is this woman to be my savior or my demise?*

***

Bitsy stirred. Her eyes opened briefly before closing again. *What's wrong with me?* Her second attempt to keep her eyes open was a success. She scanned the small room and the ceiling only a few feet above her head. Dim light from under the pilot's perch spilled into the room over her shoulder. When she wasn't able to turn her body toward the light, she realized her wrists and ankles were bound. She kicked her feet and wiggled her body. Suddenly, she felt dizzy. The room was moving. *I'm on a boat.*

She heard the even purr of an engine. She stopped thrashing about and immediately felt the bounce of the boat slicing through water. When she raised her chin and twisted her head toward the light, she saw a man's hairy leg. He wore thick soled boating shoes. She tried to sit up, but couldn't get her elbows on the thin mattress for leverage. She held up her bound wrists and raised her legs. She didn't have the strength or the space to rock into a sitting position. Her legs fell with a thud against the

199

mattress. She growled from the effort needed to rise up onto one elbow.

"Oh, my American woman," Constantine called from the deck, "You are waking."

She recognized the voice calling her an American woman.

"Have you lost your mind, Signore Verone?"

"Oh, what a sound. To hear your charming voice again." Constantine bent down far enough to see her. He kept one hand on the wheel.

"You're surprised to see me?" His laugh filled the cabin like the thundering cackle of the monsters lurking in a midway fun house.

She pushed up with the sides of her hands and managed to swing her legs over the side of the berth.

"Untie me, you fool. You must be mad." Her voice echoed back to her off the smooth white walls. Her throat was dry. She fell back onto the bed. She brought her knees to her chest.

Constantine leaned down again. "What's the purpose of your struggle? You're in the middle of an ocean. There's no escape."

Bitsy shut her eyes, knees on her chest. She stretched her arms as far as they would go over her knees. Two fingers reached the rope that bound her ankles. She tugged at the rope. The sharp fiber scraped her fingertips. She turned her head toward the door. She wasn't being watched. She tugged and jiggled the rope and then tugged and jiggled again. Blood spots dripped onto the bed sheet.

What am I doing? I need to undo my wrists first.

The repeated movements of her hands to loosen the ankle rope had stretched the rope on her wrists. She was able to bend her right hand over her left and pull a loop in the knot.

The engine noise diminished. The boat stopped. The rocking motion increased. And she hadn't untied the rope. She felt dizzy as the boat began to dip and sway in rhythm with the waves.

She watched two bare ankles above canvas shoes move down the ladder. Constantine ducked his head and entered the cabin. For a moment, he looked like he was bowing to her. She said a silent prayer.

"I've waited for this moment, Signora Bowman." His rather large white teeth gleamed under his moistened upper lip. "You didn't show me consideration, now you will."

She didn't move. She willed her mind to remain calm, to let him talk.

"You've no thought about why you're here? I can see that your face is blank. I must ask how stupid are you? " He leaned against the opposite berth. "Do you not know what you had, what you brought with you from America? Amateur! It's my luck to be stuck with an amateur."

Bitsy expected him to spit in her face. Instead he walked to the ladder and left the cabin without another word.

She swung her legs over the side of the bed again. "Constantine, please untie me. Obviously, I can't go anywhere, right?"

From the top rung, he turned and met her gaze. "You've been working, no, to undo your bindings. That's to be your job, Signora. When you're done, come topside to see the beautiful Aegean. It's likely to be a lovely morning." He touched the brim of his cap and disappeared out of sight.

Chapter 29

Ciara O'Toole slipped away from the tour group, tired of feeling like a sheep, herded onto tenders, packed with old people, and led around dusty, crumbed ruins before returning to the cruise ship. She ignored her twin sister, Claire, who motioned her back to the line. She shook her head and pointed to the small hill where several ribbons flapped in the ocean breeze, like her auburn ponytail when she danced the Greek dances on board ship.

The early morning tender from ship to Delos was another outing to another Greek island among so many other stops on the cruise. Her parents' enthusiasm to visit the birthplace of Zeus' twins bored her. What did that myth have to do with her and Claire? She had tuned her mother out when she explained the uniqueness of Delos, but remembered her using the term remarkable. Dull and meaningless information for a fifteen-year-old who had made a date with a cute Australian boy to spend the day at the ship's top deck pool.

"Come with me," she mouthed to Claire.

Claire hesitated, but moved away from the tail end of the tourist group and joined her sister on the side of the dirt path. Ciara pointed to the three stakes standing alone against the horizon. The ribbons lifted up and a circle of flowers could be seen.

"Look at that, Claire. A flower crown. Could there be nymphs on this island?" She put her arm around Claire's shoulders.

"Don't tease me Ciara. You know I like myths even if you don't." She pulled away and crossed her arms over her chest. "Let's catch up with Ma and Da."

"No, let's take a closer look up there." Ciara stepped onto a slab of marble edging the walking path. She waited for Claire to follow before she headed up the grassy hill to the stakes.

The morning sun hadn't warmed the sea breeze blowing across the island. She shivered. Delos and Mykonos were often lashed by strong winds that arrived suddenly and died down as quickly. She watched the ribbons whip into spirals. The flowers on the circlet scattered like butterflies.

She attained the crest of the hill with Claire a step or two behind. She didn't scream. Instead she took a step backward and bumped into her sister with such an impact that they both lost their balance and fell to their knees.

"Don't look, Claire, don't look," Ciara gulped back a scream. She crawled further away from the hill top.

"What's up there?" Claire turned to look back at the stakes.

"We have to tell Ma and Da," Ciara said, "We have to tell them quick." Her voice rose from a low mumble to a high pitched shriek that sounded like the clash of the metal symbols she played in her school band.

***

Claire stood frozen midway up the hill. Her sister's eyes were three times their usual size. What had she seen? She turned to the stakes and watched several flower petals fall to the ground. Something lay on the ground under the middle stake. Something that flashed in the morning sun. It shimmered with rainbow colors.

Before Ciara could stop her, Claire ran up the embankment. She stopped in front of the stake. She bent down and saw a silver beaded hoop earring. It lay in a pool of blood.

She jerked upright and looked over her shoulder toward the spot where Ciara had been. She wasn't there.

"Ciara! Where'd you go?"

***

Ciara had collapsed at the base of the hill, her legs like water and her head buzzing as if her skull was a hornet's nest. After a moment, she called back to Claire.

"I'm coming. Stay there."

Her sister pointed to the bloody earring. Ciara walked closer. The pool of blood bisected two of the three altar stones. She placed one hand on the outside of one stake and leaned forward. Her sandaled feet to the side of the square stones. Blood weaved through yellowed grass behind the altar like a snake slithering toward the sea.

"We've got to go." She grabbed one of Claire's hands to pull her back down the hill. Her pulse kept pace with her quick strides down the dirt path toward the tour group. Even though they almost fell several times, she continued to grip her sister's hand. Her mind reeled with fear and terror. *Could the bloody myths be true? Did some bloody ritual take place on that hill?*

***

The tour group wandered around a crumbled mosaic floor while their guide explained how water was made available through underground aqueducts in the 10th century B.C. Screams stopped her lecture short. Ciara panted and Claire collapsed to the ground at the edge of the group.

A few seconds after her parents had reached her; Ciara took a deep breath and leaned on her Da's shoulder. Her voice shook in his ear "I saw a woman covered in blood."

***

Down a different path from the small hill, the women who celebrated the Goddesses the night before began to wake. The screams acted like an alarm clock.

Francesca was the first to stand up.

"Who is that screaming?" She looked around her and mentally counted the bodies as they stirred, sat up or stood. Two women were missing.

"Stay here; I'll go find out what's happened. Can someone gather up my things? I think we need to be ready to leave pronto."

Chapter 30

Peter stood in the back of the auditorium. From this position he could check the lighting and placement of books to be discussed during the classes. Activities would start soon after 10:00 a.m. which would give the Delos group enough time to return from their overnight trip and dress for the day. He was glad for the delay. He stayed up late to pour over the red leather book. He didn't try to translate the entries last night. That he would do later. He only wanted to hold the book, feel each page in his gloved hand. He did spend some time searching the Internet for references to the rumored Emperor's diary.

Sometime after midnight, he became distracted with the history of the Hapsburgs and the various accounts and theories of the deaths at Mayerling. He watched one of the dozens movies made about the tragedy. There had been no time to study the small diary, but he did determine it was written at Mayerling.

The central doors of the auditorium opened behind him. Two local policemen stood in the threshold.

"May I help you?" Peter walked toward them, hands at his side.

"Mr. Gallenos," said the older of the two men, "We have some terrible news, some very terrible news for you."

The younger officer reached out to shake Peter's hand. "Sir, two women, reportedly here for your meetings, have been attacked on Delos."

Peter dropped the officer's hand. His body sagged against the back of one of the red velvet seats. "What happened?"

The older officer stepped closer. He stopped near Peter. His face was pale above his dark blue uniform. "Please, come with us to the hospital. We've been told the woman there has regained consciousness."

Peter pushed himself away from the chair.

"I must lock up before I can go and I need to leave a note on the museum door. I'll meet you at the hospital." He shimmied past the officers to the ticket office door just inside the auditorium.

"Very well, sir. There'll be a policeman there to direct you."

Peter took a placard from under the ticket counter. He found a black marker and wrote, No Classes Today, in bold block letters. He grabbed a list of attendees with their local contact information. Before the day was over, he knew he would need to contact them. He especially wanted to talk with the women who had spent the night on Delos.

The only hospital on Mykonos was further down the beach than the majority of the tourist hotels. It was on one of the hills mid-island, located in a mostly residential area. In recent years, Mykonos had developed a reputation as a party destination which had necessitated an expansion of the hospital. The new structure had a trauma unit, something many of the small Greek islands did not have.

The buildings were made of the usual whitewashed stucco surrounded by palm trees, masses of bougainvillea and tall pots of geraniums. Two tall cacti flanked the sliding double doors that led into the hospital lobby. The name across the port-a-cache was etched into a thick marble overhang in English rather than Greek, Arcadia Hospital.

Peter was familiar with the hospital. He volunteered once a month to work with geriatric patients being referred out for hospice services. He thought of this as penitence.

The hospital doors slid open without a sound. His soft sole shoes were silent on the tile flooring. He realized he didn't know the name of the woman being treated. There was no policeman in the lobby. He walked to the admissions desk. The receptionist directed him to the second floor. Room 212. She didn't offer the patient's name.

After a long wait for the elevator, he took the stairs. A guard stood outside one room door. He hurried his steps. A nurse opened the door and he saw the two police officers from the museum. They stood next to the hospital bed blocking his view of the patient. The older of two stepped away from the bed and motioned for him to come inside.

He got his first look at Pamela.

Her lips were split and purple and her head was bandaged. He could barely see her green eyes surrounded by swollen skin. It looked like she had been hit in the face.

"Come in, Peter," she said. Her usual lilt had a lisping sound to it. "I'm going to be fine, let's get that out of the way. No worries about me, okay?"

He took her small smooth hand in his large one. "What happened, Pamela?" He reached behind his back with his other hand dragged a heavy chair next to her bedside.

The officer in the room interrupted. "Miss, I think you should wait until the Police Chief gets here to give your statement. He should arrive anytime."

The door opened and a tall, muscular man in full dress uniform entered the room. His smile was as brilliant as the overhead fluorescent light. "Chief Mercori," he introduced himself to the gathering. He moved to the far side of the hospital bed. "May I?" he inquired before he leaned over Pamela and kissed her cheeks. "You're a lucky woman, Ms. Jones."

"I know." Her face flushed. She scanned the room. "But no one will tell me if Bitsy's alright."

***

Pamela asked that the head of the bed be raised. She wanted to see her audience while she gave her statement, her story of the night on Delos and of her attack. She shared details of the celebration, the dancing and singing, the Summer Solstice bonfire. She recalled that Bitsy suggested they sit around the fire embers before going to sleep and that Bitsy had told her a secret.

She asked for some water. Peter handed her a lidded plastic cup with a bendable straw in place. She twisted the straw between her fingers. The rest of the room was motionless.

"I'm kind of fuzzy about Bitsy's secret, but sometime after that she walked away from me. That's when something or somebody hit me from behind.

"I must have fallen on the stone floor of the Goddess altar. I was able to get to my knees using two of the stakes for leverage."

She took another sip of water.

"I felt warm liquid on my face and I saw Bitsy being carried to the water's edge. She was put into a boat."

Pamela blinked repeatedly as tears filled her eyes. Without saying a word, the police chief handed her a handkerchief.

"My first memory after that was being here in this room."

"So, Ms. Jones," the Chief said, "Did you recognize the person who attacked you and your friend?"

"No, but it was a man. He wore dark clothes and a cap, like a ship captain's. It was pulled down low on his head." She sniffed, blew her nose before she patted her eyes with the damp cloth.

"I do remember a name on the side of the boat. *Jason*." She let her head fall back onto the pillow. Her gaze shifted from her listeners to the acoustic tile ceiling.

"Now please answer my question about Bitsy."

***

The Hotel Apollo's desk phone hadn't stopped ringing since the early morning report of an assault on Delos. The number of people in the hotel lobby grew larger with each passing hour. After the two teenagers found Pamela, bloody and unconscious, the tour group was ferried back to their cruise ship where they would be questioned. The group from the booksellers' conference arrived at the hotel on a second ferry. Word passed from person to person that it was someone from their group who was attacked.

The police were most interested in speaking with Francesca Campelli. She was described as a close friend to both the injured Ms. Jones and missing Ms. Bowman.

In the midst of handling calls from those who had heard about the incident, the hotel staff found themselves overwhelmed with questions from hotel guests who knew nothing of the crisis, but who were concerned by the presence of two police officers who flanked the front entrance while others stood next to numerous police cars and one ambulance in the hotel's circular drive.

A new group of tourists had arrived from Piraeus only to be told that many of the usual excursions and events had been cancelled. NO SERVICE UNTIL POLICE ADVISE SAFETY was printed on placards and notepaper and placed on doors and in windows of restaurants and souvenir shops that fronted the beach.

***

Somewhere around noon, Rick left his hotel room. He had called Bitsy's room with no luck. *Where is she? Did she stay out all night?* As he stepped out of the elevator he muttered under his breath, "So I didn't have a drink with her my first night here, she goes off who knows where?"

He put his hands in his pockets and shrugged. *Maybe I should forget about her altogether.*

Once in the crowded lobby, he barreled through a group of women who seemed oblivious to anyone except themselves. *I don't need women. I don't need a certain woman for sure.*

"Excuse me, sir." A uniformed policeman stopped Rick in mid-stride. "No one's leaving the hotel. There's been an attack on tourists and precautions are made. All guests will remain in the lobby until given authority to leave the hotel or, if you prefer, you may return to your room."

Rick didn't reply. He weaved his way toward the front desk. He leaned on the wide counter. "Hey," he called.

The concierge held up a hand, but continued a phone conversation in an adjoining room next to the registration desk. Rick kept his eyes on him and thumped the counter with his right thumb.

When the concierge reached the desk, he said without preamble, "I'm sorry to inform you, Mr. Bennett, but your friend, Ms. Bowman, is missing."

"What?" Rick stepped back on his heels. "Missing?" The word sounded like a hissing bullet aimed straight between the young man's eyes. It moved the concierge away from the counter and brought his hand up to straighten his glasses. "The police are looking for her, I assure you, sir."

"When did this happen? Where?"

"She was one of the women who went to Delos last night for some ceremony. They stayed on the island overnight. I was told that early this morning, before sunrise, she was taken away on a boat. Another woman was injured and is in hospital."

Rick struggled keep his voice his normal, but was able thank the concierge for the information. He walked to the nearest policeman and tapped his shoulder. "I need to get to the hospital to see the woman who was injured in the Delos attack."

"Sorry, no one leaves the hotel. I can suggest you call."

Rick settled on a leather stool in the hotel bar and ordered a coffee. He reached inside his khaki jacket for his cell. He found the hospital number online. *Maybe I should call home first. Call Anna. Bitsy has no one else, no family or kids and Anna would want to know. And maybe I just need to hear a voice from home.* "But what can I tell her?"

The bartender placed a large mug of coffee in front of him. "You have a question?"

He shook his head. "Just talking to myself." He stared at the bright light of his cell phone. He looked up the number to the museum.

Chapter 31

Anna was lost in a daydream. Joe's case manager had called yesterday to confirm Joe's discharge plans for next week. Her mind bounced back and forth from visions of pushing him into the house in a wheelchair and setting up the bedside commode to visions of sitting under the Mediterranean sun with nothing on her mind but fun and a carafe of martinis.

The blinking light and the monotonous beep of her answering machine finally penetrated the morning daydream. Like it or not, she would need to get up into the reality of life at home in Middlecreek.

She listened to the first message from Joe. He had left it the night before.

WHEN ARE YOU PICKING ME UP? I'M READY TO COME HOME. She sighed. "Not 'til next week."

After a soft click the second message began. From Rick Bennett. His voice was muffled. If he hadn't identified himself, she wouldn't have known it was him.

ANNA, THIS IS RICK, RICK BENNETT. CALL ME AT THE HOTEL APOLLO WHEN YOU GET THIS MESSAGE. I KNOW IT'S EARLY THERE. I THOUGHT THE PHONE WOULD WAKE YOU.

She leaned closer to the answering machine. It wasn't like Rick to ramble or to call her for that matter.

ANYWAY, I NEED TO TALK TO YOU ASAP. HAVE THE HOTEL DESK PAGE ME. I DOUBT I'LL BE IN MY ROOM.

Her hand shook before her heart began to race. There didn't seem to be any oxygen in the room. She gathered Tuppence to her. "Something bad has happened," she whispered into the cat's ear.

Rick hadn't left a number.

She searched for the scrap of paper with Bitsy's contact information. A thick stack of scraps were tucked haphazardly into the pockets of her chintz covered day planner.

"Hotel Apollo," a soft female voice answered.

"I need to speak to Rick Bennett."

"I'll ring his room."

Before she could stop the operator, she heard several ear piercing clicks, then a tinny ring, ring and ring. She hung up and called back.

"Hotel Apollo."

"Please page Rick Bennett. He's not in his room." Her breath was shallow and rapid. Her pulse raced. She gripped her phone in one hand and her thigh in the other. She watched the clock on her bedside table. "Why isn't he answering the page, Tuppence?"

"Hello, this is Rick Bennett."

"Rick, its Anna. I just got your message. What's going on there?"

"Are you sitting down?"

"Yes." She held her breath.

"Bitsy's missing." She heard Rick's voice drop to a whisper. "Gone."

"What do you mean?" Anna had imagined different reasons for his call, but none of them came close to this news.

"It's a long story, Anna. Briefly, she was with other women at a sleepover, one was knocked unconscious and she was taken."

"Taken!"

She sprung up from her bed. She knocked last night's chamomile tea from its place on the nightstand. A dark, soggy tea bag fell to the floor. Tuppence pounced.

"What do you mean taken from a sleepover? Who would do this?"

Rick cut into her questions. "It's chaos here, not many answers yet."

She looked at Tuppence toying with the still wet tea bag. No answers there.

Anna was surprised to realize she had moved away from her bed. She cradled the phone under her shoulder and chin as she opened her bedroom blinds. Her sorry-we-aren't-going-to-London-after-all car sat dusty in the circular pebbled drive.

"Rick, I'm coming to Greece."

"What? Would you? You know Bitsy better than anyone and maybe you can help the authorities." There was a brief pause. "And me."

"I'll call you when I have my flight schedule. I'll be there as soon as I can and, Rick, keep me updated, text or call." Before she said goodbye, she asked one last question. "Do they think she's dead?"

"No, they believe she was kidnapped. And I may have met the kidnapper in the hotel. There was a man I confronted earlier last night. I'm trying to find out his name. I'll fill you in when you get here."

Anna snuggled Tuppence in her arms and blew into her ear. "I know Joe's scheduled to come home next week. But, it isn't next week, yet. And you, Tuppence, you'll love the kitty spa."

She pulled her soft sided carryon suitcase from the top shelf in her closet before she sat down on the bed to call the rehab hospital.

"Joe." Anna's voice was an octave higher than usual. "I'm leaving for Greece in a few hours." Her voice shifted to a lower octave. "I may not be here when you discharge. You may need to have the hospital make other arrangements for you."

"Have you lost your mind, Anna? You can't go to Greece. I'm coming home."

"Bitsy's been kidnapped." She swallowed hard. "Did you hear me, Bitsy, my best friend, is missing in Greece? You'll be fine. I'll call when I get there."

"You can't do this."

"Yes, I can and I am flying out of DFW today. Don't give me a hard time about this, Joe. I'll call Reverend Wilson. He may be able to help you."

"But..."

"I'm hanging up now." She hit the off button on the receiver.

She turned to the back of her day planner to the telephone numbers. She couldn't remember where she had written Reverend Wilson's home number. It could be under W for Wilson or H for Harold. No, not there. *Maybe*

I put it under M for minister or R for reverend. Her last choice was to look under the name of the church, F for Fellowship Christian Church. *Now why did I put his home number there?*

After her usual lengthy explanation of events, Reverend Wilson agreed to pick Joe up from the hospital, if discharged before she returned home from Greece, and take him to the parsonage.

I'm going to Greece. Me, Anna Tudor. The joy of her thoughts of a trip to a foreign destination crashed against her forehead along with the palm of her hand. *Bitsy's missing, you dotty old fool! Stay focused.*

Her reservation was confirmed. Her bright floral carryon suitcase was packed. She pulled on her Liberty of London floral crop pants. Prissy would pick her up for the drive to DFW with a quick stop at Bow Wow Kitty. She tucked her passport into an outer pocket in her tote bag. Almost immediately she pulled it out. She flipped through its blank pages. Before the weekend is over, one of these pages will have been stamped. Adrenalin pumped through her veins. Thrill mixed with fear, excitement with anxiety.

Since Bitsy's departure for Greece and her daily reminder of Joe's infirmities, longing for independence led her to rethink her choices.

I stayed when I could've left. I should've left him.

She studied her reflection in the dresser mirror. Deep lines bracketed her thinned lips. Her famous dimples had all but disappeared. Crinkled skin spread out from her eyes. *My wrinkles show years of smiles, years of laughter.* She shook her hair brush like a marimba, her head tilted to the left. *He may have lied, but he's my partner and oh, how he could dance.* She gently placed her hair brush onto the filigreed rimmed dresser tray. Will he dance again? Will he walk?

A car horn startled her. It was followed by a beep from her cell. Prissy had arrived.

Chapter 32

Hermann Bracken crammed his phone into a small inside jacket pocket. He sat in a taverna outside Piraeus located in an area where many summer homes of wealthy Americans lined the beachfront. He had been assigned the task to wait there until Constantine was within an hour of the port, then others would join him. He was the only society member who spoke Greek and as the newest member of the group was usually stuck with surveillance or other boring jobs.

The cold coffee in front of him had tasted bitter and thick. His eyes roamed around the dark room. A roughhewn shelf on one wall held different brands of beer. He had been warned to avoid any alcohol. He snorted at the thought of lager for breakfast. Now as the minutes ticked by like sand in an hourglass, his mouth watered for a taste of the rich foam head of a good German beer. He rubbed his hand across the well-worn checkered table cloth and tried to remember the text message he received from the group of men meeting in Athens. His desire for a drink increased.

***

At 3:00 a.m., in one of the well-appointed suites at the King George Hotel in Athens, Karl Fresch stood in the room's small foyer. When his colleagues entered the room, he motioned to the sitting area. He remained silent while they sat down next to a large marble-topped coffee table.

The room doorbell sounded. "We'll not speak until after refreshments have been deposited." He placed an index finger against his lips. He turned the dead bolt lock and opened the door. A hotel employee stood on the plush burgundy hallway carpet, hands on a large rolling cart of coffee carafes, cups and saucers and a basket of pastries.

He took a step backward to allow space for the cart to be rolled inside the room. When the waiter maneuvered the cart into the room's foyer, he placed a hand on his shoulder.

"I'll take the cart. We don't want to be disturbed." He placed a large tip into the waiter's hand. "*Danka*, thank you."

He turned back toward the two men seated on the large brocade couch. Two slipper chairs were on the other side of the coffee table. It was covered with numerous maps and faxes from Vienna and Piraeus. Before he sat down, Karl pushed some of the paperwork into piles to make room for the coffee service and sweet smelling pastries. Cinnamon, nutmeg and the smell of roasted pecans filled the room.

"Shall we come to order," he said. "I'm sure you're aware of the urgency of this meeting." He poured three cups of coffee. "I recently heard from Johannes regarding the whereabouts of Constantine. But, alas, no word about the diary."

The two men on the couch glanced at each other. In unison, they slumped backward, their heads thumped against the tightly tufted couch. They gazed up to the frescoed ceiling. Bert Blancl was the first to speak.

"So where is the Playboy of the Society?"

Edgar Stollenwerck harrumphed and reached for a pecan encrusted square shaped pastry. "Baklava, my favorite Greek sweet."

"Earlier this morning, Johannes dispatched Hermann to Piraeus," Karl said. "He reports Constantine is somewhere between Mykonos and Piraeus. Reportedly, he's on a boat, a boat he's piloting," With a grin, he saluted his colleagues.

227

"Hermann reported he will arrive in Piraeus around 7:00 this morning. It seems he brings something with him, but no one knows what."

"So, no diary, but something that has to do with the book?" Edgar talked around the crueler in his mouth. "Sounds fishy to me. Constantine brags about another fantastic, but bogus, lead and wastes our time."

Karl waved a finger at Edgar. "No, no, not this time. Be aware it wasn't only Constantine who watched the woman he said had possession of the diary. A friend on Mykonos slipped a hand full of coins to a clever and, perhaps, hungry bellboy at the Hotel Apollo. At last report, late yesterday, the woman left Mykonos with a group of women for Delos. Within a few hours, Johannes reported Constantine had asked for permission to disable the woman, if necessary."

"Disable? Are we now thugs?" Bert's usual flushed face turned ashy white.

Karl stood up. He walked behind a slipper chair and rested both hands on its gold raw silk upholstery.

Edgar turned to Bert. "We have clues here." He nudged Bert with his elbow. "Our Playboy Duke has the American woman with him. *Et alors, cosci ci.* Don't you see? When Constantine arrives she will be in our hands."

"And just what do we do with her?" Bert jumped up and away from Edgar. "This disabled woman with no diary." He rubbed his unshaven chin between the fingers and thumb of his right hand. He stopped next to Karl. "Has Johannes put this together? Does he know what Constantine has done?"

"Ah, my friends, he's aware and on his way to Mayerling. We're to meet him there with Constantine's, shall we say, surprise. Then we make a plan to retrieve the diary from its currently unknown location. In the meantime, we must make arrangements for travel from Piraeus to Mayerling. We'll meet Constantine at the dock."

He motioned to Edgar to remove the empty breakfast basket from the table. It was time to unfold the maps and get to work.

Long before daylight, the final plans were in place for the type of transportation, necessary clothing and quickest route from Piraeus to Vienna and a needed transfer for the trip to Mayerling.

***

Daybreak began over distant and scattered islands. The sea that tapped the hull of the boat changed from deep purple to shades of orange, blue and gold in the morning light as if a rainbow had fallen into the ocean. Bitsy had removed her restraints in the smothering darkness of the cabin. Constantine stayed on deck piloting the boat at a slow speed. She hadn't attempted to talk with him for hours and waited for daylight to leave the cabin. What was there to say or ask? She was his captive. He was in charge. At least while on the boat, she thought.

She rubbed her wrists and ankles for the hundredth time. Blood stained her fingertips, but her acrylic nails remained in place. In fact, they acted as leverage to loosen the bindings. She smiled before berating herself for her thankful praise that her nails were intact. *I must be the shallowest person on the planet. I've been kidnapped for heaven's sake, who cares about fingernails at a time like this?* She swung her legs over the side of the narrow bed. *First priority, get on solid ground. Now that will be something to be grateful for.*

When the morning light illuminated the cabin opening and the wooden stairs, she slid off the berth. She stretched her arms above her head, rolled her shoulders in circles and bent over to touch her toes. She slowly opened the door of the head not wanting to alert Constantine that she was out of her restraints and, certainly, not that she was about to use the toilet.

"I can hear you down there. Your captain grants you permission to come top side."

She heard a shrill whistle. *Is he nuts? Captain Verone now.*

Inside the head, she closed her eyes and prayed. Prayed for strength, cunning, and rescue. She prayed that this man wasn't psychotic or a psychopath, that he was someone she could reason with. *More fantasies!*

She sat on the narrow seating that edged the deck and leaned against the side of the boat. Looking across the vast expanse of water with no land in sight, her imagination fought to take over her resolve to survive no matter what Constantine had in mind for her. The middle to the ocean was no place to make a stand. She would have to wait for the optimal moment. In the meantime, she could find out more about her kidnapper, his interest in the books and who, if anyone waited for them on the mainland.

"Ah, it's beautiful, is it not, Signora?" Constantine came to stand beside her. "There's nothing like a sunrise over the Aegean." He raised his arm to the sky before he reached out to touch her shoulder.

She recoiled and felt sharp pain in her right elbow. "Ouch!" She cupped the injured area with her hand.

Constantine moved closer. He shoved his hands into the pockets of his black shorts. "No yelling, Ms. Bowman."

Don't anger him, use your well-practiced charms.

"Please, signore, don't touch me." Bitsy held out one arm, "I'm sunburned. It hurts when touched." She came close to batting her eyelids. *Charm, don't encourage.* "Will you tell me where we're going?"

"We're going on a journey with several stops along the way. It'll be a long journey, but we will reach an end."

He tipped his cap and moved away. From the wheel, he called to her.

"There're cheeses and breads in a blue and white bag under the seat near you. Please to eat all you want."

She found the canvas bag. She was hungry and thirsty. She set out some food on a table cloth that had been folded inside the bag. Before she started her meal, she offered a prayer under her breath, "Please help me stay strong in body, mind and spirit and receive nourishment from this blessed gift of food." After a pause, she added, "May I find the strength of Artemis in me."

She was surprised she enjoyed the meal, the fullness of the feta cheese mixed with richness of the Kalamata olives. She savored each bite and tried not to imagine it being her last meal. Behind her Constantine hummed a tune that sounded like *Hey Mambo, Mambo Italiano.*

Is he oblivious to the seriousness what he's done? She wrapped an olive and some feta in a piece of pita bread.

"Are you going to talk to me?" she said.

"Nothing to say."

"Well, how about giving me an idea of why you kidnapped me, what you expect to gain?"

"You're a smart woman, a smart American woman, no? How do you say, figure it out?"

"I know it has to do with the books I brought from the states, but you know I don't have them. You looked in my room, right? Where I left them. They weren't there. So, I have no clue where they are, Signore. I call you Signore; you're Italian, aren't you?"

No response.

While she worked to free herself from the bindings, she decided she would stick with the story that the books must have been stolen from her room. No need to involve Peter, not yet anyway.

"If you think I can help you find the books, you're wrong."

He began to hum what sounded like *Strangers in the Night.*

"Don't you get it? I can't help you. So, before anything else happens, how about you letting me go?"

She pulled her legs onto the bench and wrapped her arms around her knees.

Constantine turned off the engine. He took a long drink from a flask that had rested on the dashboard. He didn't walk toward her; he went to the other side of the boat. He dropped the heavy anchor overboard.

From across the deck, he spread his feet apart, put his hands on his hips and let out a guttural laugh.

"Maybe you're not so smart or maybe you think I'm stupid."

She held his gaze. She didn't believe he would harm her while on the boat. But she didn't need to test the theory that he believed she knew where the books were. Maybe she would lead him on a bit.

"No, I don't think that, no way. But maybe someone else beat you to the books. That's a possibility."

A rogue wave tipped the boat upward. Constantine teetered on his feet for a second before he raised the anchor and took a step back to the wheel.

She wanted to ask about Pamela. She wondered if she was alive. In the brief moment before she had passed out, she saw blood on Pamela's face. *If he's already killed someone...?*

She shivered and leaned over the side of the boat to wash her fingers of olive oil.

"Hey, don't think you can swim to safety! We're many miles from land and I don't think you want to die."

She leaned away from the boat railing.

"That's better."

Time passed slowly and she repeated several times that she didn't know where to find the books.

Finally, Constantine responded to her denials.

"I don't have belief in you. For one thing, Ms. Bowman, you say books, not book. Ha! I'm not one of your book worms. There's but one book that matters and I believe you know that."

Is that a clue, has he told me something I can use?

The sun remained to their east as if it were tied in place. She glanced at her watch. 6:20 a. m. Greece time.

Chapter 33

Peter didn't take his eyes off Pamela while she recounted her assault and Bitsy's abduction. His face was without expression like those found on the Greek statues in his museum. His inner response to the revelations was completely out of control. His gut churned, his fingertips and toes tingled and his silent mantra was to be still. He wanted to bolt out of the room and race back to the museum. More than anything, he wanted to check on the books. The safety of the books.

When Pamela mentioned Bitsy's concern over the importance of the books given to him, he knew he couldn't avoid being involved in the investigation. He moved a step back from her bed. The policeman in the room moved closer to him.

It's just a matter of time before they'll want me to accompany them to the police station. Did I lock the safe before I left?

He buried his hands in the front folds of his robe. He reviewed his movements after the police had told him about Pamela, before he came to the hospital. He had rushed to write the note for the door and turn off the lights. There had been no time to go his private office and check the safe.

Why did I move the books from my house? To keep them close to me. Yet, if I'm a suspect, both the museum and my home will be searched.

The difference, in Peter's mind, was if the books were in his house, he might have a chance to secure them in his cubby hole behind the fresco, where he has kept his priceless artifacts. Items he acquired due to his position at the museum. *I'd already decided those books would be mine.*

It had been obvious to him that Bitsy had no idea of their value. It wasn't likely she had any interest in the fabled history of the red leather bound diary. But he did. And she had no idea who Marta was. But he discovered her involvement in the tragedy of Maylering when he translated the first entry in the small black diary. *If the books are safe in the museum, do I turn them over? Never.*

***

"Peter." Pamela reached out for his hand. "Are you alright? You look awfully pale."

"What horror you and Bitsy have had." His voice trembled to match his shaky outstretched hand. "I suppose I was trying to not hear the details of your ordeal." He made the sign of the cross. "I'm sorry, my friend."

"Forget what I've been through, it's Bitsy we should be concerned about."

The lead policeman spoke in a deep and solemn tone, developed over years of giving terrible news to family and friends of crime victims. "We don't know exactly where she is at this time, Ms. Jones, but we do know your information is vital to Ms. Bowman's recovery."

"You've no idea where she might be?" Pamela pushed herself up from the mattress and pillows. She leaned toward the foot of the bed. She scanned the group of people who stood around her. "I told you she was put onto a boat, a blue boat, a boat with Jason painted on its side. Have you been looking for that boat?"

"The Aegean is a big sea, Ms. Jones. We've sent out many boats and helicopters, but the kidnapper had many hours on the water before you were awake and able to give us the information you mention."

"Sorry." Pamela sniffed and sighed. She lay back onto the pillow. "Can I ask if you're watching all the ports for that boat? I pray the man has done no harm to my friend. That he's taking her to some port of call."

"Ms. Jones, there are far too many ports and docks in this area of the world to have people watch all of them. I will say that we're covering all the major ports."

Peter nodded toward the two policemen who prepared to leave the room.

The lead investigator put his hand on the hospital door handle. Before he opened the door, he turned back toward Pamela and Peter.

"Mr. Gallenos, we'll need to take your information at the police station. Ms. Jones must have time to rest. Please come with us, sir."

Chapter 34

"Officer!" Rick called out in an attempt to attract the attention of a policeman. For hours, he had tried to get information about Bitsy's disappearance with no luck. The tallest policeman in the hotel lobby acknowledged his shout. May be someone would be willing to talk. He approached the officer. "Sir, can you tell me if the missing woman has been found?"

"I'm sorry, sir. We're not here to talk to hotel guests about the incident. An investigator will see you as he can."

"I'd like to give my statement at the police station. I need to reach the hospital to see about Ms. Bowman's friend. The woman who was injured in the attack."

"I have no authority, sir."

He asked if he could return to his room until the interview.

"That's permissible."

Rick pushed the button for the third floor and the one for the basement. He knew how to exit the hotel from the lowest level. His Cadillac was in the underground parking.

When he checked to make sure it was in a protected area of the garage, he had gotten lost. He found himself in the hotel basement among large stainless steel pipes, rows and rows of locker-like closets and one door with a red lighted sign above it that said Exit in Greek and English. What had irritated him then was his way out now.

The afternoon had changed to early evening. He walked around the lush landscaping at the back of the hotel. Hands in his pockets, a whistle on his lips. Soon he had made his way several blocks away from the hotel grounds. A taxi driver sat on the front fender of a beat up cab, a cigarette between his lips. Rick raised a hand. The cabbie tossed his smoke on the ground. Rick slid onto the back seat.

"The hospital, please."

"Okie dokie." A wide grin showed tobacco browned teeth. "You're American, no?"

"Yes, I'm American and a friend has been hurt. Can you hurry it up a bit?"

"I drive fast. It will take no time to get you there."

Rick sat back against cracked and yellowed plastic seat covers. Out the left side window, he saw the shimmer of the sea. He shielded his eyes. The horizon glowed as if under a powerful spotlight, the sun hovered about it. *Hang in there, Bitsy. You're the strongest woman I know. I want you back, we all want you back.*

He tapped on the glass that separated him from the driver. "Sir, I've changed my mind. Take me to police headquarters."

As much as he wanted to talk with Pamela, to get the details of the attack and abduction, he needed to tell the police about the unknown man he had argued with at the hotel. The man who looked for Bitsy the night she disappeared. He hadn't seen the man in the hotel since their confrontation.

The Mykonos Police Station was made up of three small rooms in a white washed stucco building with a blue painted door. Brown shutters and flower boxes decorated the windows. The only indication this wasn't another small bungalow on the island was a large rectangular sign situated above the door. Thick painted letters spelled out, *Myconos Police.*

The main room was filled with numerous computers and sleek ergonomic chairs behind wooden desks. Ladder back chairs placed against the side of the desks didn't look very comfortable. Rick sat on a long bench at the front of the room.

After a five minute wait, a large man with a wide handlebar mustache and wearing an elaborate uniform stood in front of him. He bent forward and breathed into his ear.

"I'm the Chief of Police, Opi Mercori. I was alerted of your failure to follow the rules, Mr. Bennett. Come now into my office."

"Sure, happy to oblige you."

Seated across from the police chief, Rick told him about his encounter with the man with slicked back black hair and an Italian accent in the lobby of the Hotel Apollo. He emphasized how this man demanded information that would lead him to Bitsy the evening she had gone to Delos, the evening she was kidnapped during the night.

He stood up after he finished his story, but was told to remain seated. He angled his chair to better see what was going on in the main room. Would the man from the hotel be brought in for questioning?

"What are you going to do with my information?"

"We're questioning every guest at the Hotel Apollo. If that man's there, we'll talk to him. I'll call the concierge to confirm your story and ask if he knows the name of the man you described. Meanwhile, you're not to leave the island. Understand?"

"I do want to see Pamela Jones at the hospital. She was the last person to see my friend."

"I cannot allow that sir."

Rick jumped up from the chair and leaned over the desk. His cheeks burned as blood rushed to his face. "I've given my statement and I will see Bitsy's friend."

He turned away from the police chief. Two policemen who had entered the station walked on either side of a man he recognized. The curator of the museum. He had seen Bitsy with him after the first day of the conference, the day he tried to apologize to her. *Maybe I'll hang around here before I go to the hospital.*

He looked over his shoulder. "Changed my mind, Chief Mercori. I'll be a good boy."

***

Peter was shown to one of the straight back chairs next to an officer's desk. He slid onto the chair with his eyes cast down. He massaged his fingernails with his fingertips.

"Mr. Gallenos," the officer began, "We're aware of the relationship between you and the missing woman. We know she's part of the current group meeting at your museum. We know from Ms. Pamela Jones other information that must be discussed directly with you."

244

Peter remained mute. He rubbed his robe stretched over his legs with both hands. Still no eye contact with the officer.

"For instance, we know Ms. Bowman passed to you some books. Where are those books, Mr. Gallenos?"

The time had come. The officer reached around the corner of the desk. He tapped Peter's knee with a pen. "Mr. Gallenos?"

For the first time since he arrived, Peter straightened his spine. He cleared his throat.

"Many participants bring me books, sir. Part of my work is the study of out of print books, antiquarian books. Why do you think the books left me by Ms. Bowman are connected with her disappearance?"

"I'm the one to ask questions, sir."

"Sorry, it just seems unimportant, the books. Isn't it more likely she was mugged for her jewelry or her looks? Ms. Bowman is an attractive woman who, how shall I say, flaunts her assets."

"No, sir," the officer said. "We have firsthand knowledge from Ms. Jones that the books brought here by Ms. Bowman were valuable. Were you not there when Ms. Jones said it was you that placed importance on these books?"

Peter's shoulders sagged. His gaze returned to his fingernails.

"We know the man showed no interest in Ms. Jones' jewelry or her person," the officer continued, "When found she had on a valuable ring. And I might say, Ms. Jones is also an attractive woman, but she wasn't taken."

Peter shifted his weight on the small chair. He felt a heavy hand on his left shoulder.

"You know Bitsy?" Rick squeezed his shoulder like a vice.

"Do I know you?" He blinked rapidly at the tall man who stood over him.

***

"Excuse me, officer," Rick said, "I also want to know what this man knows about Bitsy's disappearance."

"Be my guest." The officer leaned back in his chair.

Rick pulled up one of the small chairs. Out of the corner of his eye, he saw the Police Chief standing in his office doorway, combing the mustache that topped his smile like a fuzzy beret.

"So, Mr. Gallenos," he said, "I heard this officer call you by that name. Tell me about your relationship with my lifelong friend, Ms. Bowman. And tell me about the books she brought to you."

***

When Peter rushed out of the museum to see Pamela, he hadn't changed from his heavy black robe and high necked shirt. Under the fluorescent lights and the glare of this new interrogator, beads of sweat ran down his clean shaven cheeks to rest along the ridge of his collar. His thoughts were rapid and confused. *I don't want to let go of those books. But how can I not help with the investigation? Bitsy trusts me. Has my passion corrupted my character? What will become of Bitsy, of the books, of me?*

"How about some answers?" Rick had shoved his chair closer to him. They sat knee to knee.

Peter pulled a large handkerchief from under his robe. "Please, sir, please back away."

"Not until I get some answers."

"Okay, I do believe Bitsy was kidnapped because of the books she brought to the island."

He rubbed the damp handkerchief across his forehead.

"She brought them here for a friend in Texas and asked if I would look at them. She wanted to know if they have value beyond being very old. She didn't know their value, but she does now."

"And how valuable are they?" The Police Chief had joined the group of men at the small desk.

"Priceless," whispered Peter.

Chapter 35

The drive to the Dallas Ft. Worth International Airport was uneventful. No traffic jams, no accidents, no bad weather, little conversation. Anna's right hand gripped the overhead handle as if she was in a race car taking a sharp curve. Her forehead touched the window.

It was nice of Prissy to act as chauffeur. She was worried about Bitsy, too.

"So, Ms. Tudor, will you call me when you know something? I mean know something about Bitsy. Missing sounds scary anytime, but she's in a foreign land."

"We'll find her. I'm sure the police are doing everything in their power and Bitsy has many friends there at the conference. A posse to look for her."

"Well, I guess she couldn't have gone far, after all she's on an island, right?"

"Oh, Prissy, Bitsy will be so grateful for your concern." Anna kept her eyes out the window. Prissy knew nothing about the man Rick had described. Missing meant lost in a crowd like at the State Fair where many people get lost from their family members each year. She wouldn't dissuade her of that notion.

They exited the highway and merged into the south airport entrance traffic.

"Ms. Tudor, are you alright? You've been so quiet since we got onto Highway 183."

"What?" She blinked away tears.

"I mean you haven't said much all the way here."

"I'll be fine, Prissy. I'll be fine." She had said that to herself for hours alternating with thoughts that Joe would be fine and Bitsy would be fine. She hated the word fine. Meaningless, easy word to avoid reality.

"Well, here we are, Ms. Tudor. Do you want me to go in with you?"

"No, just drop me off at the curb." She was about to say she would be fine, but instead managed a small smile. "Thank you for bringing me at such short notice. Keep up your good work at the bookshop, stay busy and I'll call when I've more information about Bitsy."

She opened her door as soon as the car stopped. Prissy popped the trunk from inside the car and a waiting porter pulled out her carryon bag.

"Be careful going home."

"Bon voyage, Ms. Tudor."

Anna waved. She followed the porter to the curbside check in counter. *How I've longed to hear those words. Bon voyage. But not like this.*

She pulled off her pink plaid Easy Spirit shoes and placed them in the plastic bin on the conveyor belt. She put her tote on top and her carryon beside the bin. She stepped through the metal detector. No beep, thank goodness. She bought a Danish and a small coffee at a kiosk before making her way to the gate. She settled onto a black faux leather seat in front of double gray doors that concealed the airline's movable walkway. Her plane hadn't arrived yet and the tarmac was vacant with the exception of two baggage carriers and their drivers. With each sip of her coffee she reviewed the information Rick has shared about the man he met and confronted in the hotel. The man he suspected was the kidnapper.

Why would a total stranger kidnap Bitsy? Who was this suspect? What could he want? Is Bitsy hurt, has she been found? These thoughts circled like a whirligig, each one chasing the other and showing up again. *Bitsy's a strong and smart woman. She'll outwit this man. I need to believe that.*

She checked her watch for the hundredth time. *Where is my plane?*

She ran a hand down her crop pants. Their bright English rose print trimmed at the calf with pink plaid that matched her shoes brought a smile to her face. Her brows relaxed.

She flipped through the latest People Magazine. She stopped on the page showing the cast of Downton Abbey. It had become her second favorite English television program, edging out Poirot. Miss Marple remained number one. Further into the magazine, she began to read about an actor with a head injury. *Too close to home.* She folded the magazine and stuffed it into her tote.

When she glanced up, she saw her plane had taxied to the gate.

The plane was full. Summer travel to Greece. She wiggled past the aisle and middle seat passengers and maneuvered herself onto the window seat. She slid her carryon under the seat in front of her and tucked her tote bag next to the armrest. She kept a purse size journal on her lap. She turned to the page where she had jotted down several phone numbers. Her current support group. Prissy, Rick, Minister Wilson. No rehab hospital. Joe's needs were too great at the moment.

The revving engines and the jolting bounce of the jet as it sped down the runway brought her back to the present moment. She hugged the journal to her heart. Life lines.

A flight attendant arrived at her row of seats. She leaned in and handed her a dry martini. She barely remembered ordering the drink. She stretched her legs as much as possible and sipped the strong cocktail. The thirteen hour flight to Athens had begun and there would be the quick trip by Aegean Airlines to Mykonos.

The plane hit some turbulence. She inhaled a sharp breath.

What will I do if Joe doesn't get his independence back?

She sipped her drink. Martinis reminded her of Bitsy, but also of Joe. After they met at the college bookstore and after his almost daily need for her assistance there and after she had agreed to a date, he told her he was a martini aficionado. They were at a charming bistro styled restaurant in the Turtle Creek area of Dallas and he explained he could name the vodka or gin used by any restaurant in town. She was barely old enough to drink.

He was so handsome, worldly and sophisticated. I was swept off my small town feet. Martinis in Big D with an educated man of means.

When the engagement was announced her hometown friends asked if she would drop out of college. Women went to college to find a husband and she was about to have one. Her college friends reminded her she was at the forefront of women's liberation. College was imperative.

Joe sided with Middlecreek friends. He was ready for a wife at home. I had other dreams. What did my degree do for me? Nothing.

She finished her drink and asked for a pillow. No more thoughts of Joe, of what was or wasn't meant to be. Bitsy's top priority.

Head nestled against the seat, she looked out the window. She couldn't see the ground.

***

The plane seemed to float through a pitch black sky. She turned away from the window not wanting to see the flashes of lightning pierce a bank of storm clouds. Her eyebrows shot up and under her fringe bangs. She was the only one on the plane. *Where is everyone?* She jumped out of her seat and stumbled toward the front of the plane. Blocking the cockpit door stood a large Mastiff, teeth bared and making the most terrifying sound she had ever heard. A low growl like the hum of a large thrasher machine. There was no

254

way around the dog. She turned and fled toward the back of the empty plane. When she reached the last row of seats, she saw sunlight pooled at her feet. She bent down and looked out the window. A giant butterfly pierced an angry looking cloud. Its wing span was as wide as the plane was long. With each graceful movement of the large wings, rich colors fell away to disappear into the dark sky. She sat down in the seat and pressed her face against the window. The clouds had separated to reveal crystal blue water and under the shade of the butterfly's wings she saw a rainbow bleed into the sea and form a circle. In the center she saw Bitsy waving an outstretched hand and smiling up at her. The water's reflection bounced off her purple nails and danced through her strawberry blonde hair. She wore a life vest.

Anna's eyelids fluttered. *Caterpillar, chrysalis, butterfly. Transformation..*

"Miss, miss, would you like chicken or beef for dinner?" The flight attendant gently touched Anna's shoulder.

"What?" She blinked her eyes open.

"You were asleep, Miss."

She rubbed her cheeks with both hands, her head against the headrest. *A dream.* Bitsy safe and well. Suddenly, she was very hungry.

Chapter 36

Karl poured another coffee. Edgar and Bert had left for Piraeus. He took a few sips of the tepid drink before he placed the cup onto a small saucer. The cup rattled as it tipped over. *What a mess, but one I can clean up.* He twisted his Society signet ring with his left hand. To transport a hostage from the port at Piraeus to Vienna wouldn't be an easy task. His major concern was moving her from Vienna to Maylering. The small out of the way dock near Piraeus was likely to be deserted, but Vienna wouldn't be.

He rested his head on the back of the brocade sofa. *Then on to Mayerling.* With eyes closed against the light of the crystal chandelier, he remembered the first time his father took him to the cottage.

He was special, the first born son, and he would inherit a special mission to protect the history, the legacy of the Hapsburg dynasty. That meant finding the Emperor's diary. The personal diary that disappeared from the possession of his highly trusted Grand Master of the

Horse, Karl's grandfather, Helmut Fresch. The rumor of a smaller diary kept by a young Austrian undermaid, who lived at Mayerling and served the Crown Prince and his guests had been dismissed as a romantic notion by commoners. Without the Emperor's diary, the true story of Mayerling and the deaths of Rudolph and his mistress, Marie, remained a mystery. Karl reviewed again the multiple versions of the event of January 30, 1889, which included several conspiracy theories.

He stretched both arms over his head. How had the Society's glorious mission come to this disastrous day?

He stood up and removed his jacket. He leaned closer to the coffee table and stacked the papers and faxes into one neat pile. His thoughts remained on Maylering. By chance and circumstance his family became intimately involved in the splendor and tragedy of the days when Mayerling was filled with royalty from many countries.

He rubbed his forehead with his fingertips. His yawn was a heavy sigh. *A quick nap that's what I need before going to Piraeus.*

His eyes closed. He noticed flickering spots on his eyelids and he imagined the Vienna of his childhood. His beloved metal horses kept in the wooden humpbacked chest at the foot of his small bed. If he was to visit relatives in Salzburg, he would carefully pack them in his knapsack for the journey. He took them to the Vienna Woods on picnics and to local beergartens filled with pipe smoke and the smell of sausages. As he fell closer to sleep, he saw himself play his favorite game. He would pretend the circular rug under the family dining table was the Ringstrasse and his horses were Lipizzaners.

Chapter 37

The dark mahogany paneled room where Marta sat folding and refolding her tattered lace handkerchief was larger than her home in Vienna. The meager light coming through small openings in the heavy velvet curtains covering the room's three windows did little to illuminate hanging tapestries the size of floor rugs. She didn't see a wall clock and she had no timepiece. Her thirst and hunger told her it must be mid-day. The small meal she ate hurriedly after waking wasn't enough to sustain her for the long drive to Mayerling and this long wait, alone, in the reception room.

She was barely eighteen, from a local Viennese family. Her father was a cobbler. Her mother was ill with consumption and wasn't expected to live. Her older brother, in the military, never contacted the family. Their common status embarrassed him. The day he began his military career he boasted of his importance to the glory of the Austria-Hungary Empire. With her mother near death and her father aging, she sought employment rather than marriage.

Who would be interested in me? She wrapped her arms around her growling stomach. When she borrowed books from the library last week, the librarian told her about the position as an undermaid at Mayerling. All the imagination contained in the thousands of books in the library couldn't match her immediate fantasy about employment at Mayerling, in the Vienna Woods, where the Crown Prince enjoyed hunting with royal friends. She quickly sent an inquiry along with a recent picture.

"Young miss."

She looked in the direction of the soft voice. A pretty blonde haired girl stood on the edge of the shadows. Marta stood so quickly her crumpled handkerchief dropped to the floor.

"Yes," she said. Not wanting to appear clumsy, she ignored the handkerchief that rested on the toe of her shoe.

The girl merely pointed toward the floor. Marta squatted down and retrieved the handkerchief.

"Please come with me, my name is Britta, and I will take you to my supervisor."

Marta followed the older girl down a long hallway. She held her small black handbag against her chest along with a sheave of papers, numerous recommendations from local merchants who had known her all her life and from the two families for whom she once worked as a babysitter and tutor. She also carried two small books. Her love of books provided her with an education and sparked a desire to be a writer. Inside her handbag, she had wrapped a new diary in a pale lavender handkerchief trimmed with hand tatted lace. The handkerchief belonged to her mother, the only prized possession she owned. Marta feared she wouldn't see her mother again.

Britta explained that Mayerling had been built as a convent, but the Crown Prince wanted a hunting lodge in the Vienna Woods. His father, the Emperor, turned Maylering into a place where heads of state and family members could enjoy hunting parties for the men and garden parties for the women. She pointed out the rich wood paneling and the ornate chandeliers which reminded visitors that this place, too, was part of the Hapsburg Empire, an empire known for elaborate and undeniably sumptuous homes, palaces and guest houses.

"If you're hired, you will live here in the Lodge along with other servants."

Marta nodded her head.

Britta continued down the hallway a few steps in front of her. Abruptly, she stopped.

Marta came close to running into her.

Instead, Britta took her by the arm and leaned closer. She whispered, "If you work here, you must sign a document to never tell tales. Do you understand, miss?"

Startled by being touched and her so close to her face, Marta hesitated in her response.

"Perhaps, we stop here, young miss, if you're unsure of your ability to be silent."

"Oh, no, Miss Britta, I can be silent. I was only taken by surprise. I've never spoken out of place. I do not gossip."

Britta continued with the tour and provided additional information about the royal family.

"You will not see the Empress here often, but the Emperor comes frequently. Mostly, you will see the Crown Prince, his attendants and, may I now say to you, some lady friends who come, not for gardening, but for other things."

At the end of the hall, a tall beveled glass window overlooked well groomed grounds. A small stone wishing well was surrounded by a flower bed protected from wild life by a low wrought iron fence. Elaborate evergreen topiaries stood like sentinels in empty beds stripped of visible life by the cold winter weather and the latest snow cover. A massive sculpture of a five point buck at the feet of a hunter stood on the edge of the woods behind the manicured garden.

"Oh, what a sight!" Marta pressed her body against the thick wood paneled wall, her chin raised and eyes downcast toward the flagstone walkway lined with small pine trees and decorated with strings of berries.

"Come, young miss, Herr Schmidt, awaits you."

After her interview, she was shown her quarters in the lower level of the lodge. She would share the room with two other girls. Her duties would center on serving meals, either in the main dining room or in individual apartments, to both guests and the Crown Prince. Herr Schmidt had seemed especially taken by the fact the she was literate and he gave her a stack of papers, including the floor plan of the lodge, a list of specific duties and a page titled Rules of Residence.

Alone in her room, she opened the small valise she had left at the front door of the lodge. On top of her neatly folded nightgown was a list of things to be brought from her home in Vienna. Herr Schmidt said a carriage would bring her things within a few days.

When there was a knock on her door, she quickly closed her suitcase

I must not show my fear or anxiety. This is my home now.

"Enter, please."

Britta balanced a plate of cheese and bread in one hand, and pushed the door open with her hips. She held a carafe of wine by its slim neck.

"Welcome to Mayerling, Miss, I will leave you to settle in and have some sustenance."

Marta sat on the thin blanket that covered her bed. She took a quick sip of the golden colored wine. It warmed her throat and chest with its spicy tart taste unlike the dark lager served at home. After another sip, she removed her diary from her purse and unwrapped it. She took a small ink bottle and rough handled pen from her valise.

26 December 1888

Today my life changed. I'm surrounded by those who are educated and who have money, power, and a lively life. No drudgery here. I promise to make entries that will remind me of what I am learning. About life, our country, our royal family. Nothing will escape me. Conversations and menus, whispers and names of the handsome guards and attendants to the Royal Family. Things that become part of me by my writing. Oh, my mother, I wish you could be here to hug me good-night. I will be a good recorder for you if you can be able to ever know my new life. I am to meet the Crown Prince tomorrow. My heart flutters in my chest. Good-night to Mayerling, good-night to my Wien.

She ran her right hand across the top of the small book, and then placed it under her mattress. She couldn't have imagined the events she would witness and document. Or the efforts made to covert the truth. Within five weeks of her arrival, the Crown Prince would be dead along with his mistress. She would be removed from the lodge in the dark of night with the weight of several gold coins folded into her gloved hand. Deposited at the door of her parents' home, she would be told her knowledge, her truth, was not to be breathed to anyone on threat of her life.

***

At the same time Marta was writing in her diary, Emperor Franz Joseph made another entry into his personal diary. Only his Master of the Horse, Helmut Fresch, knew he kept two diaries. The official one and the one in which he now wrote. The one in which he could bare his troubled soul, for it was troubled.

In the event the diary fell into enemies' hands, the Emperor had devised his own code. Should some catastrophic event occur which required the Emperor's personal writings to be revealed; Helmut Fresch was given the means to decode the entries.

He felt he had covered all possibilities and felt comfortable expressing his deepest fears and concerns. Cathartic and revealing, the written words allowed him to maintain his formal persona while sorting through his private anguish about his son.

He focus was on the escalating and humiliating behavior of the Crown Prince. Not only his promiscuousness, but the growing rumors of his association with the Freemasons, a group banned by the Vatican and therefore by the Hapsburg Empire.

The Emperor knew political enemies wanted his son to denounce the royal dynasty. This was not going to happen even if it meant disowning the heir to the throne. But how to accomplish this task was his bane.

Today is the day after Christmas, the day after the celebration of the birth of our Lord and I plot the downfall of my own son. How can this be done? I will not, by my hand, harm him, but he must be stopped. His health is compromised, but is that enough to declare him unfit to stand in line for the crown? He has angered too many political groups and thus an assassination is not out of the question. These thoughts spin around and around in my head. Soon I will need to come to a decision. I pray God will guide me.

When he was told of his son's fate on January 30, 1889, he collapsed onto his bed. Had his covert meetings with his son's enemies, primarily those opposed to Rudolph's liberalism, hastened his death? *It must be made to look like a suicide.*

He didn't yet know there were two bodies at Mayerling. Had he set in motion not only the death of his son, but that of a seventeen year old girl? Could a few innocent meetings among peers and patriotic Austrians be seen as sanctioning this tragedy?

When told about the girl, Franz Joseph only asked if she had committed suicide, too.

Chapter 38

Francesca paced the well-worn tile floor of her Mykonos friend's kitchen. Her eyes were rimmed in red from stinging tears. Earlier, at the hospital, she was turned away from Pamela's room. No visitors allowed. An officer directed her to go home and wait for a call from the police station. When she emerged from the hospital elevator, she saw Peter Gallenos walk past at a rapid clip. She failed to get his attention before he disappeared around a corner.

Surely, he'll call me when he knows anything.

Closed doors were foreign to her. Helplessness was never acceptable. She reached for the drip coffee pot on the stove top. The dark espresso coffee had cooled. She spit a mouthful of tepid liquid into the wide sink. Out the kitchen window she watched the slow spin of the iconic island windmills. A picture postcard of Mykonos.

Was it just this morning that she had been awakened by the screams of the teenage girls? She followed them to the pool of blood under the Summer Solstice stakes. She had moved beyond the stakes to see her friend unconscious

269

and bloody. There was no sign of Bitsy. Sundried grass behind the altar was marked by shoe prints to the shore. Only one foot size was visible. Bitsy had been carried off.

Due to these crimes, she wanted to reveal her true identity, to jump into the middle of the investigation. To do what she knew she could do better than the local authorities. But her job required she remain under the cover of her professor persona, not just on Mykonos, but elsewhere. This wasn't the time to alert anyone.

After I collect more information about the abduction, I'll call Washington. It's time to share what I know about the location of the diary and my concern for Bitsy. Then I'll request permission to tell a few people about my real work.

"And get marching orders," she said. She put the empty coffee carafe on the blue ceramic tile counter.

In the adjacent living room, the phone rang. She waited in the doorway threshold to see if her friend, Petra, would answer.

The front door opened and Petra came in, a pot of ever present geraniums in one hand. Before she answered the phone, she placed them on a small mantel.

"This is Petra."

She winked at Francesca. "Yes, she's here. Please hold for her."

"Hello." Francesca held the phone receiver in both hands.

"Ms. Campelli, my name is Police Chief Mercori. I'm pleased to tell you your friend Ms. Jones is able to have visitors; however, it's necessary that we visit with you first to get your statement. Please can you come immediately to the police station?"

"I'm on my way."

Her thoughts bounced back and forth from Pamela and her recovery to the call she would make later in the day. She had information central to the attack and kidnapping, but she didn't know if she would be permitted to share it.

Chapter 39

Rick relaxed his grip on Peter's shoulder and nodded to the Police Chief.

"You know what to do, Chief."

"Yes, I do. We'll put out a bulletin for the man who was so interested in the whereabouts of Ms. Bowman. Between your description and that of Ms. Jones, it's only a matter of time before we know who we're looking for." The Chief paused before he patted Peter on the back. "And you, you'll provide us the priceless books."

"Right," Rick said. "Now I need to see Ms. Jones before I return to my hotel."

A visit with Pamela came first, but he really wanted to question the hotel night manager and to check his messages. Anna may have called. She was due to arrive at 7:00 a. m.

"Chief, if you need me later, I'll be at my hotel or at the airport tomorrow morning. A friend from home is expected to arrive there early."

"Ah, Mr. Bennett, who is this friend?" The police chief put his hands on his hips. "Tell me more."

Peter turned toward Rick and mouthed, "DON'T."

"Sorry, I don't understand, Chief."

"Sir, you've been here for some time, but failed to mention this friend until now. Do you expect this person will advance the search for Ms. Bowman?"

"No, she's just a friend of mine from my home."

"A friend of Ms. Bowman, too?"

"Yes, we all live in the same town, a small town, near Dallas. But Ms. Tudor and I are better friends, if you know what I mean." He winked and smiled a practiced smile. "She has nothing to do with this." He spread both hands to his sides, palms up. "In fact, she knows nothing about what's been going on. Just a quick trip to enjoy your beautiful island before I take her to Milan."

"So perhaps she isn't the owner of the books?"

"She never mentioned any books although she knows Ms. Bowman. As I said, we live in a small town where everybody knows everybody." His fingers were crossed behind his back.

He had tacitly agreed with Peter. Anna didn't need to be interrogated by the police. She was half a world away when Bitsy was taken. But, why did Peter, who didn't know Anna, want her relationship with Bitsy kept secret. *What's in it for him?* A question he would ask Pamela, along with other questions for the hotel employees.

He walked out the door. The same shabby cab sat in front of the police station. The driver flicked a cigarette out the window. "Where to Mister American?"

***

After the door closed behind Rick, Peter stood up and asked if he could leave. He mentioned the ongoing conference and his responsibilities to the attendees.

"Go as you may, Mr. Gallenos."

"What about the books?" he dared to ask when he reached to open the door. He was anxious to have all interactions with the police behind him. He hoped to avoid the woman Rick mentioned. No need to have another person scrutinize him. And, if she was the owner of the diaries, she would likely demand their return. *I need time to make a plan to keep them from those who would take them from me.*

"Oh, sir, you'll be accompanied by one of my men back to the museum, where we'll take those books into, what do they call it on television, protective custody." The men who stood around the room laughed. The police chief laughed the loudest.

274

"Stefano," he said. "Take two other officers with you and go with Mr. Gallenos."

***

Francesca pulled into the police station's parking lot in Petra's little yellow Citron. She tapped on the horn and motioned to Peter and a policeman who walked her way. Peter tucked his chin down into his collar and went past her. Was the interview grueling for him?

She swung open the blue station door with more force than she intended. Slow down; keep the lowest of profiles while in here.

"Oh, Signora Campelli, you've arrived." Chief Mercori motioned for her to follow him to a desk at the back of the room, just outside his own office.

"Of course," she said. "I'm very happy to help the police in any way I can. Both Ms. Jones and Ms. Bowman are friends of mine."

The police chief pointed toward a chair next to a cluttered desk. He introduced her to the young officer who stood next to it. She extended her hand for a handshake, but the officer kissed it.

"Officer Kapra, please never do that again." The police chief lightly slapped the young officer's cheek.

275

His face flushed pink from the sting of the slap or embarrassment. "I thought kissing a lady's hand was the standard greeting in Europe. Please accept my apology, madam."

"Not to worry, young man. I'm flattered. Shall we get started?"

She planned to focus her statement on her relationship with Pamela and Bitsy as fellow women interested in the feminine in Greek mythology. She would offer as many denials as necessary regarding knowledge of the books and their importance. *Better a feminist than a spy.*

***

A small crowd milled around the entrance to the museum. A sign on the front door read, *Closed today. Meetings will resume tomorrow at regular time.* While conference attendees at the Hotel Apollo remained detained, others from other hotels knew nothing about the events of the morning. At least they knew nothing until word began to spread from locals to tourists as they arrived at the museum. The gossip shared was that one bookseller was missing and another had been assaulted.

A cry rang out. A few people in the group saw Peter step from a police car.

"What's going on, Peter?"

"Is it true someone died?"

"Are you going to cancel the conference?"

One of the officers blew the gold whistle he wore around his neck. The shrill sound drowned out the questions.

"Make way. There will be no one allowed in the museum at this time. Return to your homes or hotels, please."

***

Francesca's shoulders dropped to their usual relaxed position. The interview with the police officer had gone well. She was cooperative, pleasant and forthcoming with the information she wanted or needed to share. She related the events of the trip and evening ceremonies, the location chosen for sleeping and the time the group of women called it a night.

When the questions began, her responses were often in the negative. No, she didn't know her friends had left the sleeping area. No, she heard nothing unusual until she and the others were awakened by the screams of the Irish teenagers. No, she had never seen Bitsy Bowman with anyone other than other those attending the conference. No, she didn't know Richard Bennett although Bitsy had mentioned him. She knew nothing about important books.

277

She looked over the shoulder of the young officer questioning her toward the police chief. He nodded. She winked, then rubbed her eye as if something was in it. All seemed to be going well without need for additional interrogation.

The young officer thanked her for her cooperation. She stood up and shook his hand.

"Let me know if I can be of further help."

The police chief escorted her to the station door. He put his big hand on her shoulder and kept it there for just a second or two too long. In spite of his admonishment to his young officer, she almost expected the chief to bow or give her an air kiss cheek to cheek.

She crossed the parking lot and smiled. The bright yellow car stood out among the gray mopeds and mostly, black or blue sedans like sunshine among storm clouds. She exhaled through her mouth, her lips blowing mental clouds away. *My charm's intact. Now back to Petra's and the call to Washington.*

Chapter 40

The day had been unusual for the local police. The typical round up of inebriated, unruly, tourists was easily trumped by a kidnapping. Other than local family disputes, teenage vandalism, and those few misbehaving tourists, Mykonos was a peaceful, sun-loving, place to relax, party and leave troubles behind.

Two policemen dispersed the crowd at the museum. Stefano and Peter waited at the double doors.

When the majority of the crowd had left, Stefano ushered him across the threshold.

"It's time."

He nodded to the officer. Over his shoulder, he shouted to the few stragglers on the walkway. "Tomorrow we'll return to schedule."

He hoped he would be around tomorrow to open the doors. He hoped he would still be the curator, the coveted position that had given him years of opportunity to add to ill-gotten, looted antique ephemera and books. The position that could be lost along with the diaries.

It was only a matter of minutes before he would have to turn over the books. The exquisite red leather diary and the humble black one. Important and priceless additions to his collection even though he could never acknowledge his ownership.

He barely registered the fact that the front doors of the museum had been unlocked as he led Stefano and the other officers down a dimly lit hallway toward his office. Suddenly, it sunk in. The unlocked front door could mean he had also forgotten to lock his office safe. He put his right hand against the wall to keep from falling to the ground in instant despair. *What if I left the safe unlocked?*

After one more step, his legs gave way.

"Sir, are you alright?" Officer Cosmos said. He bent down to put his muscular arm underneath Peter's slumped shoulder.

"I'm okay. Just worried about my friend."

"You said the books are in the safe," Officer Yanni said. "Let's not delay, sir."

His sparsely furnished office was cooler than the hallway. Thick tapestries hung on two of the thick stone walls. A small window air conditioner hummed behind his well-organized desk. He touched the silver cross around his neck before he knelt in front of a rusted black safe wedged tightly between two wooden lateral file cabinets.

Several seconds passed. Slow for the officers, rapid for him.

"Mr. Gallenos?" Cosmos said. "You must open the safe."

"I'm trying to recall the numbers. My mind goes blank when I worry." He was telling the truth. He quickly added, "I'm very worried about Ms. Bowman." *But more so about losing the diaries.* Taken away, put in another museum somewhere or in a local library in Texas of all places.

Sweat underneath his collar spread to his chest. *Yia sou, goodbye my new treasures.* He opened the safe door. A musty smell hit his nose, but the sight in front of him was like a punch in his stomach. The books were gone.

"No, it can't be!"

He fell back into a squat. Stefano stopped his fall with a knee to his back.

The policemen gathered around the opened safe. There were two shelves covered with leather pouches, rolls of stamps and what looked like ledgers.

"Please give me some room." Peter grasped the open safe door with both hands. He pulled himself up then leaned against the door for a few moments before he turned to face his audience. He lurched to his desk chair where he fell against the worn leather back. No one spoke.

The fading sunlight passed through ancient beveled glass windows on the west wall. Sun spots danced across the top of the desk. Peter absently picked up one file folder after another as if the missing books were lost in one of the neat stacks of papers. He rearranged several gold paperweights.

"Mister Gallenos?" Stefano cleared his throat. He walked toward Peter. "Are you feigning surprise? Perhaps you haven't been honest with us regarding the books?"

Cosmos shuffled his feet against the well-worn stone floor and scanned the room.

"I've no idea where the books are." Peter's voice cracked. He didn't look up from a folder he had opened. "I've no idea."

Cosmos pulled out his cell phone. "I'll call the police chief for orders."

Stefano gestured toward the room door. "You might need to go outside to get a good signal."

Cosmos eyed the phone on Peter's desk.

"We mustn't touch anything in this room. Go outside," Stefano said.

When Cosmos moved toward the door, Peter seemed to wake from a dream. He closed the folder and put it on top of the shortest stack of papers.

"You think you can find fingerprints on the safe and in this room that will lead to the books?"

"Perhaps, but I think we haven't finished searching for them, Mr. Gallenos. I think we'll also need to search your home. I think we will accompany you there very shortly."

Chapter 41

Constantine eased the boat close to the rocky shoreline a few miles west of the Port of Piraeus where most cruise ships were docked. He didn't expect many tourists to be at the small locally used dock he had chosen. And if anyone noticed his cruiser, they wouldn't question the choice to anchor away from the congestion of Piraeus. He counted on it.

Before arriving in mainland waters, he had bound Bitsy's wrists and ankles and this time he blindfolded her with a cotton bandana. He had lost the small rounded bottle of chloroform when he carried it to the boat deck to hide it away from her. He had stumbled on the anchor chain and watched it sail into the black water of a night sea.

Under his breath, he cursed his clumsiness. He checked the rope bindings a second time and twisted the knot at the back of the bandana until he saw her grimace.

He would have to explain his actions soon. Bitsy hadn't provided any useful information about the diary. She only repeated her story again and again. She hadn't shown anyone the books. She planned to ask about them and get an appraisal the last day of the conference. If the books weren't in her room, she was mystified as to where they could be. *She actually said mystified!*

He cut the motor. Before he leaped ashore, he called down to Bitsy in the cabin. "Not a sound or I'll gag you."

He tied the boat to the weathered dock piling. He spit into the oil slicked water.

When he looked up the rocky cliff, he saw the headlights he was hoping for. Three flashes. "All is well," he said under his breath. He stepped back into the boat to retrieve Bitsy.

She didn't struggle. Instead she went limp, dead weight.

"Make it harder for yourself. I'll drag you if I have to."

He lifted her by her waist and towed her like a flour sack up the stairs. Once on deck he pushed her onto the dock. With one foot on the boat and one on the dock, he pulled her legs over the side of the boat. He pulled her to a standing position. She didn't cry out when he threw her over his shoulder.

"Did you think I'd toss you into the sea?" he whispered. "In my fantasies maybe."

He carried her to the end of the pier, where he was met by a colleague. Two others stood at different spots on the hill. They passed her from one to another. When everyone reached the top of the hill, she was placed in the back of the dark green van. ST. WALLEN'S BEERGARTEN was painted on each side in black script with purple grapes hanging from the apostrophe. A frothy rimmed beer stein bracketed the tavern's name. His colleagues wore putty colored overalls and Greek styled caps bearing the same logo. Karl handed him the same outfit and told him he would stay with the woman.

"Where're we going?" he said. He slipped off his boating shoes before he tossed the captain's hat into a proffered canvas bag. "We're in Greece and you have us in a German van. How will that work, my friends?"

Karl closed double doors and moved a few feet away, a finger to his lips.

"We must get the woman to Mayerling as quick as possible," Karl snapped. "We have cases of beer in the rear of this vehicle and if stopped can easily say we're delivering to local tavernas. Ones that serve the better German beer!"

"So we're driving directly to Austria, to Mayerling?"

"Where did you think we would keep your woman? We must have privacy and time to get from her the information you don't have. And, I add, we need to learn more about her, who she is, where she got the books, etcetera, and etcetera." Karl dusted his cap against his hip. "And, we must decide about you, Constantine!" He moved closer to the van and pounded his fist on the double doors.

***

Rough carpet covered the floor and rubbed against Bitsy's face. She could smell beer and cardboard. She heard the men's voices and strained to make out their words. She recognized the language as German, one she didn't understand. Her relief to be off the boat turned to fear when she heard one of the men yell Constantine's name.

Tears welled up behind the blindfold. She didn't know where she was, mainland Greece, Turkey, Crete. She visualized a map of all the possible ports and failed to make a connection with Germany except the origin of the diaries. *These guys are taking me to Germany.*

Her resolve to escape once on solid ground shifted from possible to impossible. Her level of helplessness had multiplied by the number of men who were holding her. And she couldn't understand them. She knew Constantine wouldn't translate for her. It sounded like he was in serious trouble himself. She was glad she hadn't revealed Peter's name and felt sure the books were safe with him. *When Peter finds out I'm missing will he connect my abduction to the books?*

In that moment, she realized a lot of people would be worried about her, both on Mykonos and at home. She wondered if Rick had seen Constantine at the hotel. Peter knew possession of the books might be dangerous. *He'll connect the dots, he'll alert the police. Not to worry.*

She managed to roll over. She kicked the side of the van in hopes it would attract the attention of someone who might rescue her. She heard a shout and kicked harder.

***

"Get in there and shut her up." Karl pointed his index finger toward Constantine. He swung his shoulders and added, "You, too, Hermann."

"I could use some rest from her, Karl…" Constantine began.

"You do as I say," Karl said, fists at his sides.

"Okay, let's just get out of here."

Bert climbed into the driver's seat. Karl motioned Hermann to follow Constantine into the back of the van.

288

"I'm riding up front with Bert. Edgar's flying to Vienna to meet with Johannes. Then Johannes will travel to Mayerling to meet us. The plan is to have the woman there by 7:00 or 8:00 tonight. Drivers will rotate, those in the passenger's seat will sleep and, those in the back will keep the woman quiet."

***

Bitsy wrinkled her nose. The smell of male sweat mixed with the pungent beer and box smell was thick and irritating. Constantine was the one who sat her up. She knew his smell.

She leaned her head against the metal wall. She wasn't ready to talk to him; the only one she knew spoke English. Her mind had shifted away from Peter and Rick and was filled with the image of Pamela lying on the Solstice altar. While on the boat, Constantine told her he had struck her with a mallet he found in the cabin closet. He refused to tell her anything else. She fought against thoughts that her friend was dead.

The road from the dock was rough and rattled everything in the back of the van. Her stomach lurched forward and back when the van stopped. Her head bounced against the siding when it took corners. There was a strange silence for many miles with only the sound of an occasional yawn or cough. After a while someone turned on a fan that whined. She turned her face toward the breeze whenever it passed her way.

What do they have in mind for me wherever we are going? How long before we get there?

She kept her questions inside and waited. If they were travelling to Germany by van, there would be stops along the way. Restroom stops. There would be a chance or chances to alert someone or even escape.

Her wrist and ankle bones ached. Her back hurt. She needed a toothbrush. Taking inventory of her physical state kept her emotions from showing. She would not cry, she would show no fear. *I have the qualities of Artemis and the love of God. I am courageous.*

"Do we speak English so your woman will know we mean business?" Hermann said.

Bitsy licked her dry lips. *Yes, do, please.*

***

The thirteen hour drive to Vienna seemed endless. The group stopped for gasoline at off-the-main-road service stations and after filling the tank, the van was parked in the back where Bitsy was walked to the restrooms. Dire consequences were threatened if she screamed or attracted

290

attention. Her blindfold was removed inside the restroom and the door was kept ajar.

Each time she finished, she shoved the restroom door. Constantine would hurry to replace the blindfold. After the last stop, he didn't notice she could see her surroundings if she lowered her eyes and raised her chin.

Food and water, offered periodically during the trip, consisted of small sausage sandwiches she could eat blindfolded and bottled water. The taste of the meat and brown mustard coated in her throat even after she finished eating.

It was during one of the meals, she heard Constantine insist that she was the only one who knew the location of the diary and stated his actions were necessary. It was all about the red leather diary like he had said to her earlier. No mention was made about the small black book.

After Constantine and Hermann moved to the front of the van, she squinted her eyes and raised her chin, she saw, under the gap between the blindfold and her cheekbones, that two different men had crawled into the back of the van.

After the double doors closed, one of the men clicked on a small LED flashlight and poured over several newspapers. With the turn of each page, he grunted or growled. *He must be searching for information about the kidnapping. The police must be looking for me.* Has anyone come forward about the books or Constantine? Have they found Pamela?

"Is all well back there?" She recognized Hermann's voice. She raised her chin higher to see what Karl and Bert were doing.

"Yeah, all's well." Bert's face didn't mirror his words. He spoke through gritted teeth. He crumpled the paper he held and tossed it against a large box of beer.

His frustration could be my opening.

"What's in this for you?" She leaned closer to Bert. "I've lots of influential friends who could make your life better." She whispered into his ear. "Will you help me?"

"Be silent." He scooted away from her. He retrieved the crumpled paper and buried his face between the open pages.

Karl heard the exchange. He struggled to his feet holding on to a short stack of beer crates for leverage. He stood up. His head angled away from the headliner of the van. Lips pursed, he let out a long hiss like the sound of a deflating balloon. "You've no idea who we are, Frau Bowman or you wouldn't ask such a question. Better you stay silent until we reach our destination."

***

Constantine was in the passenger's seat. Time to plan his defense. *How will I save face, maybe save my life? It isn't my fault this American woman was so careless with the priceless diary. I should've found a way to question her, evaluate her, right away, the first day I saw her in the elevator.*

Too late he recognized her ignorance about the diary. Who carries such items in a canvas bag? Too late he understood her flirtations were easily made and frivolous. How many men did she pursue? The book was always in danger of being lost while in her possession. *What a fool I was. My fate may be banishment from the society or into the deep dark Vienna Woods.*

Chapter 42

Peter sat in one of the straight back chairs in the police station. It was after 8:00 p.m. and the paperwork was finally completed. He was handed a search warrant issued for his home and automobile. In spite of agreeing to the searches, the police chief insisted a warrant be obtained.

"Everything must be done by the book," he said. Peter watched him tweak his mustache. "We play by the book, for the book, you see?" With that pronouncement, several officers escorted Peter to a waiting patrol car.

He stepped aside to allow the group of police officers into his living room. He couldn't remember if he had cleared out his altar area of the morning ritual items. The remnants of a purging rite he practiced daily. He watched the officers fan out across his living room, into his kitchen and down his hallway. He clutched his hands together inside the front of his robe. *What if they find my cubby hole? Please to all the gods, let them see only what is safe for me."*

Before he had left his home that morning, before he heard the news about Bitsy and Pamela, he had opened the camouflaged door in the fresco panel. His need to see his treasures compelled him to spend time each morning and evening in front of the hidden compartment. First, he would scan the items stored there, and then after he closed the small door, he would kneel at his home altar, light three candles and make a sacrifice to the gods. Often he would burn various texts he found personally offense, those opposed to his rigid beliefs about ancient Greece and the supremacy of gods over goddesses. This particular morning he had offered up an out of print book on Turkish dominance of the Dardanelles and a moldy Hindu diary with images of Eastern Goddesses.

He moved further into the living room now empty of officers. He could see the constant movement of the sea out his patio door. He took a deep breath. He reviewed his movements before everything crashed down on him in front of his office safe. He closed his eyes and pulled his hands out of the robe.

The silence of the search party vanished with the shout of one of the officers.

"What have we here?"

What have they found?

295

"Mister Gallenos, come join us, please."

He walked to the small area next to his patio door. Two officers held up the large brass platter he used in his sacrificial rituals. A pile of ashes covered the platter. Remnants of a gold lettered book spine shone neon under the hall lighting.

"I can explain." Peter backed away two steps. "I burned an old book, an old diary, but not the books of Ms. Bowman." He gulped and his next words were strangled at the back of his throat. "You can see…there's no red leather…It was part of a ritual… to rid the universe of lies." He put his hands in front of him toward the platter.

"Oh, no, sir, this will be taken to the station."

At least my cubby hole has not been discovered.

"Go ahead, take them. You'll see I'm telling the truth." He turned away from staring eyes. He pulled his rosary from under his robe.

Maybe the ashes will satisfy them. Maybe they'll leave now.

***

"Chief, we found a burned book at Mr. Gallenos' house. Do you want us to bring him with us when we return with the ashes?"

296

"Have you searched the entire house?" the police chief said. He motioned for an officer to come into his office. "Stay there and look everywhere. Remember we have a missing American tourist and an injured English tourist and both were associated with Mr. Gallenos and his museum. We need to make sure he's not involved in the assault and kidnapping. I'll send an officer to pick up the ashes."

***

The officer a few feet away from Peter folded his cell phone and put it into his shirt pocket.

"Mr. Gallenos, please sit here in this room with my partner while I continue the search of your premises." The officer's stare bore into him.

He sat down on the edge of a blue and white painted chair near his patio door. From this vantage point he could see Stefano standing at the edge of the fresco to the left of his altar. His stomach cramped. He bolted up toward the hallway and was restrained by an outstretched hand that clamped down on his wrist.

"Where are you going?"

"I need to use the bathroom, its urgent!"

The officer kept a hand on his left wrist and walked him toward the bathroom. A small window set high on the back wall of the bathroom. The officer hesitated in closing the door even though Peter had immediately dropped down on the floor in front of the toilet.

"I'll not leave you long and I can hear everything from outside this door."

Less than an hour later Peter sat relaxed in his favorite chair. He had forgotten his nausea and his fear. His cubby hole hadn't been found. His prayer was answered, he thought.

He watched Yanni, the oldest officer place his right hand on the corner of the fresco. *Not now after all this time!* He held his breath. From the corner of his eye he could see his terra cotta pots filled with pink geraniums, so beautiful and unchanged from yesterday.

Yanni drummed his fingers against the fresco. Peter saw him straighten his shoulders and shake his head.

"Something's not right here?" he called to Stefano. "I can feel it in my old bones." He stepped back from the wall. "You paint this, Mr. Gallenos?"

"Yes, officer." Peter wiped his brow.

"Strange place to paint this elaborate scene of ancient ruins. You can't see it from anywhere in the house, except in this narrow hallway."

"I wasn't interested in sharing it, sir."

"Ah, but, it seems an unusual spot."

Yanni pulled a large wooden bully stick from its leather holder and gently tapped it against the painting. He walked the length of the fresco. Tap, tap, tap-tap.

"I believe this wall is hollow in some places and not in others. I have the authority to tear it down, Mr. Gallenos. Shall I do that?"

Chapter 43

A transfer in Vienna, from the van to a limousine, put the Society members at risk of discovery, but a beer truck at Mayerling would raise questions if noticed. Limousines often made their way there with tourists who wanted to see where the Crown Prince and his mistress died. Hunters who often rented the adjacent cottage from the nuns usually came by automobile or the occasional truck. The biggest transfer issue was to keep Bitsy's presence a secret.

The city's roadways and streets were full of dog legs, changes in names and many of them flowed to the Danube and away from the mountain roads. Small streets cut across the main roads to the center of the city. A quick exit from the Vienna, using back roads, was impossible.

Bitsy was placed in the back seat of the silver BMW limousine. The darkened windows designed for anonymity of celebrities, honeymooning couples and others wanting to be out of the public eye would keep her invisible to anyone who looked her way. Her hands and ankles were bound with plastic ties and the bandana blind fold was replaced by a sleeping mask. Before the limousine left its garage, a wide tape was put across her mouth.

Bitsy's sore limbs relaxed against the soft leather interior of the automobile. Cooled air from the air conditioning vents wafted across her dry face. She tried to move her lips behind the padded tape. She strained to hear the whispered conversation of the men who sat at the back of the limousine. She had been placed next to the partitioned glass nearest Karl, the driver. *The speed has increased. We must be outside Vienna.* She had overheard bits and pieces of conversation during the trip from Piraeus to know this transfer would be take place in Austria.

She felt the car climb as it made its way into the foothills of the Vienna Woods. An hour is what she heard Karl say before he closed the limousine door. *An hour. Then what? And where can we get to in an hour?*

"We're nearing our destination, Ms. Bowman."

Karl's voice was muffled by the closed window partition.

She heard the window slide open.

"You may take the tape off her mouth now."

Someone sat down beside her. She felt clammy fingers, pulling at the tape. She squeezed her eyes tight and gritted her teeth.

"Ump," she moaned through closed lips. She shook her head from side to side, jaw still rigid.

"This would be a good time for you to talk, Ms. Bowman. The next stop won't be as pleasant as this luxury ride, I assure you." Karl said over his shoulder.

She bit her lip and tasted blood. She said nothing. "Mayerling awaits, Ms. Bowman, as does the cottage still used for hunts. Predator and prey come together in the woods. Something for you to think about, eh?" She recognized Constantine's voice and smelled his mint freshened breath.

A window near her opened. She heard what sounded like heavy raindrops pound against the side of the car. *Mayerling is my destination.* She closed her eyes behind the sleeping mask. She always closed her eyes when she prayed. *Dear God, how can anyone find me in such a remote place as the Vienna Woods? Is anyone looking in this direction? Why would they? By your grace, I believe there will be a way to remain unharmed and escape.*

Before she could complete her prayer, the limousine came to a stop and a hand grasped her arm.

"Don't make a sound. We're merely changing drivers." Constantine whispered in her ear.

Chapter 44

Nose pressed against the oval window, Anna looked down on the Aegean Sea bathed in the first light of day. The water looked like an indigo gown trimmed in lace. Small white caps rippled in and out of the surface. She arrived at the Athens airport a half hour earlier and quickly made her way to the departure gate for Mykonos. With carryon in the overhead compartment and her tote held close to her body, she watched the ocean below. *Where are you Bitsy?* She imagined her friend on one of the small boats that bobbed among the waves. *Is she looking up at the plane right now?*

She didn't call Joe from the Athens airport. She told herself there wasn't enough time. She leaned her forehead on the window. "Nothing to tell him," she whispered. The man next to her tapped her right arm.

"Sorry, did you say something?"

She shook her head and reached deep into her tote. She retrieved her cell phone and reread a text from Rick.

NO NEWS IS GOOD NEWS.

***

Rick was surprised to see the Mykonos airport was designed in a sleek modern style. No marble columns or statuary. Instead the floors were wide Italian tile in a checkerboard design of black and white. One walkway could be seen off the circular entrance area that led to the security check in. Smaller hallways were designated for airport personnel. Silver streamers looking like Mylar hung between expanses of large windows with views of the runway. They shimmered in the morning light that spilled into the terminal. He was reminded of Star Trek and the Jetsons. Not ancient Greece.

He walked to the end of the non-ticketed area. A string of black leather seats bolted to the tile floor were positioned in front of a bank of automatic doors designed to let arriving passengers out, but no one in. He called the Hotel Apollo to set up a meeting with the hotel manager for 8:00 o'clock.

Anna's plane was due to arrive in less than ten minutes. He found no Sunday newspaper, but purchased an English edition of the Saturday newspaper to check coverage of the kidnapping and assault. No article on the front page. A short article on the back page titled *Unfortunate Incident on Delos* merely described the injury of a tourist. The last sentence reported no further information available at press time, but that the police department planned an announcement after further investigation.

Talk about keeping a lid on things. Tourism is the name of the game here.

He dropped the newspaper on the vacant seat next to him. Two legs covered in bright floral print pants stepped near the chair. He looked up to see Anna looking down at him.

She collapsed next to him, ignoring the paper on the seat and she threw her arms around his neck.

"I'm so glad to see you." Tears fell from under oversized dark glasses with pink flowers on the ear piece. They left damp tracks down her lightly powered cheeks. "Any news?"

"No, no news, but we have an appointment with one of the hotel managers. The one who knew the name of the man I suspect was involved in Bitsy's disappearance. I've made my statement to the police, so I can move about without some of the restrictions on tourists here. "

He stood up and reached for her hand and pulled her out of the chair. With his other hand, he picked up her carryon bag.

"Let's do it, Anna, let's find our friend."

They began the long walk to the terminal exit. He put an arm around her shoulder and drew her close. Her head rested against him.

"There is a taxis stand outside, so we can be at the hotel in a matter of minutes."

The highly polished automatic glass doors slid open. The relative quiet inside the airport disappeared. Horns honked, taxi drivers shouted for fares, and different groups of travelers called out greetings to each other.

Anna pushed her sun glasses to the top of her head, took a tissue from her tote and rubbed away the stains on her cheeks.

"We'll find her, Rick." Her eyes sparked with determination. "We will."

He winked his agreement.

Chapter 45

Francesca pushed the end button on her cell phone and reached for her espresso. Conversations with her handler in Washington, D.C. always left her rethinking her life choices. She sipped the cooled drink. What would her life be like if she hadn't med Daniel Smith at university and fallen in love with him and with his obsession for Papal history and Church doctrine?

She scrolled through pictures on her phone and found several from those years when they were a couple. She scrolled down to one of him standing outside a monastery on the coast of Brazil where he had taken a vow of celibacy. She could still remember the letter than had accompanied the picture, the Dear Francesca letter. *And here I am, looking at uploaded pictures decades old. But I was intrigued by more than Daniel.*

She was hooked. The ongoing work of the Church to recover lost religious ephemera and objects d'art and the mission to protect, defend and glorify the Church had become her work. As a single woman she could juggle her position as a history professor in Milan with clandestine meetings around the world with a raft of informants, which included dealers in artifacts, museum procurers, traffickers in stolen art and occasional out and out mobsters. Fluent in several languages, a legitimate doctorate degree and a lack of family obligations, made her perfect for her job.

It all began in Washington, D.C. where she continued to report to another operative for the Vatican. It would never do to report to those who reside in Rome or Vatican City. Distance was an important part of remaining safe from forces against the restoration work and especially work designed to keep Church secrets.

I'm so glad to have that conversation behind me. She poured a splash of cognac into the small demitasse cup. Her movement drew her eyes to the mirror behind the hotel bar.

"Now I can speak to Bitsy's friends and share the plan I have to rescue her." She toasted her image in the mirror. There should be minimal danger to her or her friends if all goes according to plans set in motion.

She reached for her crocodile tote. Time to find Rick Bennett.

No one was in the Hotel Apollo lobby. She planned to plant herself in one of the numerous club chairs and wait for an opportunity to talk with him. She had been told to control him, to make sure he didn't call attention to the kidnapping, the missing diaries or those attending the bookseller's conference. She knew little about him other than what Bitsy had told her and what she had seen during his interaction with Constantine. She ticked off information in her head. Handsome, silver hair, trim, rich, a take charge kind of man. She circled the lobby floor before she found the best vantage point to wait. *I think involvement in Bitsy's rescue should satisfy Mr. Bennett's need for action.*

Several police officers stepped out of the gold-lined elevator. Their presence in the lobby continued. She fidgeted in the chair. She had seen no one in the lobby except the police and hotel staff and it was almost 8:00 a.m. No one had entered the hotel from the street.

Enough of this.

She walked toward the reservation desk. It was empty. She turned back toward the front lobby doors. A tall man stepped through the entrance. He had his arm around a petite woman with a short white bob. She held onto his arm with one hand and carried floral tote with the other. Francesca waved a hand over her head, shouting "Mr. Bennett!" Her stiletto heels made a clicking sound on the marble floors, a sound that echoed off the Doric columns scattered throughout the lobby like the sound of a ping pong ball in play.

"I'm sorry if I startle you," she said. She put out her right hand. "I know Bitsy and I was on the island when she was kidnapped. My name is Francesca Campelli."

Rick shook her outstretched hand. He introduced Anna.

"I'm happy to meet you both."

"Have you heard anything about Bitsy?" Anna said.

"Let's take this conversation into the bar, please." She pointed over her shoulder toward the cocktail bar which was dimly lit. It offered several intimate booths near the back of the room which would provide some level of privacy from the cadre of police officers.

"Sure," Rick said. He put his left hand under Anna's elbow. "We can check you into your room later. Needless to say, Bitsy's top priority."

Anna pulled free. "The meeting with the hotel manager?"

"It can wait." Francesca said. "Come, let's not waste a moment."

It was difficult to see clearly in the dimmed bar and the newly formed group of three stumbled against a few chairs before they reached the last booth in the back of the room. A group of officers sat at the circular bar off the lobby, but none of the booths were occupied.

A waiter had followed behind the trio.

After they were seated, Francesca ordered espresso to be brought in a carafe with three demitasse cups. She didn't want interruptions or listening ears.

"So, Anna, you know Bitsy and came all the way from Texas to find her?"

"She's my best friend. There was no way I could stay home." She reached out for Rick's hand.

"And you, Rick, you've known Bitsy for a long while."

"For longer than I can remember, but let's get down to business. What's with the secrecy?"

She hesitated for a moment. She knew the time had arrived to trust others with her identity and to enlist them on this journey to find their friend. For her part, she looked forward to putting the search for the Mayerling diaries to rest.

"While I've met Bitsy several times at bookseller conferences, I myself am not a bookseller. I teach history at the University of Milano, on a semester by semester basis. I travel many times and miles during a year because

I also work for the Vatican. You might call me a spy for the Holy See." She propped her elbows on the table and clasp her hands together. Her audience was silent.

"In all parts of the world, important missing or stolen documents and artifacts can found that either belong to the Vatican or would present, shall we say, an embarrassment to those in power or to the Church itself. My job is to find those objects and bring them back to the Holy See." She removed her arms from the table top and placed her hands on her lap.

"I'll try to answer your questions now." She leaned back against the black leather booth. Time stopped. No one spoke or moved for several seconds. She placed her right hand on the black and gold tiled table top and tapped her middle finger on the tile. The sound was like the sound her stiletto heels had made on the marble floor.

Rick was the first to speak.

"That's some story, Signora. So we're supposed to believe you're a spy for the Pope. Is this an action movie starring Tom Hanks?" Sweat beaded on his forehead. He took a handkerchief from his trouser pocket and shook it open. He wiped his entire face.

Anna pressed back against the leather of the booth to put as much distance as she could between her and Francesca.

"Some fiction has fact based story lines, Mr. Bennett." Francesca smiled a tight smile. "I'm sure you both are aware of the efforts to find and return, to the rightful owners, art plundered during World War II, including many items stolen from the Vatican. Most often these items are found by those of us who are contracted to search and find. We travel to places where we hear and see things, useful things."

"And Bitsy is useful to you?" Anna spoke up and leaned her body into the table, gripping the rim with both hands.

"Yes, she is. She brought to Mykonos two diaries searched for for over one hundred and twenty-five years by various groups. Always by the Vatican and by a group of men who call themselves the Grand Dukes Society. These men meet twice a year in a cottage adjoining Mayerling in Austria. Are you familiar with Mayerling, Ms. Tudor?"

"I know it's where Crown Prince Rudolph and his mistress died." She turned toward Rick. "I saw the movie with Catherine Deneuve and Omar Sharif." When no one spoke, she added, "I've always liked foreign mysteries."

"So, Francesca," Rick said. "Bitsy brought old dairies from Texas and they're the very ones no one has been able to find for over a hundred years."

"I know it sounds preposterous, but it's true."

Anna brushed her fringe bangs to the side. "Ms. Campelli, I gave those books to Bitsy; they belonged to my husband's family." Her eyes shone and she moistened her lips. "Only recently did I find out he isn't English, but German and Austrian." She put her left hand on her chest and heaved a deep sigh.

Rick scooted closer to Anna. "Tell us more, signora."

Francesca settled back against the leather booth for the second time. She knew her story was long and complicated and, likely, to sound fictional.

"Where to begin?" She turned her face up to the ceiling fans before meeting Anna and Rick's stares. "When Crown Prince Rudolph died at Mayerling along with his alleged mistress, Marie Vetsera, the Hapsburgs ruled Austria-Hungary. In 1889 there was only one heir to the empire, Rudolph. It was common knowledge that he was unfaithful to his wife, Crown Princess Stephanie of Belgium and that he was usually at odds with his father, the Emperor. They disagreed about many things, including

Rudolph's threat to dissolve the Hapsburg dynasty when he came into power.

"Even more troubling for the Emperor and the ruling class of Austria-Hungary, was Rudolph's interest in becoming a free mason. You may not be aware of this, but, still to this day, Catholics are prohibited from becoming Masons. This is, of course, where the Vatican comes into the story.

"Over the past hundred or so years there've been numerous theories about what happened in the bedchamber that January night. Did Rudolph kill his mistress and then commit suicide? That was the final ruling by those in control at the time, with the caveat that Rudolph had a mental disorder. This diagnosis was needed in order to bury him in consecrated ground. Other theories suggest Franz Joseph turned a blind eye to the trouble brewing over Rudolph's political leanings and that he was assassinated by monarchists. Other theories were born from reports that Rudolph poisoned his mistress and then shot her to cover up the poisoning or drunk he accidently shot her and remorseful shot himself.

"Ms. Tudor, the diaries you gave to Bitsy are believed to be those of Franz Joseph and an undermaid to Rudolph, named Marta. They are purported to contain the unvarnished, untold truth of the events of that night in 1889. Find the diaries and the mystery of Mayerling will be solved."

She took a sip of cold espresso. "However, the Vatican isn't willing for the world to find out the truth, if that truth is that Rudolph had actually joined the free masons and was, perhaps, assassinated by orders from the Church. You can see how that would be unacceptable."

She picked up the carafe and poured the last of the coffee into the three cups that rested on their small saucers.

After a long silence, Rick slid out of the booth and stood near the table edge.

"Wow, what a story." He touched Anna's shoulder. "You buy this?"

"Actually, I'd no idea there was an ongoing mystery about the deaths. Mainly, I'm stunned to hear that those old books, diaries, left to gather dust in an old trunk in my attic, are the missing links to solve such a mystery."

"They are, believe me, they are," Francesca said, "But, for now the focus must be your friend, the diaries can wait a little while longer."

"So what do you suggest we do now?" Anna said.

"We go to Vienna."

Rick and Anna shared a surprised look, eyes wide and eyebrows raised.

Francesca gathered up her purse and slide out of the booth.

"Come on, you two, I've a plane waiting at the airport. There's no need to check into the hotel here, Anna. And Rick I've had your items removed from your room and taken to the plane."

"Anything else?" Rick shook his head toward Anna.

"Of course. You're checked out of the hotel. Come, come."

She motioned for them to follow her to the back of the bar rather than the lobby. "We'll leave without notice. A taxi waits for us and travel bags, including Bitsy's, are safely in the trunk. I have collected all passports, except for yours Ms. Tudor. You may give that to me for safe keeping until you leave Austria."

Chapter 46

A thunderstorm slowed the drive through the Vienna Woods. Narrow two lane roads were difficult to manage when wet and there were many sharp curves and steep grades up the mountain side. Without sunlight filtering through the thick pines, the way was dark. There was no light at all except for the headlights on the limousine. Bert, who took over as driver, once out of Vienna, stretched out his legs in the roomy BMW, but gripped the steering wheel with his fingernails cutting into his palms.

"This is misery," he shouted to those in the back of the limo.

"Can't you go any faster?" A mixture of anger and fear was evident in Constantine's guttural complaint.

Bert lowered the partition.

"You want to get there alive, don't you?"

"I want to get as far away from here as possible," he said. He swung his legs onto the long limo seat next to him. "I never want to hear about the retched diary again and I certainly don't want to deal with this woman."

"I'm right here." Bitsy turned in the direction of Constantine's voice.

"Enough!" Karl's voice filled the interior of the limousine. "What's done is done."

"And what should I have done, I ask you?" Constantine's voice was high pitched. "I took this woman to show her our seriousness, our dedication, so she would tell us where the diary is. We're the Grand Dukes Society. Our purpose is to find the diary. Have you forgotten our pledge to do whatever's necessary to find it?"

"Your reasoning astounds me." Karl heaved a sigh and shook his head. "Can you not see the problems you have created? The diary has become the least of our worries."

The road veered to the left. In the ground mist reflected in the headlight beams, an opening could be seen between the overgrown foliage lining the road. A one lane path cut through a thick stand of pine trees to the back entrance of Mayerling used by vendors who delivered supplies to the convent nuns. At the end of the path was the cottage. The underground quarters of the main building, once used by the Imperial family's servants, was also available to the Society if needed. Over the years the servant quarters were used by the first born sons of members before they were old enough to be inducted into the society.

Karl, Johannes and Bert had spent time in those rooms as preteen boys. There was only one outside entrance to the quarters on the back wall of Mayerling. It could be seen from the cottage and could be used without notice of the nuns. Johannes had prepared a small sparsely furnished room to house Bitsy until decisions could be made by all the society members.

Bert turned off the headlights and the ignition.

"He we are," he said to no one in particular. His eyes remained on the cottage at the end of the dirt and gravel path.

Hermann opened the back door.

"It's muddy outside and we've no rain gear."

"A little rain won't kill you," Karl said. He pushed Hermann out the door.

"Should I go and open the door over there?" Constantine asked, his finger pointed to the back of Mayerling.

"Not yet. Let's get Ms. Bowman in the cottage first," Karl said. He stepped out of the car. "Stay with her while I open the cottage door."

"I'm getting soaked, Karl." Hermann pulled his wet shirt up around his ears.

"Then get back into the car, Hermann."

Bert and Karl walked side by side up the stone edged path to the cottage. The squish of their boots echoed among the tall pine, oak, and beech trees that surrounded the car. Enormous raindrops slid down the closed windows and a mist bubbled off the car's hot hood.

***

Bitsy wanted to stretch out on the sofa where one of the men had deposited her. She had been pushed and pulled through the rain and into the welcomed warmth of this room. She remained tied up, but without the sleeping mask.

She glanced at her reflection in an ornate gilt framed mirror that hung next to a large stone fireplace. Her eyes had small pillows underneath them and her face was pale in spite of her spray tan and the few hours in the Mykonos sun. *Look at me. A mess. But alive, right?* On the fireplace mantle several tankards, each centered with an enameled medallion, caught her eye. A sweet faced deer, a fluffy squirrel and white hare so lifelike. *Spoils of a hunt. Now it's me, the hunted and the caught.*

She wanted to sleep, but she also wanted to keep her attention on these men now huddled around a dark stained dining table adjacent to the green plaid couch where she sat. A massive elk's head on the dining room wall watched her through very realistic glass eyes. She wished she could wrap her arms around her chest. She cleared her throat.

"Hey, you guys, now that we're here, how about untying me?"

Constantine looked over his shoulder. He smiled the smarmy smile that turned her stomach. "My American woman, I don't trust you. I prefer you stay bound."

"Constantine," Karl said, "You know her name, what's this American woman thing?"

"I like to remind myself that she's very different from the women I'm used to, the ones quick to please a man. American women have too much independence for my taste."

"Our Playboy is old fashioned." Johannes stood in the threshold of the front door.

Constantine straightened his spine. "You're here, Johannes."

"Yes, I arrived earlier to prepare the lodging for our guest." He nodded his head in Bitsy's direction.

"Is it time to transport Ms. Bowman to her quarters?" Karl got up from the table.

"Where're you going to take me now?" her voice cracked. "I need to use the bathroom before we go anywhere."

"Where you're going, you'll be untied and will have your own facilities." Karl pushed his chair under the table.

"Constantine, since you're responsible for Ms. Bowman's presence among us, you can escort her across the property." Johannes moved away from the door to stand next to Karl.

***

The rain had stopped. The rough ground outside the cottage was dotted with puddles of water glistening in the dappled sunlight that shown on wet branches of the trees before it dipped to the ground. Bitsy noticed pine cones scattered here and there, some settled on top of fallen branches and soggy needles, some were almost covered in rainwater. The air was pungent with the scent of pine, cedar, and decomposing leaves from the assortment of trees struggling for air and light the dense woods.

She faced a large building with few windows and only one visible door. *What is this place? A prison. A medieval dungeon.*

She listened for any sounds. There were few. She heard their footsteps on the slushy ground, their breathing and the timid sound of a few birds that had come out to welcome the soft but failing sunlight. *What a strange old place. Who can find me here? Think Bitsy, you have to think.*

With one hand, Constantine fiddled with a large rust colored key. He held her bound wrists with the other. She didn't fight him. She would wait and plan when left alone for the first time since this man kidnapped her.

"Here we go," he said as the thick metal door was pulled open.

You'll get yours, signore; it's only a matter of time. The song, *I Am Woman,* flew into her head. *I am invincible, I am woman.*

Constantine walked her down stone steps. A hallway in front of them was lit with evenly spaced lantern-like lights attached to the walls. Cobwebs and dust were illuminated by the small bulbs.

They passed several doors on either side before he stopped in front of a door with a red ribbon tied to the hammered door handle.

He pulled a folding knife from his pocket and with one quick movement cut through her bindings. The plastic strips fell to the ground.

"Your room awaits."

She had barely stepped into the unlighted room before he slammed the door behind her and she heard a bolt slide into place. Still she couldn't stop herself from tugging on the door. Locked. She kicked her foot over the smooth concrete floor.

She stood in place. Eventually, her eyes grew accustomed to the dark. She saw a wall sconce near a small bed. It had a light bulb that on closer inspection looked new.

"Let there be light," she said with a hand on the pull chain.

She sat on a thin mattress covered with blue ticking. A stack of clean linen had been left on the end of the cot. *I hate making a bed.*

Fruit, cheese and hard bread sat on a small round table. *I don't think I can digest food although I am hungry.*

She rubbed one wrist after the other. The room was windowless with only a small slit of an opening near the ceiling. With the rain clouds dispersed, the small opening allowed a slender shaft of light to fall on one of the bare walls. *You can do this, Bitsy girl. Things are better; you can move freely and you're resourceful.*

She stood up and danced round and round like she had done at the Solstice celebration with her friends. She began to chant, "I was a Brownie, I was a Girl Scout, and I'm a modern day Artemis." She laughed and then, then she began to cry.

A hot anger that flushed her cheeks followed the tears. *I will not die here. Those diary fanatics will not win. Peter has the books. He'll turn them over to the police. This will all be over soon.* She stiffened her posture. The story will be in the papers. *These men will have no reason to keep me.* They won't be able to get the diary. Peter would be her savior.

She spread a sheet over the top of the mattress and tried in vain to plump up the small pillow at the head of the bed. More relaxed with hopeful thoughts of Peter, she let sleep overtake her.

***

At eight o'clock Sunday morning, approximately 30 hours after Bitsy's kidnapping, the reporters had a story that made its way to the front page of not only Greek newspapers and news programs, but would be read in newspapers and on electronic sites around the world. The headline in the Late English Edition of the Athens paper was repeated time and time again.

CURATOR OF MYKONOS MUSEUM
ARRESTED FOR THEFT

An accompanying article mentioned the burning of two books reportedly associated with the injury of a British citizen and the kidnapping of an American woman who were visiting Mykonos.

News of Peter's arrest had spread across the small island in record time. Each conference attendee received an early morning call from a police officer. There would be no further meetings at the museum. Almost immediately, a large crowd gathered in front of the police station. Several reporters jostled for position inside the station, cameras and microphones at the ready.

Peter sat with his back to them. He ignored calls to turn around. He ignored questions shouted by members of the press. On the desk next to him was the brass platter covered with ashes. On the floor next to the desk were several boxes that contained his collection of artifacts stolen from museums across the Mediterranean. All items were small and when he took them they had been archived, rather than on display. Stored in places a curator would know to look as a visiting colleague.

He looked at the stack of boxes. *It's over for me.* He moaned. "What's next for me?" he said his gaze on the ceiling.

Police Chief Mercori, who had been at the station since Saturday morning when the news broke of the assault and kidnapping, pulled a chair up next to him. He waved a hand toward the labeled boxes before he answered Peter's lament.

"These items will be returned to their rightful owners, you'll not see them again and, I'm afraid, your new surroundings will be devoid of beauty, but they'll be ancient." His belly laugh echoed throughout the crowded room.

Chapter 47

Constantine and his cohorts were at odds as to what to do with Bitsy. The men seated around the cottage table found they couldn't agree about the next step.

Karl tried to gain control of the discussion. "We cannot walk away now. After all these years, over one hundred and twenty-five years, the Emperor's diary still exists and the previous rumor of a maid's diary appears true. We must persevere."

Johannes, who had remained silent while the other men argued about how to force Bitsy to talk and how far they were willing to go to make her, spoke up. "Since you," he pointed to Constantine, "brought this dilemma to us and since you are the only one who can be identified by any number of people on Mykonos, it seems appropriate that you be responsible for the outcome, no?"

"But, I acted on your orders to get the diary at any cost."

Karl snorted.

Hermann and Bert looked at each other.

"Do you hear yourself?" Johannes put both his hands on the well-worn table top. "We're talking about undoing a kidnapping and you're bringing up the diary. The diary we don't have."

Hermann, who never wanted any part of this enterprise and who wished he had not been the oldest son, said, "But, the woman doesn't have the diary either, Johannes, and she hasn't shown much fear of us."

"That's the problem," Constantine said. "This woman, this infuriating woman doesn't act the way she should. She seems to think this is a joke, a movie plot, I don't know what she thinks, but she's offered nothing.

"But," he took a quick breath, "we haven't threatened her, we haven't pushed her, we have made no demands!"

Karl stood up and walked around the table. He touched the shoulders of three men, and then stood behind Constantine. He put both hands loosely around his neck. "Wake up, you're at fault. Because of you we have this woman here among us."

"Stop it, Karl." Constantine pulled away. "At least, we know the diary has survived and that's thanks to me." He pointed to his chest.

Karl put his hands into his pockets.

Johannes got up from the table. "We have a group of loyal Austrians on their way to Mykonos to search for the books at the Hotel Apollo, the local museum, and among Ms. Bowman's friends."

A branch slammed against the window next to dining room. All five men jumped.

The wind had picked up and its strong whistle through the pine trees carried debris from the storm. A small radio was set to the weather station and the men knew more storms were forecasted for overnight and part of the next day.

"We have the rest of the evening and the tomorrow morning to come up with a plan." Johannes continued. "The nuns expect us to leave the cottage sometime tomorrow."

He slid his chair under the table. "Since we remain here tonight, Edgar has been instructed to join us from Vienna in the morning with any news he has from Mykonos. No one else knows where we are and he won't provide that information to our Mykonos search party. I suggest we get some sleep."

He saluted his companions, made a brief bow, and turned toward the short hallway off the dining room.

He stopped in front on one of the bedroom doors.

"Let Ms. Bowman spend a night in the most uncomfortable underground cell. Then we'll give her an opportunity to talk."

Chapter 48

On the two hour flight to Vienna, Francesca had time to explain how she determined where Bitsy was most likely being held. Rick and Anna remained skeptical about her credentials, not to mention her demand that they accompany her away from the location of the abduction and the authorities who searched for their friend. She wanted to decrease their fears, if she could.

"If you'll allow me more story-telling time, I believe your anxiety will vanish to be replaced by relief."

Rick nodded his assent. Anna followed his lead.

Francesca took a sip of mineral water before she made eye contact with them.

"I became aware of Constantine Verone's presence on Mykonos when Bitsy brought up her encounter with him in the Hotel Apollo elevator. He's a known member of the Grand Dukes Society. Before I left the hotel for the Delos trip, I witnessed the confrontation between you, Rick, and Constantine in the hotel lobby. It was clear he was desperate to find Bitsy."

"Why didn't you do something right then?" Rick slammed a hand against his arm rest.

"It never occurred to me she would be harmed. The society isn't known for violence, in fact, the group has maintained a low profile for almost a hundred years."

"This is too much to take in." Anna shivered. She covered a yawn with both hands.

"Anna," Francesca said, "You might want to get some sleep. You've been up for many hours and we have hours to go before we reach our destination."

"It must be after midnight in Texas," Rick chimed in.

"I think it's the worry. I'm overrun with worry." Anna tucked a small down pillow under her head, her hands folded under her chin. "Tell Rick your story. He can tell me later."

Francesca lowered the interior lights and suggested she and Rick move to the back of the small plane.

"To continue, as I mentioned to you earlier, the society meets at a secluded cottage at Mayerling on a regular basis. Most of the members are from Austria and reside in that country when not actively searching for the diary across the world. Where else would they feel safe to take a hostage? I'll bet my reputation that she is there. And I

334

expect the group will find it difficult to decide what to do with her."

"That's my fear; they'll just get rid of her."

"No, Rick, I trust they'll not harm her. She is with more leveled headed members than Constantine. He may be trouble, but he wouldn't hurt her. Believe it or not, these men are dedicated to their mission as I am to mine. And I wouldn't hurt anyone." She touched Rick's hand. "I promise."

Rick put up a hand as if in surrender.

"I'll go sit next to Anna, if you don't mind."

***

Anna woke up when the steady drone of the plane's engines changed and it began its descent toward the Vienna airport. Her eyelids fluttered in the shafts of sunlight that peeked through small puffy clouds in a cerulean blue sky. She saw distant mountain tops covered with June snow. She reached for Rick's hand. She surprised herself with the wish that it was Joe's.

Francesca was across the aisle on her computer.

"Can we use cell phones?" she said. "I want to call Joe."

Without waiting for an answer, she dug deep into a side pocket of her tote.

335

"Sorry, Anna," Rick said, "I forgot to tell you, I got a text from him before you arrived on Mykonos."

"That's okay; we've been in a whirlwind since I stepped off the plane from Athens."

"Please, signora." Francesca looked up from her computer. "It's better if you say nothing of where we're going or who's responsible for your friend's disappearance. Not yet."

"Why not?" Anna put her cell on her lap.

"The men we're dealing with have eyes and ears everywhere and they are very tech savvy. I don't want to alert them of our location or our coming."

"Fine, I'll wait." Her voice dropped to a whisper. She dropped her cell back into the tote and she leaned closer to Rick.

"What do you think of all this?"

"As farfetched as it sounds, I believe this woman knows where Bitsy is and I want us to be there when she's found."

The jet touched down on the tarmac with a slow shudder. Light through the small round windows created large polka dots on the cabin seats. Anna took one last look outside the plane. She couldn't see the mountains now, only the Vienna skyline and several international jets lined up for departure.

Their private jet turned away from the main airport terminal. It came to a stop inside a massive silver hanger on the opposite side of the runway. Their pilot tipped his cap toward Francesca before he opened the exit door.

***

Francesca put out her hand to stop Anna from leaving her seat.

"We must talk before we exit. We'll be traveling to the Vienna Woods by private auto."

"How far from Vienna?" Rick looked toward Anna. "Is Maylering deep in the woods?" He imagined twisting roads traversing the woods in endless loops.

"It should take no more than an hour to get there."

"Can we just walk right in and say, 'Is Bitsy Bowman here?' We don't want to put her in any added danger."

"As I said before these men are, for the most part, intellectuals, not criminals per se. Only Constantine has shown a violent side and, believe me, his colleagues will handle him."

Francesca stood up and twirled her sunglasses in her right hand. She motioned for Rick and Anna to move toward the exit door.

"Besides, our driver is a very big man as you will see." It was the first time Francesca offered a brilliant smile to them. "Follow me." She walked toward a solid door on the back wall of the hanger. "Our driver knows the Woods like his own home. He'll take us there *veloce*, fast."

She handed their passports, which she held during the flight, to a uniformed man who stood behind a glass sliding window inside the exit door of the hanger.

"I forgot about entrance and exit stamps." Anna looked at Rick.

Rick shrugged his shoulders. "Apparently, Francesca has taken care of all the necessities to get us in and out of multiple countries."

Chapter 49

Karl made a pot of coffee before the others were up. He tuned in a classical radio station that played Andre Rieu's music on a regular basis. He felt better after a good night's sleep and believed that after her night in the basement cell, Bitsy would break her silence. *The diary will be found and our society will have completed our mission.*

"*Gutten morgen*," he said to each of his colleagues as they slid their chairs up to the table. "Where shall we start?"

"Shouldn't we wait for Johannes to join us?" Hermann said.

"I think we should wait for Edgar to come up from Vienna," Bert chimed in. "Let's eat. I'm hungry."

Constantine cocked his head toward the convent. "*D'accordo*, a new face may persuade the woman that we're a very large number of men who'll keep her here forever."

"I suppose we can wait for the others before we get down to the business," Karl said. He retrieved a box of pastries from the kitchen counter. "Nice of the nuns to furnished such homemade treats."

Before they finished even one cruller, the rumble of a motorcycle brought them all to their feet.

"Herr Edgar has arrived," Johannes said from the hallway. He walked past the table. He opened the front door and stepped onto the stone porch slippery from overnight storms that were gone, but had left hundreds of raindrops to slide off overhanging trees limbs. He stayed on the porch.

"Johannes, Johannes!" Edgar shouted from behind the motorcycle's wide Plexiglas windshield. He jumped off and let his bike fall to the wet ground.

"Quiet, Edgar." Johannes put a finger against his lips. "Your shout could raise the nuns."

"No, no Johannes, I can't be quiet, something's happened, something that changes everything." He waved a newspaper above his head and sprinted up the path to the cottage.

By now all the men crowded the cottage doorway.

"Move away, move back in," Johannes said.

Inside, the group of six men huddled around the table. In silence, they read and reread the headline of the Vienna newspaper. The arrest of Peter Gallenos had made the front page. The article reported details of numerous thefts of ancient and antiquarian items as well as the destruction of evidence thought to be connected to the kidnapping of an American tourist. It reported the police found residue from the burning of two valuable books, thought to be missing diaries, in Mr. Gallenos' home. Reportedly, the curator stated he routinely burned books he found distasteful. The article concluded that authorities were unsure if he had participated in the disappearance of the American woman or if her kidnapping was a random act by an unknown assailant who remained at large.

The only sound in the cottage was the rustle of the newspaper pages.

After several minutes, Karl said, "We must leave immediately. It's over, all is over." Tears rested on the rim of his eyes. "The books are gone. We no longer have a purpose."

"But what if…?" Bert began. He looked at Johannes. "What if this is a scam?"

"No, my dear friend." Johannes put an arm around his trembling frame. "This is an international story. Look at the byline. The article wouldn't be printed if not confirmed. It seems the little curator of the little museum fooled us all."

"Do you think the deaths, the murder at Mayerling offended him?" Edgar said.

"Who knows what goes on in such a mind?"

"What do we do about the woman?" Constantine said.

"I'm afraid the last deed of the Grand Dukes Society is to scatter. To rid ourselves of each other and of this place immediately." Johannes folded the newspaper and tossed it across the table.

"But what about the woman?" Hermann said.

"Yeah, what about her?" Bert said.

"After we settle in our own homes, someone on Mykonos will call in a tip to the Vienna police station. She'll be found alive and well by tomorrow. Now let's go, we can say our goodbyes after we reach Salzburg."

"But she knows our names," Constantine said.

"Perhaps, she knows our first names, Constantine, but, unfortunately for you, she knows your last name, too. I suggest you lay low for some time, stay away from your Vienna apartment, your usual haunts, the women you so fancy."

"Make yourself scarce." Karl snapped his fingers. "As they say in America, right?"

Chapter 50

"We'll reach Mayerling in a short time," the hired driver said to his backseat passengers. The black 1960s Cadillac touring car sported silver flag holders on the front fenders.

"This car's really a museum piece," Rick said. He ran his hands across the back of the leather seat. "Cars can be an expensive hobby." It was the first time he had thought about his Cadillac left on Mykonos.

"It was used by your President Kennedy during a visit to Vienna," the driver said over his shoulder. "My father drove him. I inherited the car."

"Why are we talking about cars?" Anna said. "How much longer is a short time?"

"Do you see that building through the trees, on the rise?" Francesca pointed out the side window next to Anna. "That's Mayerling. The cottage is behind the convent. A back road will take us there."

***

Bitsy lay on her back. She covered her eyes with an arm. She had fallen asleep with the naked light bulb on and the glare hurt her morning eyes.

A new day, maybe the day they let me go.

She sat straight up as her mind shifted to a dark idea. What if they left her here? What if they had left for parts unknown or back to Mykonos to threaten Peter or her friends?

She put her feet on the cold concrete floor. She bent down to find her shoes. Under the bed she saw a notebook. On her knees she pulled it out.

What have we here? The writing inside was simple print like child's block letters in what she thought was German. There were some drawings of trees, deer with large antlers and horses with short manes. Most of the notebook was blank.

Bitsy sat back on the bed and opened the drawer of the small nightstand.

"A pencil!" she shouted. *The good Lord provides, now I can write a letter to Anna and one to Rick and one to Peter.* There was relief in the idea of putting her feelings on paper and, although she avoided the thought, if she wasn't found, now she could say goodbye to the people she loved.

DEAR ANNA, THANK YOU FOR YOUR UNWAVERING
FRIENDSHIP NO MATTER MY FAULTS. YOU HAVE
BEEN MY BLESSING. AND ANNA, YOU'RE SO LUCKY TO
HAVE JOE REGARDLESS OF HIS SHORTCOMINGS. MANY A
NIGHT I HAVE PRAYED FOR A LIFE LIKE YOURS, WITH
SOMEONE TO LOVE WHO LOVES YOU BACK. LOVE HIM,
ANNA, EVEN IF HE NEEDS TO LEAN ON YOU. IT'S GOT TO
BEAT THE EMPTINESS MANY OF US FEEL. SORRY, I DIDN'T
MEAN FOR THIS TO BE A PITY PARTY. I HAVEN'T GIVEN UP
HOPE OR FAITH, BUT IN THE EVENT THINGS GO FROM BAD
TO WORSE, I WANTED TO THANK YOU FOR YOUR LOVE,
SUPPORT AND STEADFASTNESS. LOVE, YOUR BFF, BITSY.
XOXOXO

She put the notebook on the bed. She patted the tattered cover with her right hand before placing it over her heart. With eyes closed, she counted her exhales to slow her breath and relax shoulders that had crept up to her ears.

Now some stretches and then a letter to Rick.

***

When the car pulled to a stop at the end of the dirt road, there were no signs that anyone was there. No vehicles in sight.

Francesca was the first of the group to step into the empty living room. She walked to the dining room where remnants of crullers, strudel and cinnamon cookies littered the round table. A coffee pot was filled with dried grounds. She picked up the folded Vienna newspaper without reading it and put it into her tote.

She and Anna searched the rooms, under the beds, and in closets. Rick checked the cramped attic space. They found no evidence that Bitsy had been in the cottage.

"I know she was brought here." Francesca slammed the front door behind her. She ran a hand through her hair and adjusted her sunglasses. "We need to search the grounds. We must split up.

"Rick, you search the woods behind the cottage. Anna, you check the grounds toward the convent. I'll search the storage buildings to the right."

Once she was alone, she stepped back into the cottage. She returned to one of the bedrooms and removed a black canvas bag from a night table. Inside were a scroll and a metal disk. A *tablua recta* and a cipher wheel. Alphabet and numbers. The ciphers to the Emperor's diary. The Grand Dukes had been so close. *C'est la vie.*

***

After a few minutes of moving back and forth over the soggy ground that led to the back of Mayerling, Anna stopped. A small oval object glinted in the sunlight on top of a mound of rain flattened leaves.

"I've found something!" she shouted. "I've found something." She started to head back to the cottage, but quickly decided she should stay where she was.

Rick reached her first.

"What is it?"

"It's one of Bitsy's acrylic nails. I know it's hers. It's one of her favorite shades, Plum Sparkle." She held out her hand, the nail rested in her palm. "Do you think she left a trail of these?" She was reminded of her friend's love of folklore and fairytales. "It's like Hansel and Gretel, isn't it?"

Francesca joined them. She took the small acrylic nail from Anna's hand.

"We must walk with caution so as not to bury any others that may direct us to Bitsy. We need to be vigilant."

A careful search of the ground from the site of the nail toward the back of Mayerling yielded another nail several feet away, and then another and another. The group stood a few feet from a metal door recessed in a windowless stone wall.

Francesca rattled the thick iron door handle, but the door didn't open.

"We may have to disturb the nuns."

She was about to turn away when Rick suggested he try the door.

He placed both hands on the handle and pressed down. He shoved his right shoulder against the rust covered door. Nothing. He yanked the handle toward him. The door opened. Stone stairs led down to a concrete floor. He helped Anna down the sloping stair steps and Francesca followed.

"So many doors!" Anna's voice echoed off the stone walls. She turned toward Francesca, a thousand questions unspoken.

"She's here, I'm sure of it." Francesca said.

"What are we waiting for?" Rick started down the long hallway. The scattering of small creatures could be heard. "Don't look down." He looked back at the women.

Midway down the hall, Anna was the first to call out. "Bitsy! Bitsy, are you here? Bitsy!!"

Francesca touched Anna's shoulder. She put a finger over her lips.

There was a moment of silence before everyone smiled.

"Here, here, I'm here!" a familiar voice called out.

A key hung on a brass hook outside the room where Bitsy pounded against the door. "Anna, is that really you?"

349

"It is, it is, Bitsy."

Rick's hand shook as he tried to insert the key into the lock.

"Hang on, Bitsy," he said."Francesca, this may be a task for you. I can't seem to make this key fit."

"Rick, oh, Rick, you're here." Bitsy said.

"Yes, Bitsy, I'm here."

Francesca took the key and slid it into the old lock. They heard a thud when the dead bolt sprang into its open position.

Anna got to Bitsy first only because Rick stepped aside for her.

"How are you, are you hurt?"

"I'm fine, really." Bitsy wrapped her arms around Anna's shoulders. She looked at Rick standing in the doorway. "I can't believe you're both here."

Francesca leaned around Rick. "We must leave. Bitsy, my heart swells to see you doing well without harm, but we must leave."

"Not soon enough for me." Bitsy grabbed the notebook from the end of the bed.

"By the way, what are you doing here, Francesca and what about Pamela?"

"In good time, I'll answer your questions." Francesca waited until the others had left the room before turning off the light and locking the door. The rusty key swung on its hook as everyone left the basement.

***

Anna and Bitsy talked nonstop on the drive away from Mayerling. Tears flowed. Bitsy sat between her friends. Francesca sat in the jump seat, her cell phone held to her ear.

At the Vienna air terminal, Bitsy was reunited with her tote bag removed from the trunk of the Cadillac touring car. Her large suitcase would be checked in by Francesca's driver. Rick and Anna grabbed their carry-ons.

Tears turned to laughter which was magnified once in the cavernous Vienna air terminal. Rick and Francesca walked behind the two friends.

"Your reservations are made," she said to Rick. "Your flight leaves in about an hour and a half. You'll fly directly to DFW International. I leave you here as I must return to Milano pronto." She handed Rick the tickets and three passports.

"So this is it? No police to talk to? Bitsy was kidnapped, remember?" He put the tickets and passports in his jacket pocket.

351

"The Greek police have been informed of her rescue and made aware of those suspected of the kidnapping. She'll be able to give her statement by Skype after she's home. There is a small possibility she may need to return here or to Greece in the event the men responsible are found and prosecuted."

"You do have powerful friends, Signora Campelli. Good luck to you."

They caught up with Anna and Bitsy in front of the security check-in. Francesca hugged Bitsy. "You're a brave and strong woman; your Artemis stood you in good stead, my friend."

"Thanks for that, Francesca. I did call on her several times as well as praying to the Lord for my safety and wellbeing."

Rick reached out for Bitsy's hand.

Francesca turned to Anna and held out her hand.

"Bitsy's lucky to have such wonderful and fearless friends. It has been my pleasure to spend some time with you. Safe travels."

"Thank you. It certainly has been an adventure. I'm grateful for your help in finding my best friend."

Francesca watched as they queued up to go through the metal detectors before she turned toward the terminal exit.

***

Rick settled onto a sleek grey tweed chair in one of the concourse bars next to Bitsy and across from Anna. He signaled a waiter.

"Is champagne alright?"

No objections were offered.

***

Francesca removed her sunglasses and replaced them with her professorial horned rimmed bifocals. Her tote bag, heavy with her laptop in its outside pocket, cut into her shoulder. The concierge at the Hotel Imperial placed her room key in her outstretched right hand.

"*Bitte*," she said. "Please send a carafe of espresso to my room. *Danka.*"

She passed through the ground floor of the hotel, once a Viennese palace. The marble floors, paneled wood walls, massive crystal chandeliers, and the thick Persian wool rugs paid homage to the Hapsburgs. She hesitated a moment before she walked to the elevators to admire the Bel-Etage, the main staircase, above which a life sized portrait of Emperor Franz Joseph in full imperial uniform gazed down on a life sized marble statue of the Danube Nymph.

The epitome of the masculine and the feminine. I must come here when I have leisure time.

She leaned against the back wall of the elevator. She hugged her tote bag to her side. A stack of gold bangles jangled when she reached for the polished button panel. *Times have changed, even here, no elevator attendant.*

Tomorrow there would be a meeting in Milan. Eyes closed she visualized her small apartment on its cobblestone street. She could almost smell the rich soil she had packed loosely in terra cotta pots and the scents of her beloved flowers; freesia, bougainvillea and roses. The buzz of the bees and the flutter of butterfly wings against her cheek would welcome her home.

Her hotel suite was only a few steps away from the elevator. No one was in the hallway. She slid the large brass key into the door lock. At least no plastic room card here. She heard the elevator begin its descent.

She placed her tote bag on the crimson toile bedspread. *I'll wait for the espresso before I make the call.*

She opened the tall paned window that overlooked a small courtyard that reminded her of the square outside her apartment. A few patrons were having a late lunch.

The room doorbell rang. She placed a hand on the window pane before she turned away from the window. Such a peaceful sight.

She entered the sitting room as the bell rang again.

"Your espresso, Madame." The young waiter swung the silver tray from shoulder height to place it on a round table in the center of the room.

"If you are in need of anything else?"

"Thank you, no." She handed him a tip in U.S. dollars. A smile crossed his face, but he didn't thank her. He backed out of the room and nodded in her direction at the door.

She looked beyond the table into the adjoining bedroom. She saw her reflection in a gold leaf trimmed mirror that hung over a delicate dresser hand painted with rose buds and ribbons around its legs like a May Day pole.

"Don't distract yourself, Francesca." She poured an espresso.

Time for the call to Washington.

Sitting on the edge of the bed, she pulled a throw away cell from her tote. Phones that were discarded after one use. This call was to James Kent, her U.S. contact. He was the agent cleared to meet with the Vatican committee dedicated to the retrieval of lost artifacts and ephemera belonging to or denigrating the Church. *As usual, he'll meet me in Milan, obtain my report, and then deliver it in Rome. No faxing or emails of confidential Church papers.*

"James, it's me, Francesca. My work's done."

"Should I come for a visit?"

"If you can be at my apartment tomorrow, I'll cook you my famous paella."

"I'll be there for the evening meal."

"*Ciao*, James."

"*Ciao, bella.*"

She pushed the end button on the cell with her right hand. She tugged her tote bag toward her with her left. She took out a shiny silver flask of Courvoisier and poured a small amount into her espresso. She slowly stirred the drink with a small demitasse spoon. With the first sip, she felt the warmth of the liqueur travel down her throat.

Nice, just what I needed.

She put the cup down on the marble topped nightstand. She placed her tote on her lap. She unfolded her curator gloves from a small inside pocket and put them on.

After another sip of her espresso, she reached into the tote and pulled out the smaller of the two diaries. The larger could wait; she was most interested to read the entries of the young undermaid who had no reason to doctor the truth of her experience at Mayerling. She turned to the first page written in a young girl's flowery script, *26 December 1888.*

Chapter 51

The view out the large glass window in the airport cocktail lounge was a living painting of the Austrian flowers Bitsy, Anna and Rick had seen before entering the terminal. The undeveloped field around the airport runways was covered in a rainbow of color. Western spiderwort, black yarrow and blue cornflower blooms danced in the warm late spring. Summer would arrive in a few days, but the stilled life of winter had already disappeared.

"Spectacular," Anna said.

"She sure is," Rick nodded toward Bitsy.

Anna winked at him.

"You guys. There's no way I'm spectacular. I'm a mess. I think Anna meant the view out there." She pointed to the window.

"Well, Bitsy, I see a spectacularly, wonderfully, attractive woman whose beauty is more than skin deep."

"How much champagne have you had?" She put her hand to her cheek.

"I agree with Rick." Anna reached for her hand. "I've never seen you look better."

"I guess you all thought I was a goner."

"No, I know you. I know your determination." Anna said.

"And, I'm getting to know that quality, too." Rick took Bitsy's other hand.

"Okay, you two. Enough about me. It's time for a trip to the girl's room where I can freshen up some."

"I'll join you." Anna was the first to let go of Bitsy's hand.

"I'll order us another bottle of champagne and some fruit and cheese." Rick stood, as the women turned to leave the bar. "This is a celebration if there ever was one."

Bitsy placed her powder compact, favorite lipstick and hair brush on the restroom counter. She used one the portable spearmint mini brushes she kept in her tote to clean her teeth and breath before she washed her face and put on makeup.

"I'm back," she said. "Back to the old me. No, that's not right. I'm a better me."

"Just don't go missing again, okay?" Anna gave her a bear hug.

The plane sat in line on the tarmac. Conversation was suspended while a flight attendant read safety rules and how to survive a water landing. She also passed out a list of food and drink choices, the times meals would be served and inflight movies available during the eleven hour flight.

When the plane was cleared for takeoff, attempts to make sense of the weekend and events were renewed. An annual conference in a beautiful location turned into the place for a kidnapping, an assault, the discovery of an unsuspected thief, the surprise that several groups of people continued to search for a century old diary that documented a cold case of murder and suicide or something more sinister.

The talk died down when any one of the group reached for a pillow and blanket. The chatter started again when everyone was awake. Rick kept his arm around Bitsy for hours and Anna held her hand for most of the flight home.

When the pilot announced that the east coast of the United States was visible, Anna reached for her tote bag.

"Time to call Joe."

"Do you want us to give you privacy?" Bitsy said

"We could get up and stretch." Rick swung his long legs into the aisle.

"No, stay here. It will be a short call. I just think I should touch base."

She punched in Joe's cell number. He answered on the first ring.

"Hello."

"Joe." The word caught in her throat. "Lots to tell you, but, most importantly, we found Bitsy. She's alright. We're about to pass over the east coast. I'm coming home."

There was a moment of silence. She caught Bitsy eye and mouthed "He hasn't said anything."

"When will you touch down at DFW?"

"Oh, you sound almost normal. I mean back to your old voice. Oh, you know what I mean."

"I have a lot to tell you, too, Anna, and you're right, I'm almost normal."

"Let me ask a flight attendant about our arrival time. But, Joe, whatever time it is, it won't be soon enough." Had she really said that? Was she actually looking forward to being home? Time heals or, maybe, threat of loss through death illuminated what was most important. Love.

"I feel the same. Today may be the best day of my life. Our life."

He told her he would order a car service to pick them up at DFW. He didn't tell her he would meet her there.

"Quickly, I know this call will cost a fortune, where are you?" She held her breath. Was he still at the hospital? Was he at Minister Wilson's? Had he been transferred somewhere else?

"I'm still in the hospital, but my discharge date is in a couple of days. And don't worry, I've come a long way since you left. You'll see."

"I'll call you again when we land." She hesitated, let out a deep sigh and continued. "I love you."

***

Baggage claim was crowded. Bitsy had the only checked bag and Rick stood with her as the carousel began to turn. Anna stood outside the circle of passengers. She hadn't seen anyone with her name on a placard and she wasn't sure where to go to find their hired driver.

"Hey, you beautiful woman."

She twisted her head over her shoulder at the sound of the most familiar voice in her life.

Joe waved from a spot a few feet away. A second later he dropped his hand to the rubber grip on a silver walker.

"You're walking!"

"Getting there."

362

She leaned over the front of the walker and kissed him.

"Wait 'til Bitsy and Rick see you. You're up, you're talking." She felt everyone around them could hear her heart beat. Fear and anger gave way to joy and gratitude.

"By the way, thank you for the compliment. And may I say you are one handsome man."

"Who are the others?"

"Oh, Joe. I've always loved to banter with you."

She heard footsteps coming up behind her.

"Let's get out of here and go home. Can you go home with me, Joe?" She slipped her arm under Bitsy's. Rick stood beside Joe.

"I got a pass from the hospital, but I have to be back tomorrow morning."

Anna squeezed Bitsy's arm. Rick walked with Joe.

In the back of the pearl gray Lincoln limousine, the talk of the weekend continued. Joe wanted to hear all about it. Bitsy was in her element, holding court and nestled on the back seat with Rick.

When she ended her tale of Constantine, Peter, Maylering and Francesca, she suggested Anna take over.

"The books or diaries, I should say, belonged to Joe. I think you should fill him in on what we learned. After all it's your family, Joe, who played a large part in Austria's history."

"Thanks, Bitsy," Joe said, "But I'd rather get into all that when we're home. For now, I just want to be here with the three of you. And to share a surprise for my wife."

"You've already surprised me by coming to the airport. Nothing could be better than seeing you near normal."

Joe reached into his jacket pocket and pulled out an envelope with Anna's name written across it. "For you after all these years together."

She cocked her head to the right before she held out her hand.

Bitsy and Rick had leaned forward to see what was in the envelope.

"Oh, my!" Anna almost knocked Joe over onto the wide leather seat as she wrapped her arms around his neck.

"Anna, what is it?" Bitsy strained to see what was in her hand. "Are those airline tickets?"

Joe answered while Anna kissed his cheeks.

"Two tickets to London next month, with an open return. I've rented a flat in Notting Hill."

The Lincoln neared Middlecreek. Familiar landmarks were visible out the windows.

Anna snuggled next to her husband. He squeezed her hand. His grip was strong.

Rick's fingers were intertwined with Bitsy's. She leaned against his shoulder. Suddenly, she sat straight up and turned toward him.

"Dickie Bird," she said, "I just had a thought, where's your Cadillac?"

Everyone laughed.

Author's Note:

If some of the information provided in this book sparked your interest in the murder-suicide at Maylering, Austrian history of that time or the different Greek Goddesses, the following suggested reading list is for you.

Bolen, M.D., Jean Shinoda. *Goddesses in Everywoman: A New Psychology of Women.* New York: Harper Colophon Books.

Bolen, M.D., Jean Shinoda. *Goddesses in Older Woman: Archetypes in Women over Fifty.* New York: HarperCollins. Print

Markus, Georg. *Crime at Mayerling: The Life and Death of Mary Vetsera.* Translated from the German. California: Ariadne Press. Print.

Morton, Frederic. *A Nervous Splendor: Vienna 1888/1889.* New York: Penguin Books. Print.

Also by Elizabeth Lueda Amerine
The Way We Were: A Poetry Memoir

About the Author

Elizabeth Lueda Amerine earned her doctorate degree in Clinical Psychology from the California School of Professional Psychology in 1990 and she maintains a consulting psychology and neuropsychology practice in Dallas, Texas. Previously, she enjoyed careers as a travel agent and a real estate broker. She has been an adjunct professor at St. Mary's University in San Antonio, Texas and an adjunct instructor at Richland College in Dallas, Texas. She was a guest poetry instructor for an adult education writing class at Southern Methodist University in University Park, Texas. She is the author of a poetry memoir, *The Way We Were,* and has been published in several poetry anthologies and other publications. She lives in Red Oak, Texas with her Bichon Frise, Gigi. This is her first novel.